# NORTHERN LIGHTS

# Northern Lights

---

## *The Druid of Black Lake*

### ELIZABETH MENZIE

Elizabeth Menzie

For my father, Darryl Senecal.
My hero, my biggest champion, my role model.
I love you dad.

# | 1 |

## Chapter 1

Temperatures in Saskatchewan get pretty cold, especially in the winter months. I was in our family room, reading the latest copy of National Geographic which had arrived in the mail the previous day. The weather outside was cold, ice cold. It wasn't snowing at the moment but it had snowed for the majority of the weekend, now it was Tuesday, I don't think I had stepped outside for five days. I wasn't complaining about it; I would rather be inside our warm house when it was minus thirty degrees outside. However, I wanted it be warm up just a little so my skin wouldn't freeze when I stepped outside for more then ten minutes at a time.

I had been sick for two days. It wasn't anything serious, just a cold. Warm camomile tea with honey was my grandmother's trick. Grandma Daisy had all kinds of remedies for all kinds of things. Most of which involved food, drink, kind words and good company. That woman could fix anything. The honey helped sooth my throat, the home remedy also helped to calm my nerves.

My National Geographic magazine was not holding my attention like it usually did. I stared at the cover, it read March edition. The month of March, which meant there was only one more month until the big exhibition. I had been dreading it for the past two years, but since Christmas time I had begun to have trouble sleeping and concentrating. It was almost time for the exhibition that every unmated werewolf between the ages of seventeen to twenty-five in our treaty territory knew was coming. It was the Mating Exhibition.

I know what you are thinking, and yes there are werewolves in Canada. It's not a silly story like your friend's imaginary girlfriend who lives in Canada. You know, the one he met at "summer camp" last year. We are real, we are numerous and we hide in plain sight up here.

There are four territories, the West Coast, Central Prairie, Eastern Coalition and Maritime Fellowship. I happen to live in the Central Prairie Territory, which makes up half of Alberta, Saskatchewan, Manitoba, Nunavut, and half of the Northwest Territories. It is the largest land mass werewolf territory in Canada, but not the largest population by far. That belongs to the Eastern Coalition. We do, however have the most ground to cover, which can be problematic with rogue packs but our pack leaders do the best they can to work together within the territories.

I was born here in Saskatchewan to my mother and father, Dorothy and James Gillies. My father is the Delta of our pack, the Red Rose Pack which is active in the Prince Albert National Park area. We are not a huge pack, only about three hundred members, but for a Saskatchewan pack that is a fair size. We are the third largest in the province after the Riverbed Pack in Saskatoon and the True Dawn Pack in Regina. I have been all over the province with my family, and I can safely say no other pack territory is as beautiful as ours here in Red Rose. The humans created a provincial park here in 1927, long after our pack was already in the area for generations. We are conservationists, hunters, trappers, geologists, anthropologists, and botanists. We live off the land, work the land, respect it and the life it gives us. In return, the land here has turned our pack into a healthy group of wolves. We are blessed. The river runs through our territory, the trees are high and thick. The game is plentiful and delicious. I have everything I could ever need here. I love it and I want to stay. However, I know that isn't possible. I know my time at Red Rose is coming to and end, and there is very little I can do to stop it.

My sister Marie knocked on the door and opened it, sliding her hand to the inside of the handle on the other side and peeking her head in. She smiles at me, her green eyes and strawberry hair mirror mine. She lifts her chin to gesture that I need to follow her and she points her thumb out the door behind herself. I nod knowingly, tossing the magazine down with a sigh. I want to read it but National Geographic will have to wait for another day. I rise off the sofa, fold the blanket that I had been wearing like a poncho and set it back on the sofa. I gaze outside one final time, it has started to snow again. I follow Marie out the door, down the hall and into our family's living room where everyone in our home is gathered, waiting for us.

My father, James and my mother, Dorothy are both sitting in his and her club chairs. My younger brother Byron was sitting on the floor and my older brother, Michael was sitting on the sofa. He gestured for Marie and I to take a seat with him. We sat on either side. I could hear the hiss of the flames in the fire place, my mother must have just put a new log on. My entire family was in this room, we all sat in silence for several minutes. I suppose we all were waiting for everything to sink in before we spoke about it aloud. I turned to look at Marie, she was smiling at our mother. Mother and Marie were very similar; I was the odd female out in my family.

Finally, my father shifted his weight, cleared his throat and pulled an envelope out from beside his thigh which I hadn't noticed was there. I recognized the red stamp on the large manila envelope. It was from the exhibition. My father opened it and read the letter aloud:

"Greetings Delta Gillies of the Red Rose Pack,

It is our honor to request that your unmated daughters, Marie and Charlotte Gillies attend the 110th Mating Exhibition of the Central Prairie Territory to be held in Brandon, Manitoba this year. Registration will be at 9am on April 4th, followed by three days of activities, concluding on April 8th at 10am. Please find the complete itinerary included in this invitation. Please find a copy of this letter has also been sent on to your alpha. Failure to comply with this invitation will have consequences for your family and your pack. Thank you, and may the Moon Goddess be with you."

My father tossed the letter to me and stood up. He linked his hands behind his back and stepped up to the fireplace. My mother smiled knowingly, raised behind him and rubbed his shoulder blades. She whispered to him, "I know it is hard my love, but they must go. We all must do our duties."

"I don't understand why both my girls aren't mated within Red Rose. One maybe, but not both. It's hard enough to let go of them to anther house, but another pack all together. Another province maybe. It's so far from home, how can I protect them?" my father asked her, loud enough so we could hear the pain in his voice. My father adored his children, each of us is very loved and cherished. I know he has been praying for us to find our mates here, within our pack so we can stay here and he can protect us. As a Delta, he is the Beta's second. He is strong and protective. He wants the best for my sister and I, I know that.

"I am so excited to go!" Marie finally giggles, I peer around Michael to see her face. She is beaming. Marie is over the moon that it is finally time to go to the exhibition. My mother goes to her and cups her face. She kisses Marie's cheeks and her forehead, "I know my sweet angel, you will find a handsome mate. He will sweep you off your feet and you will be so in love."

I roll my eyes. My arms cross instinctively and so do my legs. Michael chuckles at me, "You know Charlotte, with that posture I am sure they will just return you after the exhibition. Maybe that's your way out." I sneer at him, but then I nod. Perhaps he has an idea there. Michael puts his hand on my arm and smiles.

"Charlotte, Marie... this is the tradition. I know it isn't ideal but it is the way our packs have been circulating and keeping bloodlines strong for centuries. I met your mother at the Mating Exhibition when I was twenty-one and she was twenty. I could not have imagined a more beautiful mate, a more perfect mother or a happier marriage. I sincerely wish the same for both of you." My father said, returning to his comfortable chair. He let out a sigh before he continued, "I do wish you both had found your mates here in Red Rose. It would have made everything easier. I am going to have a terrible time letting my girls go to new packs."

"What happens if I don't want to go?" I ask loudly. Everyone looks at me, my mother gasps and pulls Marie close to her. Byron shifts his body to turn around to watch as father's eyes go black.

"Well, I have seen it happen a handful of times where an unmated young adult is held back and refuses to go to the exhibition. It usually ends with the execution of the individual, the ejection from the pack of the rest of their immediate family and all land and capital titles are revoked by the pack from the family line." Father said calmly. He wasn't angry, I could read his face. He didn't want us to go any more then I wanted to go. If I wanted to stay he would go to the alpha, request that I stay. It would be refused of course. If I ran away or refused to go, I would be hunted and executed. Or I would spend my life on the run as a rogue, dying young anyway. My family would be turned out and I would ruin six lives in the process. It is selfish of me, but in reality it is an archaic system of mating practices which only makes it seem as though I am being selfish.

"Charlotte, I understand how you are feeling," my mother began, kneeling in front of me. "I know you see this as some sort of prehistoric tradition. You are right, it is. But this is our tradition, it is not meant to hurt you. It is bigger then you, bigger then one family and one pack. These traditions are meant to protect all of us and to ensure the continuation of our species. This isn't going to be the end for you, it is a new beginning."

I throw my hands in the air, the invitation falls slowly to the ground. I am in tears now, hot messy tears that are coming down my face faster then I can wipe them away. "That is easy for you to say mom, you wanted to be mated. You wanted to find someone to be your everything. You wanted to have children and tow the pack line. I don't want someone to complete me, I am complete on my own."

"Of course you are sweetheart," my father told me. "There is nothing that says that if your mate is not at the exhibition you can't come back home. If he isn't there, then you return to us. You can stay here forever then. No one will bother you."

I stared at him, I hadn't even considered that. Perhaps there wouldn't be a mate for me at the exhibition. I certainly wasn't looking for one. I left the room and went back to the study. The snow was falling much harder now, almost a flurry. I listened to the wind outside whistle through the trees around our house. If I went to the exhibition and there was no mate there, I could just come back home unmated for the rest of my life. It sounded so simple, maybe it would be possible.

## Chapter 2

The rest of March slipped by without much incident. I never did finish my National Geographic magazine. Once we had received our registration packages for the exhibition we had to figure out all kinds of details for the trip. Brandon was ten hours away from our territory, so we had to arrange accommodations. My mother took us into Prince Albert to get some new outfits for the events. There were three classes to attend each day and one lecture. Each evening there were supervised mixers. On the first night there was a ball. According to traditions that is where people usually paired off, then pairs would spend the remainder of the exhibition together. It was meant to basically be a massive speed dating event that included classes on mating, marriage, pack politics, family planning and economics. While my mother and Marie were looking at skirts Michael came over to me and pulled me out of the store.

"Charlotte, you should know that this exhibition event can be very serious. If we do find our mates there, we are allowed to combine rooms and finish the mating process on site. I have heard that some of us have even conceived children at the exhibition." He told me with a slight laugh.

"I don't want to know this, Michael. I don't want to mate with someone I just met. I couldn't." I told him in a hushed gasp.

My brother just laughs in my face, "It's not like you really can control it. If you meet him, he will be irresistible to you. Nothing else will matter. Mother, father, Marie, Byron, me, Red Rose will all be a distant memory when you see him."

I roll my eyes, "Is that what happened to Stella when you met her last year?" Michael laughed even louder at me. "No, she kind of hid from me in her room for three days. She said she was sick. I had to bribe the staff to let me in. Stella didn't know how she felt about me, sometimes she still doesn't come to think of it."

I smiled. My brother and his mate had been together for about a year now. It was still very new. She didn't like Red Rose very much, she visited her mother and father a lot who were in the True Dawn Pack out of Regina. Michael was patient though. He loved Stella, she was his everything. I looked at him and thought that maybe if my mate thought that way, it might not be so bad.

My mother called us back into the store and informed us we had to go and get our dresses for the ball. I didn't want to go but Marie was over the moon. Michael carried the majority of the bags and we all shuffled down the halls of the mall to the bridal store. Dresses everywhere. So expensive, for only one day and they all looked uncomfortable and itchy. My brother sat down in the designated "sitting section", he was carrying so many bags. Marie ran up the stairs to a rainbow of colors and fabrics. Mother went to the right and I went to the back, discount racks are more my speed.

I looked for twenty minutes and I found a lot of sparkles, animal print and lace. Too much fluff or not long enough. I was moving to the end of the line when I found a green long dress with a sweetheart neckline. It was forest green, soft flowing. I liked it. The price was reasonable and it was in my size, perhaps it was fate. I called to my mother. She dashed to me and ushered me into the fitting room. I pulled the dress on, it felt perfect for me. I stepped out and Marie gasped. She was wearing a hot pink short thing; I don't know what she was thinking. "I think I like this one mom." I said as I turned around.

"Oh darling it is perfect. Just so you. Simple, elegant, classic. I love you in that dress." My mom clapped as she spoke. I spun around a bit, the green dress flowed around me, lifting slightly but showing nothing. The fabric was so soft; I wasn't expecting to like it. Michael turn around kind of to look at me, he nodded and said, "Looking good Char."

"Alright, I'll get this one then." I agreed and smiled at myself in the mirror. I did look very nice in it. My eyes popped against the green fabric, my hair, being strawberry red seemed to glow against the dress. I pictured myself wearing it down then I wore it. It would probably be one of the simpler dresses at the ball, as it is a last season dress. I didn't care, it made me feel good and I wanted to attend this archaic event in something I felt comfortable in.

"Shoes? Maybe heals?" my mother asked. I shook my head, "No mom, I have black flats that I will wear. We can shorten the dress at home to just touch the floor in them. I don't want to buy shoes as well that I will never wear again."

My mother held my shoulders tight and hugged me close. She kissed my cheek, "My practical girl." Marie smiled at me, she knew I loved the dress. She wanted me to be excited with her for this event. I know she has been looking forward to it all year. When Marie realized her mate wasn't in Red Rose she was excited because she wanted to leave and travel the world. She wanted to go somewhere else that wasn't the middle of a forest. Do not get me wrong, Marie loved our home and our family, but she wanted out. She wanted to be more then a Delta's daughter.

"Ok, let's find you one now honey. I don't think that pink one leaves anything to the imagination." My mother said turning to Marie. Marie sighed in agreement. They went off together to discuss different dresses. I changed out of my green one and took it to the till. I went back to Michael and we waited another hour and half before Marie found one she liked. I am pretty sure I fell asleep on my brother's shoulder at some point.

When we arrived home Byron was playing a game on the TV and my father was reading a book. Michael carried in about two dozen bags from the van. My father looked at my mother, "How much Dorothy?"

She took his hand and kissed his forehead, "Less then you think." He smiled at her and nodded. "One more week girls. Only one."

I gathered up my bags and took them to my room. I pulled out the dress and held it up to my body. I looked into the mirror and let my ponytail down. It did make me look radiant. Such a simple piece of sewn fabric had so much power. I smiled at myself. I would get to wear my simple dress, my comfortable shoes, my glasses and I might not even find this mate. Then I could come back home and continue to read, track and live the life I love here in the forests of Red Rose.

I slept well that night, first time in a while. I woke up at five in the morning though. I felt the sudden urge to run. I needed fresh air and I needed it now. I crept out of my room and went to my sister's. Marie was sleep still, but I jumped onto her bed and pulled the covers off.

"Charlotte, what!?" she yawned, pulling the covers back over her shoulders.

"Come run with me!" I demanded. She rolled over, almost off her bed, "No, I'm still sleeping."

"Come run with me and after I'll make you a smoothie for break-fast." My bribe seems to have perked her interest, she opens one eye to look at me, "Strawberry banana?"

I nodded. She groaned and pulled herself up and out of bed. I smiled in triumph. We crept downstairs and outside, it was still very cold, but once she shifted we shook the snow off. Marie's wolf is brown; my wolf is dark grey. We tumble through the snow together, around the back yard just beyond the tree line. We don't go too far just in case, but we run out our energy. I wanted to do this with her one last time, just in case one of us doesn't come back from the exhibition. I know I will see my sister again, talk to her often but we might never be here in Red Rose together in the snow again. It makes my heart hurt, but it is the reality of where we are going. Marie can smell my sadness and she rubs up against me. She links with me soft wordless comforts. I love her for that. We jog back to the house and I made Marie her smoothie.

## Chapter 3

The drive to Brandon was long. Marie and mother played and sang Taylor Swift for the majority of the drive much to mine and father's dismay. Michael and Byron stayed behind at Red Rose. My father was sullen the entire drive. He doesn't nap, he doesn't read, he just starred off into space with a deep sadness in his eyes. With Marie and mother in the front seat singing I touch my father's hand to pull him out of his trance. He turned his head to face me, "Yes sweetheart?" I look into his face and I manage a small smile, "I know you want to protect us dad. This is out of your control. I know that. We will be alright. I will be alright."

"Please listen Charlotte," he whispered quietly, "don't search it out. Just try to pass the days without making any kind of contact. If you float by and no one catches scent of you, then we will take you home to be safe. Just be a fly on the wall sweetheart." I nodded. I truly was my father's daughter. That was my plan, for what little I could plan for it. I turned and looked out the window again. Marie smacked my hand while singing along to the song, I just smiled at her and looked away again.

I could feel my wolf getting more active as we got closer to Brandon. She wasn't excited per say, more like she was very aware of something. She could sense something.

We pulled into the large event centre, there must have been over one hundred vehicles in the parking lot. Brandon was huge compared to our city. The hotel was attached to the event centre and we saw it was also large and it looked very fancy. I guess the territories like to put on the dog. We parked the van, got out our luggage and walked into the hotel. My dad carried our garment bags for us so the dresses wouldn't touch the ground. In the lobby of the hotel I had never seen so many young wolves in my life. All around my age, most looking so excited to be here. I gulped a bit when I saw how some of the girls were dressed, they were showing mid drift, wearing a lot of make-up and long fake nails. I looked like a dumpy country wolf for sure.

Father and mother led us to the front desk and we waited in line for our turn to check in. Marie's head suddenly shot up and she looked around. I glanced at her and asked her what was up without words. "Mate." She whispered. I looked around, there were probably fifty young wolves in this lobby alone, plus parents and event personal. She smelled the air deeply, looking around franticly. My father caught her and sighed heavily. It was finally our turn, he pulled Marie in front of him and stepped up to the desk.

"Marie, honey, just settle please. You will meet him tomorrow." My father whispered to her. She whimpered slightly, and her head fell. My mother pushed her hair behind her ears while father checked us in. I looked around again to see if anyone was coming towards us. I could tell there were many males who were looking around, but none that settled on us specifically. I subconsciously sniffed the air, annoyed immediately at myself for doing it. Nothing, no one particular. I exhaled happily. Maybe he wasn't here. Maybe I could go home.

My parents got an adjoining room to Marie and I, mainly so that they could keep an eye on us in case anything happened like what just had in the lobby. Marie put her bags down and sulked on the bed. My father was not amused.

"Why can't I just go and find him daddy? Isn't this the whole reason we are here? You knew I would probably find my mate here, just let me go find him, please?!" Marie whined. My father was annoyed; I could see he was agitated. He walked around to the other room and back again, I have never seen him this annoyed.

"Dorothy would you please explain it to her." My father finally requested before rising, going to their hotel room and closing the door behind himself. My mother sighed and sat down next to Marie on her bed.

"Alright girls, you both need to hear this right now. Charlotte sit with us please." She began, I sat down on my bed across from them to hear what my mother had to say. "I am sure that the pull is strong Marie, even though you don't have a face to go with it. I know, I have been there. My sweet girls, it is our duty to make sure your virtue stays in tact as your parents. Not every pack and family feels that this is important but at Red Rose it is. It is our responsibility to ensure that un-mated males do not take a special interest in you two. There is a reason this entire exhibition is chaperoned, because there have been incidents in the past where unmated females have been hurt by unmated males. Your father and I will protect you both until the end of time. So please, don't leave the room Marie. I know you want to, believe me I under-stand, but just trust us until the time is right please."

My body shook with what my mother just said. Where had they brought us? How barbaric are these males? What would they do? What could they do? I couldn't stop shaking. I looked at my mother, her eyes were very stern. Marie was also shaking; my mother was holding her tightly. I went to both of them and wrapped my arms around my mother's shoulders. She rocked us back and forth for a while. It calmed us down, I didn't want to leave this room now.

Marie and I went to sleep that night in silence. It was the first time we didn't talk before bed for as long as I could remember. The hotel sounds echo laughter, shouting and passion. I can hear people my own age having fun, but I am paralyzed to even get up to go to the bath-room. I eventually drift off to sleep but it is restless. When I wake the next morning I see Marie is up on her phone already. I sigh and wave at her, going to the bathroom. She waved back as I went by, putting her phone down and pulling up a piece of paper and beginning to read it aloud:

"Today we have the welcome brunch at 10am in Hall A. Then we have introduction to Mate Bonding Etiquette, that's a two-hour class at 1pm in Conference Room 2. Then we have the banquet at 5pm fol-lowed by the ball at 7pm in the Oak Ballroom…"

"Sounds good I guess." I managed to say as I yawned.

"I think they separate the males and female for the class this afternoon." Marie sighed through the bathroom door. I nodded, then remembered she couldn't see me.

"Probably, I am sure if we were all together there would be some of us that wouldn't be able to keep our hands to ourselves." I muttered. I heard Marie giggle through the door. I started to brush my teeth as she opened the door and came in. She crossed behind me and sat down on the edge of the bathtub. Her face was smiling so broadly I don't think I had ever seen her face so bright.

"I wonder what he is like…" she said wistfully. I put the toothbrush in my mouth and started moving it around. I raised my eyebrows at her and said nothing. Marie started to giggle.

"I hope he is tall, and strong, and handsome, and hung!" she started to laugh as she spoke. I turned to her, laughing through the toothpaste suds. My eyes were coming out of my head. "What Char? It's important!" she told me.

I spit and rinsed my mouth. "I don't think that is important. You should hope he is kind and gentle." Marie nodded, "Of course all that too. I want a mate that is soft and kind as well, but strength is very attractive."

"I think you are looking for an Alpha by the sounds of it." I tease her. Marie's eyes widen and she smiles again. She shrugs tilts her head to the side playfully.

Alphas are a league of their own. As the leaders of all leaders they are notorious in many different ways. Alphas tend to be strong, brave, fearless and intimidating. They can have very short fuses and be very controlling and possessive of their mates. The qualities that make for a great leader such as confidence and control also make for a difficult love life. Personally I have always found Alphas rather intimidating and I have avoided spending too much time in their prescience in the past. Of course, many females find that power and control attractive. It's one of the reasons why it often takes Alphas so long to settle down sometimes with mates, they tend to sew a lot of wild oats with females before choosing just one.

"I know you don't like Alphas, Charlotte. You have to admit though, they have an aura that is hard to ignore." Marie finally said. I shook my head and stared at her, "Not so much for me. I don't like that kind of intensity. It's too much."

I heard a knock at our adjoining room door and our mother's voice, "Girls, time to get up and ready, we have brunch in half and hour!"

We made it down to brunch just in time to grab our seats before the welcoming speeches started. We were seated with another family from Red Rose, John Bushly and his parents. He was a year older then Marie and myself, a nice boy, quiet Omega. He enjoyed cooking at our pack house. I didn't know him very well but he seemed nice. Marie was smelling the air around us and she caught something. "He is in this room." She whispered to me. My father's whole body went ridged, he knew he could smell her too. My mother touched his hand and gave him a knowing smile. I nodded and sighed as she continued to swivel her head.

"Welcome everyone to the 111th Central Prairie Mating Exhibition. We are so thrilled to have a total of seventy-two young unmated men and women here with us today in this room. We are excited to host you on your journey and continue to strengthen our bloodlines, treaties and ties to make our communities stronger. Please enjoy the meal and remember to mind the chaperones." an older blonde woman made a lovely welcome speech. Everyone clapped. We waited for our turn to go to the buffet.

I looked at the spread of food before me. Scrambled and poached eggs, bacon, back bacon, sausage, ham, hash browns, various toasts, crepes and fruits. It was an amazing assortment of food. I took in a deep breath when I got to the bacon, when I caught it. I closed my eyes and breathed in as deep as possible. It was apple pie, a mouth watering smell that filled my whole body with warmth and I sighed heavily. I looked around, who was it that smelled like apple pie? My sister was taking a second helping of eggs; my parents were talking to each other. No one noticed that I had caught it. I shuffled along, trying to compose my-self and return to my seat. I got all the way back to the table before

I realized I forgot to grab cutlery. I rolled my eyes at myself, turning and going back to the buffet table. I was almost back when I smelt it again, so strongly, apple pie. I raised my eyes with a whimper, he was there in front of me. Black jeans, navy sneakers, tan t-shirt. He has dark brown hair, blue eyes, tan skin, sweet rose lips and a small scar on his left cheek. He smiled at me without opening his lips. I couldn't move. I didn't smile, I didn't speak, I just stared up at him, he was at least four inches taller then me.

"Here." He whispered to me, handing me a set of cutlery. I took them from his hands, almost unable to stop shaking. I tried not to make eye contact, "Thank you." I moved away quickly and almost ran back to our table. He didn't follow me, he didn't try to join our table, he just let me go. I sat down with a quiet sigh and started eating. Everything tasted so good, I didn't realize how hungry I was. I didn't look up from my food until there was nothing left on the plate. My parents seemed surprised I ate as much as I did, but no one said anything.

"Dad, I think I know who he is. Can we go and talk to him?" Marie asked, hopefully. Father looked at her face and around the room. He sighed and nodded, "Well this is a safe environment, with chaperones and parents here. I suppose it is as good a time as any. Come my darling, lets go meet your mate." Marie shrieked and hugged him tightly around his neck. My father hugged her back so hard she exhaled unexpectedly. He looked so torn, as only the father of a daughter can know. He rose and took her hand in his, taking a step away from the table. Marie looked around and started to walk off in the direction of the far corner. Mother and I watched as a tall, strong blonde man stood up and smiled at them approaching him. He shook my father's hand and then Marie's. His parents stood with him. "Here we go." My mother whispered to me. I smiled after her, knowing this was what she wanted. I was happy for her.

I turned around, looking for mine. I sniffed the air and I could still smell apple pie. I shifted my eyes to my mother, she was engrossed with the scene with my sister, so I was able to stand and slip away from the table. I decided to go and get a small plate of fruit, so I walked to the buffet and took the plate. Strawberries, melons and… apples. The scent was coming. I froze again. I closed my eyes and took a very deep breath, it was the most amazing smell in the world. "Mate." I whispered to myself as I opened my eyes. I looked to my left and I saw black jeans and navy sneakers. My heart stopped in my chest for a moment. It took all my courage to look to my left and let my eyes rise up to his face. "Mate." He whispered back to me, a small smile spread across his lips. He had kind eyes, very kind eyes. I smiled at him, I was so nervous but I wanted to let him know that I was also kind.

"Hello," he said softly to me. "my name is Clark Duffey from Black Lake Pack in North West Territories. What is your name?"

"My name is Charlotte Gillies from Red Rose Pack in Saskatchewan. It is nice to meet you." I said, just above a whisper.

Clark smiled broadly at me, I smiled back at him, unsure of what to say or do at this point.

"Would you like to meet my family?" he asked me. I looked around at all the people in the room, I realized I had completely forgotten there was anyone else here except he and I. I looked back at him and nodded slowly. Clark reached out to me, he waited for me to take his hand. He didn't rush me, he just smiled at me and waited until I took another deep breath. I reached out and touched his fingers, it was electric. He felt it too, I could tell. I squeezed his fingers in mine and he fulling took my hand in his. Clark gently pulled me with him to a table two in from the buffet. I looked around and saw five people at the table, two sets of parents and another young man.

"Well, Clark who is this lovely vision?" one of the men asked. I blushed slightly and glanced at my feet.

"Mom, dad, this is Charlotte Gillies from Red Rose Pack in Saskatchewan. She is the one." He looked at me with excitement when he said that. "Charlotte, these are my parents, Beta Samuel and Cheryl Duffey of Black Lake Pack in North West Territories."

"Hello." I manage to say with a very small wave.

The mother and father both stand and hug Clark tightly. Then the mother turned to me and hugged me tightly. "Welcome to Black Lake my dear. You will love it, and welcome to the family. Where are your parents?"

I pointed to our table, where my mother was still sitting watching Maria and my father.

The Duffey's all gathered around me and Clark gently squeezed my hand, I started to move forward towards my mother. It felt like it took me an hour to cross the room, when I did I touched my mother's shoulder. She turned around and she saw the small group of the Duffey's with me, she looked shocked, then she started to smile. My mother rose and pulled me in as close as possible. I felt like I was going to explode with excitement and nerves. She turned and began introductions with the Duffey's. I turned towards the table where Marie and my father were. He was staring back at us, he realized he had missed it. He had a profound sadness that I couldn't begin to comprehend. I smiled at my father and mouthed the words, "I love you daddy."

After my father returned and had introductions with the Duffey's we all enjoyed a cup of coffee together. Marie was at the table across the room still with her mate and his family. I couldn't stop smiling, I wanted to relax so badly, I thought my heart would explode. Clark held my hand tightly. He couldn't keep his eyes off me. I wanted to be alone with him to talk to him about anything and everything. I wanted to let him hold me and be close. I wanted to see what it was like to kiss him. I wanted to do so many things, but I couldn't move. We had to wait. Clark pulled my hand to his face and kissed the back of it, almost as if he could read my mind. I smiled at him and did the same. He blushed, smiling a huge smile with such open blue eyes.

"Well, Charlotte I believe we should get going to the classes. You and Clark will see each other at the ball, we may even be able to pull some strings and sit together at the banquet. I'll see what we can do." My father said, looking at his wrist watch. The Duffey's sighed in agreement.

"I'll go and get Marie." My mother said, and she excused herself from the table. Beta and Mrs. Duffey shock my father's hands again and both hugged me warmly.

Clark held both my hands tightly and pressed his forehead to mine, he inhaled my hair deeply, I closed my eyes and inhaled his scent too, "These next few hours will be painful, but I can't wait to see you tonight."

"I will save you a seat." I managed to say in a sweet teasing tone.

"I'll take that seat, and I'll fill your dance card for the evening." He whispered, giggling. Clark kissed my head and my hands before he turned and walked out of the room, smiling at me one last time as he stepped foot out the door.

I turned to my father, he looked at me and pushed my hair behind my ears, "He is kind baby, and his family is good. I know about this pack; they are family oriented like us. He will be good to you; I just wish it wasn't so far."

I hadn't even thought about that; the North West Territories was so far away. I would be so far from home; it was like another world up there. I had never been to the territories. It was all so overwhelming. Marie and my mother returned momentarily and we went back to our rooms. We had to get to the classes but I wanted to use the bathroom first. Marie talked on and on about her mate nonstop. I went into the bathroom, looked in the mirror and I couldn't stop myself. I lurched at the toilet and threw up all of my brunch. It hurt so much, I couldn't stop it. I kept lurching until I emptied my stomach. I started to cry as I leaned back against the wall.

"Charlotte, what happened?!" Marie yelled through the door. "Mom, dad, I think she is sick."

My mother came into the bathroom and found me on the floor. She flushed the toilet and wet a face cloth, she started to wipe down my face and mouth. "Marie, please go to the class. Your father will take you. I will be along with Char in a bit." My mother said softly.

Marie left, though she looked very concerned. I took my glasses off; they were covered in vomit. My mother took them and washed them in the sink for me. After she cleaned me up, my mother sat on the floor with me and held me close. We didn't talk for a bit, she just breathed and let me breathe with her.

"Mom, it's so far away. It's so fast. My heart is beating so fast I can't stand it. I want to hold him and kiss him but I don't know what any of that means or feels like. What if I do it wrong?" I start to blubber on. She doesn't say anything; she just listens to me. I continued, "How do I leave Red Rose and go that far away? I have always loved it at home. I can't imagine leaving you and father, Byron, Michael and Marie. We will never be together again. My life as I know it is over."

I am sobbing now; I can not stop crying. My mother remained silent, she knew what I was saying and how hard it would be. We were never to be the same after today.

"My darling Charlotte, my sweet gentle baby. I have been here where you are. I know exactly how you feel. When I met your father, I moved all the way across two provinces to come to his pack. I was nineteen at the time. I was already with child when I arrived, we had conceived Michael while we were at the exhibition. I know it is scary and overwhelming and it feels like light and dark, life and death all at the same time. You are not alone, you are loved and you are cared for." She said to me, rubbing my back with our heads together.

"Clark Duffey is kind, his family is kind. Your father has a great deal of respect for the Black Lake pack. I believe you will be taken care of there. I believe you will be happy with him. He is the kind of mate we all want our daughters to have." My mother continued. I nodded. I would be alright, it was so far, but I would be alright. I took a deep breath and said, "I suppose I should go and learn about werewolf love and sex."

We both laughed. I felt better. I pulled myself up and brushed my teeth again. My mother walked me down to the class, which I was late for. I apologized when I arrived and hurried to sit with Marie. She linked her arm in mine and squeezed tight. I knew she didn't understand my fear of leaving home. Marie and I were different on that front; she was excited where I was scared. I wanted to be brave, I really did.

"His name is Anthony Martins, his parents are Alpha Antonio Martins and Luna Juliana Martins from Rocky Mountain Pack in Alberta. He is so handsome, Charlotte, I can hardly stand it." Marie whispered in my ear. An alpha, I smirked at her words. I squeezed her arm with my own, she is happy and I am happy for her.

"Now, how many of you know about the marking and how it effects us?" the instructor asked the room. A few wolves raised their hands, most of us nodded. "As you know there is a very personal and each of us will experience it slightly differently. For some, the actual act of sex is not connected to the marking process. Some of you will have sex without marking or have sex with someone who is not your mate. Though we do not advocate this, it is the reality of life. For some, the marking occurs when they are having sexual relations with their mate for the first time. For others yet, the act of being marked or marking a mate occurs separately from the act of sex all together. Everyone is different and there is no right or wrong way to experience marking."

I was listening to the instructor carefully. I didn't realize that marking and sex didn't have to go together at the same time. She continued, "The bite of a marking is painful for a moment, but once it is over there is a wave of pleasure and endorphins that hit both the biter and the receiver of the bite. Also at that time, a mind link between the two mates is established, which will also increase the desire to have sex with each other. This is one of the reasons why sex and marking are often associated with being one in the same."

She continued on for a while on different styles of markings, how to mark if your mate doesn't like to be bitten, establishing consent with marking and so on. Some of it was basic sexual education, but some of it was new to me.

"I hope Anthony wants to mark me tonight at the ball. I plan to mate with him tonight." Marie whispered to me. I grabbed her arm and squeezed it hard, she yelped out slightly. I glared at her, "Are you serious? You just met him today!"

"He is my mate, I am excited. We want to bond right away. I would sneak off if I thought I wouldn't get caught." She hissed. I wouldn't let her go, she knew I would rat her out.

I stared at my sister, she was playing with fire. I thought to myself, how can she want to do this so fast? "Give it some time, maybe learn about him before you jump into that. We have lots of time for all of this." I tell her, I sound like our father. Marie rolls her eyes at me, "I've got the rest of our lives to do that, right now I am so intoxicated by him. I want him so bad."

I understood that. Clark was intoxicating. I thought about what his body looked like with clothes on, it seemed toned and muscular. I am sure he was very healthy and strong. I blushed as I imagined him without clothes on. At this point I don't think the instructor's voice could have touched my mind.

## Chapter 4

My mother was in our room with Marie and I getting ready for the banquet and ball. My father was in the adjoining room waiting for us to get ready. He was already in his suit. There was a knock at my parent's door. My father answered it, I heard the door close and he came in to our room and tapped me on the shoulder. I turned and he handed me a box with a card. I opened the box and it was a red rose wrist corsage on a dark black lace ribbon. I was amazed, the red rose was so perfect and beautiful. I opened the card, it read:

"Dearest Charlotte,

I would be honored if you would wear this red rose to match me, as a token of my commitment to your honoring heritage. I have placed it on a black band to signify my pack heritage as well. This is the joining of our two packs together, as one.

With Love, Clark"

Marie and my mother read over my shoulder. I started to tear up, this was so touching. I put the corsage on my wrist and admired it.

"I can't believe he would do such a thoughtful thing, what a wonderful young man." My mother said, handing the card for my father to read. He read it, smiled and gave the card back to me, "I like him."

I smiled at my father, I liked him too. My dress was done, my hair was done, light make-up was done. Marie was doing some finishing touches on her hair. We were ready to head downstairs.

My father escorted my mother into the hall, Marie and I linked in arms behind them. We found our table, I was pleased to see the Duffey's already there. Clark stood up, walked over to me and took my hand, he kissed it and smiled at the corsage. He had a matching red rose boutonniere in the lapel of his suit. "My goodness Charlotte, you look absolutely beautiful." He said gently. I smiled at him, "thank you, you look very handsome."

He smiled and winked at me, "I clean up ok, but you are a vision." He pulled my chair out for me, after I was seated Clark moved over to my sister's chair and pulled it out for her as well. Marie smiled at him, as he pushed it in for her a hand ripped his off of her chair and held it up with a growl. I turned to see Anthony starring daggers at Clark and growling.

"What do you think you are doing Beta? You keep your hands to yourself." Anthony bellowed at him. I was taken aback by this display of dominance. Clark stared back into Anthony's face, he didn't cow to him, he simply took a small step to the side. "I was only helping my mate's sister with her chair Anthony. There is no disrespect for you here, only respect for my mate and my in-laws."

Clark removed his hand slowly from Anthony's grip and sat down between myself and his father. Anthony glared at him, sitting down next to Marie with a hard grunt. I turned to Clark and rolled my eyes, "Alpha blood is too intense." Clark smiled at me. My hand was resting on the table, he gently took it and stroked my fingers with his. As he leaned forward to kiss my forehead, Clark said in a low voice, "Not all Alphas are like that. Possession does not have to mean aggression. I have met many Alphas who would never pick a fight over something as minor as good manners."

Once the Martin's joined us everything seemed to settle down into place. People were still pouring into the ballroom. There was much excitement in the air. My father stood and raised his glass of wine in the air, "A toast to my two beautiful daughters. Marie and Charlotte, you are both such beautiful, thoughtful and kind young women. Your mother and I are so proud of you both. As a father, it is terribly hard to let my girls go so far from home, but I trust the Moon Goddess you are going on to your everlasting happiness. These two young men you have found seem to be upstanding and well suited. I wish you all the best."

Samuel raised his glass and stood next to my father with respect. Antonio remained in his seated position but still raised his glass. We all drank to my father's toast. I noticed that Marie and Anthony were very close at the table, he was rubbing her back with his hand going lower and lower each time. I knew she did not mind it, but I could see it was making my parents uncomfortable. My father looked as though he was about to say something when Antonio chuckled loudly, "Oh calm yourself father dearest, my son isn't up to anything disrespectful. Anthony is looking forward to claiming what is his. He's been waiting for your little wisp of a daughter for a while now."

My mother and father looked at each other with wide eyes. I shifted in my seat, Clark sensed I was uncomfortable and he squeezed my hand gently. My father looked back to Antonio with a cold face, "I understand he is looking forward to this, we all have been in his place. However, my wife and I would appreciate if your son would show us some respect as Marie's parents as well as respect for the room."

Antonio's face flushed, "As I said, he is not being disrespectful. He is claiming what is his." My eyes shifted to his Luna, she said nothing, in fact she only looked to her husband. She was completely subservient to him. I could read that his word was law, that he was in charge of their pack and their home. There was no partnership in that pack house.

My father's eyes shifted to Marie, she was looking at Anthony's face, not even noticing the intense exchange going on at our table. He sighed and sat back in his chair, father turned to Antonio again and swallowed hard before opening his mouth, "As a father, I would hope you would understand it makes my wife and I uncomfortable to see our daughter being handled like that." Antonio stared back at my father, he took a slow sip of his wine before leaning forward slightly and whispering, "And I would hope that you, as a Delta would recognize your place and respect what an Alpha and future Alpha's words when we say that nothing is amiss here. Look James, you and I both know you are not going to win this discussion so why don't you just be a good boy and back down."

My father's eyes went black; it was the first time I saw absolute rage in his face in my entire life. Without realizing it, I pulled my hand away from Clark and slid back in my chair. I held my breath, the entire room faded away and I was acutely aware of how much anger was at this table. I had to leave, I had to run away from it and I had to take Marie with me. I rose quickly from the table, everyone stared at me. I forced my feet to move and went to Marie's side, I looped my arm through hers and pulled her up with me. I couldn't even hear what she was saying, I am sure she was yelling at me to let her go, but I dragged her with me from the ballroom and down the hall towards the elevators. I realized I still wasn't breathing, I sucked a deep breath into my lungs and slowed down my pace. I could finally hear Marie.

"Charlotte! Why did you do that? Are you crazy?" she yelled at me, trying to pry her arm from mine. I held on to her, I couldn't let her go. We had keep each other safe. "Char, you are crazy, let me go!"

Marie wiggled and pulled her arm until I was unable to hold on. She starred at me, her eyes were angry. "Why did you do that?" she asked me.

I couldn't answer, I just wanted to protect both of us. I am not sure at what point I had stopped moving. I crouched down against the wall, I was breathing hard. My chest was hurting, I wanted to go back to the room. I wanted to go home.

Marie knelt down in front of me, she hugged me tightly and signed, "I love you, Charlotte. I have to go back to Anthony. He will be so disappointed if I don't come back. I don't want him to be angry with me." I searched her face. How could she want to go back in there? I had just taken us away from it. I wasn't going back there. I watched Marie walk back to the ballroom. The elevator dinged and I slowly rose and went inside it. I pushed the button to our floor and went to the room. I couldn't go back to the ball now. I had gotten so upset with the argument between the fathers and I had run out of there like a child. I had a panic attack by the elevators and I had embarrassed myself completely. I was sure everyone in the entire room had seem me leave in a hurry.

I looked at myself in the mirror. My dress looked so nice, my hair and make-up were done and I didn't even get to enjoy it. My mother had done such a wonderful job of my hair, it was all curled and elegant. I sighed heavily and started to take the bobby pins out one by one, setting them on the sink. I was sure I would get to go back to Red Rose after all. There was no way Clark would want me for a mate after that display. I was unstable, sensitive, childish and weak. I couldn't even handle a little bit of arguing without running away and making a scene. I could feel the tears coming from my eyes. I let them fall, first just a few then a sob. I sat down on the floor in the bathroom, a sobbing mess. "I'm sorry." I whispered to myself.

Clark was going to reject me. I was sure of it. I could feel it in my heart. I was too weak to be a Beta mate; I was not a fighter. I was a coward to ran away from conflict, I wasn't strong. I would go back to Red Rose with a broken heart, but at least I knew it. I could prepare for it. I had wanted to go back to Red Rose anyway, that had been the plan since before I arrived here at the exhibition. At least I had the corsage to remember our brief romance. I pulled tissue after tissue out of the box, making a nest around myself on the floor of the used ones. My shoes came off at some point and I ruined my make-up completely.

I wasn't sure how long I had been sitting on the floor when I heard a knock at the door. I was sure it was just my mother making sure I was alright. I got up, not bothering to fix my hair or make-up. I shuffled to the door and opened it. I was shocked to see Clark there with a huge tub of ice-cream and a bottle of chocolate sauce. My eyes were popping from my head and my mouth fell open. He looked at my shyly and shuffled his feet a bit before he spoke.

"I thought you might want some company, and when I am feeling sad I like ice-cream. I hope that is ok. I have to admit I really just wanted an excuse to see you." He said.

I looked at him, he was so handsome. His blue eyes were so soft and kind. I wanted to let him in to the room. I looked around, we didn't have a chaperone. My eyes fell to the ice-cream and I smiled at him, "I like ice-cream. Come in."

Clark exhaled like he had been holding his breath. He stepped inside my room and kicked his shoes off. We sat down next to each other against the bed. He handed me a spoon and put the ice-cream pail between us. I took a bite; the vanilla was delicious. Clark lifted the chocolate syrup bottle up and told me to tilt by head back. I did, and he squirted a small amount right into my mouth. I laughed out loud and so did he.

"I asked your parents if it was ok that I came to visit you unsupervised. They agreed as long as I promised nothing would happen." He told me, taking his own bite of ice-cream and squirt of syrup. I nodded. They trusted him. My family does not trust outsiders easily.

"Charlotte, I wanted to talk to you about our bond." He began, "I want to talk to you about who you are and I want to tell you who I am. I want us to get to know each other so we are ready for the end of the exhibition when you come with me to Black Lake."

I searched his face, I was surprised he mentioned me going with him to Black Lake. "You still want me to come home with you?"

"Of course, you are my mate. You were made for me, and I for you. I would never betray that." He said matter of factly. I smiled at him.

"Shall we play twenty questions?" I asked. I hoped the ice-cream would last all night. He nodded.

"I'll go first," he offered, "how many siblings do you have? Also names."

"I have an older brother, Michael, Marie my twin sister and my younger brother Byron. You?"

"I have one older brother, Heath. He is back at the pack house now."

"Alright, my turn. What are your favorite things to do in your free time?" I asked, tucking my hair behind my ears.

Clark smiled at me, he turned his body to face mine and took another spoon of ice-cream, "I love to run my wolf. I read a lot, mostly non fiction. I love to hunt, trap, fish and track. You?"

"I read a lot, all kinds of different things but I've been getting more into poetry lately. I also like to run my wolf. I can sew and knit. My grandmother also taught me a lot about healing herbs and home remedies." I told him.

"Do you like your pack territory?" he asked me, taking a large squirt of chocolate.

"I love Red Rose. It is nestled right in a provincial park. Its full of wild game, herbs and plants. It's so peaceful and calm. I love all the seasons there; each is more beautiful then the next. I never wanted to leave…" my voice trailed off at the end. I filled the small silence with ice-cream and chocolate.

Clark noticed my face before he answered, "I love Black Lake too. There are no roads in or out so we have to fly into our territory. It is surrounded by dense forest and there is the huge lake just south of the pack house. I go out tracking every day. It is a paradise if you like the outdoors, away from too much noise and civilization."

"It sounds really nice." I whispered to him. Clark took out his cell phone and opened the photo library. He moved closer to me to show me, our shoulders met and rested together as he went through the photos of his territory. The pack house was smaller then Red Rose but it was very well built and it looked homey. The trees didn't seem to end; I could picture Clark getting lost in those woods each day. It looked amazing. I showed him some pictures of Red Rose on my cell phone as well, he leaned his head into mine as we swiped through them.

"What is your favorite colour?" I asked him. I noticed he hadn't moved away from me after we put our phones down. Our shoulders were still touching and he was very close to me. I didn't mind at all, but it did make my stomach flutter a bit.

"Red. I really like anything red." He whispered, smiling at me shyly. I smiled at him and giggled a bit. "Red? Really? Is that a line?"

He chuckled, rubbing his hand on the back of his neck before he answered, "I know you have red hair, and it does sound like a terrible line but it is the truth."

"Mine is green. I think it's because I love the forest so much." I offered. Clark nodded.

"How old are you?" he asked me. I hadn't even considered how old he was before he asked me my age, "I'm eighteen." He looked at me, exhaling slowly, "I am twenty."

I searched his face for a bit before I got the courage to ask him my question, "What did you expected when you knew you might find your mate here?"

Clark smiled brightly and chuckled, he blushed before he answered, "You are actually more beautiful then I expected. I wasn't sure what to expect. I was hoping I would find my mate here. Black Lake is so far from other packs that if we don't find our mates within the pack we all look forward to the exhibition. When I first saw you, you took my breath away."

I smiled at him, his words touched my heart and made stomach flutter, "Any you? Was I what you expected?" he asked me, his face hopeful.

I sighed and rubbed my forehead like I was thinking hard, "Well I have to say you are a lot better looking then I expected. I wasn't sure what to expect, in fact I was pretty sure I didn't want to find my mate. But I have to admit, you are pretty hot."

Clark laughed out loud and kissed my hand. I laughed with him, we were having a wonderful time bonding. It was as like talking to an old friend, as though our souls already knew each other before we could even speak. I wasn't expecting any of that.

We continued on asking various questions about music, movies, television, family and nonsense for over two hours. I liked his laugh, and his smile. Clark put me at ease with his gentle ways, which I was not expecting when I arrived here to meet a potential mate. Found him disarming, I felt a trust building with him that I wasn't planning on. At some point while we were talking he had taken my hand to hold in his. I let him, it was nice. He didn't seem in a hurry to push me which made me feel safe with him.

"Are you afraid of arguments?" he asked me. Clark looked into my face, he seemed to be concerned for me. I shook my head, "Not arguments, I don't like aggression. I don't like the peacocking that Alphas tend to do. That whole display downstairs in the ballroom made me panic. I wanted to get my sister away from them to keep her safe. I always want to keep us both safe, so I instinctually took her to hide away from it."

He seemed satisfied with that answer, he started to tell me his feelings on it as well, "Not all Alphas are aggressive. It is a trait found in many of them, but not all. Some Alphas are protective, sincere and lawful. They don't all have to throw their weight around. I, personally am not a fan of aggression either but I have learned how to deal with it since I started warrior training."

"You seem to know a lot about Alpha behavior." I mentioned, Clark turned his head towards the window and broke our eye contact. He sighed before turning back to me, "Our Alpha at Black Lake is not like most of them. None of ours have been like the typical Alphas for hundreds of years now. My brother, Heath is next in line for Alpha at our pack house. Our Alpha has no children, he and my father are very close so he has been training my brother to take over for him in a year or so."

I am not sure what possessed me to, but I rested my head on Clark's shoulder. He turned quickly to look at me. I didn't raise my head, I just rested there for a minute. I felt his face come to my hair, breathing me in and kissing my head. It was very intimate, quite and sweet.

"Have you ever been in love?" I asked him, just above a whisper. He swallowed before answering, "You mean before now?"

I raised my head to look at him, he met my gaze and smiled at me. "No, not before I met you my darling." I exhaled slowly, he smelled so good. I wanted to know what he tasted like. He read my mind and brushed my lips with his, so slowly. I felt sparks all over my body, his hand squeezed mine. I murmured against his lips, "me neither."

When we broke our soft kiss I couldn't take my eyes off of him. I was falling for this boy, sitting next to me in my room who brought me ice-cream.

"How far have you gone with another person?" he asked me, his voice almost cracked as the words came out of his mouth.

I looked down quickly and buried my face in his shoulder. I was embarrassed, "You were my first kiss, so… that is all I have got." He kissed my hair again, he sighed as though he were relieved.

"I have only kissed a few girls in my life. Nothing else. You are by far the best one though." He told me. He raised my chin to meet his eyes. Clark kissed me again, still so slowly. It was sensual and soft. We kissed for a while, he opened his mouth a little, I followed his lead. He slipped his tongue in between my lips and tickled mine with his. I had no idea what I was doing, but it felt so wonderful. He tasted so good, everything about him was perfect.

When we moved apart he ran his fingers through my long hair, pushing it behind my ears again and giving me small pecks on my forehead and cheeks. "Do you want to be mates?" I asked him.

"Very much. I want you very much." He told me breathlessly. I could feel the longing in his voice, and feel it in his touch. "Me too." I whispered against his lips as I kissed him again.

"Will you come with me to Black Lake after the exhibition is over?" he asked against my lips, refusing to stop kissing me. I smiled at his request. "Yes I will." I told him.

With my words he pulled me closer and into a more passionate kiss. I could tell he had been holding it back for a while but when I agreed to go with him and join his pack he stopped trying to control it. Clark's kisses were heavier and full of lust. I needed to slow him down before things got out of hand. I put my hands on either side of his face and kissed him slowly again. I moaned and touched his tongue with mine, gently. He followed my lead and slowed down. Clark's hands slowed down, resting on my shoulders, he let out a heavy sigh and broke the kiss, resting our foreheads together.

"Charlotte, you are so amazing. I want you to be mine." He whispered into my face. I wanted to be his, I wanted him to be mine. I wanted us to be mates forever.

"Will you mark me?" I asked him. He pulled his head back, stunned at my question. "Are you sure you want me to do that?"

"We don't need to have sex to mark. I learned that today in class actually. Though often sex and marking go hand in hand, marking doesn't have to be done during mating. It can be done in a sensual way instead. Do you want to mark me?" I explained.

"I want you to be mine, all of you. I want more then anything to mark you so everyone knows you and I belong to each other." He said, seemingly out of breath, "will you mark me too?"

I nodded. Clark slid his jacket off his shoulders and started to undo the buttons on his shirt. I started to help him, he looked at my face as I undid his buttons. I blushed slightly, I could feel his gaze on me, it was intense and full of emotions. I was focusing on what I was doing. Once he had his shirt off, Clark pulled me closer to him in between his legs facing towards him. He kissed my lips again and moved down my chin, my neck and to the crook where my shoulder meets it. I followed his example to the same spot on his body.

"You bite first darling; I want to go at your pace." He told me, I smiled and kiss his marking spot. He shivered, I licked it, he moaned. I drew my teeth out and grazed it before biting down with all my might. I tasted his blood, Clark yelped and shook as I gave him my mark. I felt his teeth bite into my flesh and I immediately felt a massive wetness in my underwear. My whole body shook and I was overcome with ecstasy as it flowed from my mark down my entire body and out my fingers and toes. I wasn't expecting to have a sexual reaction to being marked but it was intoxicating. We both let go and licked our marks to seal them.

"Charlotte, this is perfect. I can feel you everywhere inside me. You were made for me." He whispered into the crook of my neck. I nodded into his, I didn't have the words for how he made me feel. I was suddenly exhausted and I wanted to lay down. We crawled up onto my bed, laying down on top of the covers in our clothes. I drifted off with Clark behind me, forming a protective shield using his body around mine.

## Chapter 5

"Darling, wake up and kiss me goodbye." I heard a sweet whisper in my ear. My eyes were closed, I was sound asleep and I could feel my lips were dry. I snapped my mouth open and closed to gather some moisture, "What time is it, Clark?"

"A little past midnight. I shouldn't be found here by your parents. I am sure they would believe I was being inappropriate. I will talk with my father in the morning and arrange a meeting between our parents to make plans for us. I will see you in the morning my dearest." He nuzzled into my neck. I didn't want him to leave, I wanted to fall back to sleep with his scent filling my entire being. For the first time in my life, I didn't really care about the rules and expectations I just wanted him. However, Clark was right. My parents would not be pleased if they found us here sleeping next to each other, be it fully clothed. They had trusted us to be alone, I wanted to make sure we could continue to be alone throughout this exhibition until we arranged the move to Black Lake.

Clark stared down into my eyes from above me, he smiled broadly and kissed my forehead sweetly. I blushed, I wish I knew what to say in these intimate moments. "Alright, see you tomorrow." I whispered. He leaned down to my face, nuzzled my nose and kissed it lightly. I stroked his hair with my finger tips, searching his eyes as if to ask if it was all real. "Good night my darling," Clark mouthed against my lips, giving me one last passionate kiss before he crawled off the bed, slipped his shoes on and out my door.

I screamed into the pillow on the bed, it smelled like him, so sweet and delicious. I thought my heart might explode at any moment. I was so happy, how did any of this even happen. I crept out of the bed, took off my dress. Even though we didn't get to dance at the ball, I felt my dress had been a good luck charm all the same. As it hit the floor I reached for my sweatpants and t-shirt, pulled them on and hung the dress back up in the bathroom. I brushed my teeth and hair out. As I was about to pull it back I looked at my neck in the mirror and noticed the mark. Clark's mark. It was swollen and red, fresh. It hadn't been a dream, we had marked each other and by doing so promised to spend our lives together, to be partners, lovers, friends and confidants. It was an unbreakable bond.

I pulled my hair over my shoulder and braided it loosely. I was tired, it was time to sleep and let my body rest. I crawled back into the bed, turned out the light and went to sleep. I was sure I would have sweet dreams of him.

I was awoken some time later to my father yelling through the walls. My eyes shot open, at first I was sure they were yelling at me. I sat up with a shock and looked around. It was still dark out, I turned the light on and looked around, the clock next to the bed read 2:34 am. I got up quickly and opened the door between my room and my parents room, I rubbed my neck to work out the kinks of sleep and looked around.

My mother was sitting on their bed crying into her hands and my father was on his cell phone talking loudly with someone. I ran to my mother, kneeling down to her and placing my hands on her knees, "Mom, oh god, what is wrong?"

Her eyes rose to meet mine, she was sobbing uncontrollably. She wrapped her arms around my shoulders and wept into my hair. "Oh Char, she took off and we don't know where she is!" my mother managed to stutter out as she continued to weep. My eyes widened. Marie. What was happening?

I looked to my father, he was talking to someone on the phone and pacing around the room, not looking at us. I held my mother while she cried. There was nothing else I could do. My heart pounded in my chest as I waiting for my father to get off the phone. My mother couldn't talk; she didn't form words. I had never seen her like this before.

Finally, my father hung up and turned to face us. His eyes were black again. In one day I had seen his eyes go dark more times then I had ever seen before in my entire life. He was livid, furious, so angry. "Dad, what is happening?" I asked him, still holding onto my mother.

He crossed the room and sat down in the chair, his phone still in his hand, "Marie ran off with that boy Anthony. When we told her we were going to turn in at 1am, that she should come back to the room in about an hour she said she wanted to go with Anthony. I said no, she needed to come back to her own room until they were properly acquainted. Anthony got very angry and pulled her away from us and dragged her off."

I stared at him in disbelief. That wasn't like Marie, she wouldn't disregard our parents like that. She would disagree, pout and whine but never just run off and leave. I shook my head, "Where did they go?"

"I don't know. I went to follow but that damn Alpha Martins stepped in front of me and told me to respect his son's claim. That she was his now, not ours and I needed to step away. I tried to push past him and he sucker punched me in the face. Your poor mother shrieked and I was dumbstruck. We searched the whole ball and main floor but we couldn't find them. I was just on the phone with the leaders of the exhibition, they are sending out some chaperones out to look for them now." My father went on, "I tried to call the Martins' room but they didn't answer. He wouldn't even come to the door. There was no answer at the son's room either. I called Marie's phone but it went straight to voicemail."

"The Alpha hit you?!" I asked. He nodded. I couldn't believe it. That is so primal and primitive. I was shocked someone would do that to our father. Especially when he was just trying to protect his daughter. I was also shocked that Marie would go with his son, who was on the path to be like him I was sure. I listened to my mother crying her heart out, it was devastating. My heart broke a little bit.

"I called our Alpha, he is getting on the phone to the heads of the exhibition. I am hoping that helps us find her. I'm not sure what more I can do." My father whispered. He looked so embarrassed and hurt. "I am going to get some help." I rose and kissed the top of my mother's head. "I'm going to ask Clark and his father to help. They might have some ideas."

My father nodded, he crossed the room to my mother and held her close. I ran to my room, pulling on a bunny hug and out the door. I found Clark's room and knocked hard on the door. I heard movement inside, Clark came to the door. His eyes went wide when he saw me, taking my shoulders in his hands, "Darling what is wrong?"

I told him everything my father told me. Clark's face fell as I finished the story. "We need to find them; we need to find her." I whispered, the tears had started to come finally. He hugged me tightly, kissing my hair and nodded. "Come with me, we need to talk to my father."

Samuel Duffey and his wife we so kind as I told them what had happened. Cheryl rose and gave me a warm hug, "I will go to your parents and try to help your mother. I can't imagine how worried and upset she must be." With that she put on a housecoat with slippers and left the room. Samuel looked at Clark, his eyes very stern, "Son, we need to go and find out where the caves are in this city. That is probably where he's taken her." Clark nodded.

"Caves?" I asked. Clark turned to me and pursed his lips, "It's a rent by the hour hotel type of thing for our kind. They are usually full of seedy types of folks, not much good happens in the caves of a city." I turned up my nose as he explained it to me. I didn't even know there was a place like that.

Samuel nodded, "Clark get dressed and meet me downstairs in ten minutes. We will go and find out where they are. Charlotte, go back to your parents and wait for us to return. I am sure we can find her, and when we do, we will bring her back. I can promise you that."

I hugged him, I couldn't help it. He was being so good to us; I was so excited he was going to be my father in law. "Thank you so much." I felt Samuel nod into my shoulder, "Your family is our family now, we take care of our own, always."

He ushered us out of his room so he could change. Clark kissed my lips lightly and hugged me tight, "We will find her. I've heard of these places; the guys always talk about them as though they are some kind of right of passage to manhood. Trust me, we will bring her back."

"I trust you completely." I told him, staring into his eyes, "I love you so much." He pulled my face to his and kissed me hard. "I love you too, Charlotte. I will call you when I know something." He let me go, kissed my forehead again and went to his room. I sighed heavily and turned back to my own room. I sent out a silent prayer to the Goddess that they would find Marie safe and bring her back to us.

Somehow it was morning, the sun was coming through the curtains of my parents' hotel room. I was laying on the bed with my mother and Cheryl. We had all passed out at some point in the night. My father was still pacing around the room, staring at his phone. He was willing it to ring. I looked at my own phone, no calls or messages from Clark. I signed and rose, trying not to disturb the mothers on the bed.

My father looked at me with sad eyes. He was exhausted but he couldn't sleep. He felt so lost, I couldn't imagine his pain. I crossed the room and kissed the top of his head, "I'm going to order us up some coffee and breakfast, you need to eat something daddy." He could only nod. I went to the phone in my room and ordered coffee, orange juice, eggs, bacon and toast for all of us. I couldn't do much but I could make sure everyone ate.

I went to the shower, trying to distract myself long enough for something to change. The waiting was so hard. I hoped Anthony wouldn't hurt her, taking her away from her family like that, it was so wrong. No respect for us, our traditions or our values. I was starting to become less sad and angrier and I washed my hair. Who did these people think they were?

The food came, I woke up the mothers and we all ate a bit. Father only ate about three slices of bacon and coffee. I couldn't force him to eat anything else. My mother's eyes were all bloodshot from crying, her voice was gone due to the sobs. I was grateful Cheryl was there with us. She had a very soothing prescience, she was so kind. I was thrilled she was going to be my mother in law.

I looked over at the clock, it read 8:17am. I decided enough was enough. I had to try something, so I told everyone I was going to get some ice. I left the room and went to the Martins' room, I swallowed hard as I locked on the door. There was movement inside the room, I could also hear water running. The door opened and Julianna stared back at me, she seemed shocked I was standing there.

"Hello Ms. Gillies how can I help you?" she asked curtly.

"I just want to talk to my sister. I need to make sure she is ok." I told her.

"I can assure you she is safe with my son. He is not a monster, he just a young wolf in love." She attempted to placate me.

I shook my head, "I need to talk to my sister. She has never been away from me for a single night of our entire lives. I need to know she is alright for myself. I want to speak to her right now."

Julianna stared at me, she looked back into the room and stepped out into the hall with me, closing the door, "I am sure your parents are worried. They don't need to be. My son will take very good care of her."

"No Mrs. Martins. Anthony disrespected my family by taking Marie away last night without consent. Your husband hit my father when he attempted to defend his daughter, which I am sure is frowned upon by the exhibition. He wouldn't tell my father where they were last night when we were searching for her in an unfamiliar city where she knows no one but her family. You must know this is inappropriate and an absolute nightmare for my family. I want to talk to my sister, NOW!" I stood my ground, toe to toe with her. My heart was pounding, I had never been so brave in my entire life. I was not leaving until I spoke to my sister.

Julianna looked down at her feet and then back to me. She seemed defeated. Her hand went into her pocket, taking out her cell phone. She dialed a number and put the phone to her ear.

"Hi Tony, yes, can you put Marie on please. Yes, now." She looked at me, handing me the phone.

I put the phone to my ear, "Marie?" "Char? Oh god, thank god you are there. Anthony took my phone and threw it out of the car as we left last night. I'm sorry I didn't call you." It was Marie, I sighed so heavily, it was as though I had been holding my breath since last night.

"Are you alright? Where are you?" I asked.

"I'm in a hotel, it's kind of grungy but it's ok. I have so much to tell you about last night. So much happened after you left." She sounded happy. That was a good thing. Marie was safe, she sounded as though she was content. I relaxed a bit, knowing she was alright.

"What hotel?" I asked. Marie paused and it sounded like she was looking around, "It's called the Hamilton Inn." I nodded to myself, "Ok, is he bringing you back soon? You know our parents are beside themselves."

"Just tell them I am fine. Everything is fine. I will be going back with Anthony to his pack territory the day after tomorrow. Anthony wants to have our ceremony as soon as we get back. I am so excited; he is so dreamy." She told me.

"Marie, I am sending a car to get you right now. Please come back and talk to our parents. I have never seen them so upset. You must understand that how Anthony handled this was unacceptable. If you don't come with Clark when he picks you up I will be very angry with you. Come back now and talk to our parents like an adult." I told her sternly.

Marie sighed heavily. I could tell she wasn't very happy about what I said, but she agreed to come back to our hotel to talk with our parents.

I handed the phone back to Julianna, nodded curtly to her and walked away. I sent a text to Clark telling him where to find Marie. I ran back to the room and told everyone that I had talked to Marie and that she was enroute back to us. My mother started crying again, only these tears were of relief, Cheryl rubbed her back. My father hugged me so tight, I thought he would crush me, "Charlotte, you are our brave angel." I drew back to see my father's face. He was also crying.

After about half an hour later a knock came from the door, my father opened it to find Samuel, Clark and Marie. He pulled Marie close and hung on for dear life. My mother ran to the door and joined in the hug. I couldn't stop myself, I piled on, squeezing my family as hard as I could. We stayed like that for a few moments. When we all finally loosened are grip, I looked at Marie, she had a few bruises on her neck as well as a fresh bite mark.

My heart sank, he had marked her. It was done. Anthony Martins had claimed her as his, our time left together was limited. My father looked at Marie, but he spoke to me, "Charlotte, would you please go with the Duffey's so your mother and I can speak with Marie in private?"

I nodded, I gave Marie a big hug and a kiss on the cheek before I closed the door behind myself. I turned to the Duffey's and hugged them both. "Thank you for all you did for us last night. We were completely lost and you helped us so much. Thank you, thank you, thank you."

Samuel and Cheryl each hugged me and offered warm words. They were such kind people. I loved them already. I turned to Clark and smiled at him, he engulfed me in a bear hug, so tight. I never wanted to let him go. Cheryl started to speak, it took a moment for her words to echo in my ears, "Come now you two, lets get you back to Clark's room. You can rest in there, but no funny business. You are both exhausted and need to sleep." Clark took my hand and we walked to his room with his parents. They went on to their own room, Clark opened the door for me and I went inside.

His room was similar to ours except his only had one bed. Clark took off his shoes and started to undress, he took off everything but his boxer shorts. I tried not to look at him but I failed miserably. He was toned, strong and stunning. I could see that he exercised quite a bit, his muscles were tight. I was suddenly overcome with shyness when my eyes met his. Even though I was in sweat pants and a bunny hug I felt like I wanted to hide more inside my clothes.

Clark stepped forward and pulled at my bunny hug, lifting it over my shoulders and off. He kissed my lips softly, slowly again. These kisses of his were so intense, they were my favorite so far. So sensual. I always wanted more when he pulled away. "Do you want to take off more clothes to sleep? I promise I won't try anything." He offered.

I nodded. I turned and picked up my bunny hug. I put it on the chair in the corner of the room. I slowly pulled my sweats down and put them on the chair as well. I left on my underwear and my t-shirt. I let my braid out and my hair fell down my back, I shook it to let it flow. I turned to face Clark and his breath caught in his chest. We crawled into bed at the same time, I took off my glasses and placed them on the nightstand. He pulled me to his chest and kissed my forehead.

"Thank you for everything. I don't know what I would have done without you." I whispered.

"I would do anything for you my darling." Clark murmured. I could tell he was already drifting off to sleep. I nuzzled in close to his chest and let myself fall asleep in his arms. Apple pie filled my nose, I was in my happy place and I never wanted to leave it.

We slept the day away. No one disturbed us. When I woke up I glanced at the clock, it said 2:47pm. I sighed and rolled over to sit up. My movements woke Clark, he groaned as I pulled away. He opened his eyes slowly to look at me, "Hello darling." His voice was horse with sleep, I could see he wanted to return to slumber but I was restless. I wanted to know what my parents had said to Marie. I reached out and ran my hand through his hair, he purred at my touch. Clark was so sweet and gentle, I was grateful.

"They haven't come to get me yet. It's been hours." I finally pushed through the back of my throat. He nodded, "We should go back and find out what happened." I smiled at him, he knew me so well without knowing me forever. It was as though he could read my mind.

"Have I said thank you yet today?" I asked with a chuckle. Clark laughed, rolling over and sitting up in bed. He stretched his shoulders and arms, I couldn't help but stare. He was so toned and strong, stronger then the average Beta male I noticed.

"Charlotte, you are becoming my mate, my wife and my everything. One day you will give me my children. You will be coming from your home to mine and starting over. Trust me, I am the one who is thankful. Anything I can do for you is not a chore, it is a gift." He told me as he turned and tidied up his side of the bed.

My eyes widened when he said children. It hadn't registered before, but I realized I was looking at the father of my children. They were hypothetical at this point, but that realization made my breath catch in my chest and my heart immediately started to pound. Family was everything to my pack. My family had always been the highest priority, and now Clark was my family. He would give me my children; my mind began to imagine their beautiful faces. He searched my face, "Darling, shall we go?"

"Yes. Sorry, I was just thinking about children." I muttered, getting up from the bed. He giggled, "Having them or making them?"

I put on my glasses and I had to turn away so he couldn't see how much I was blushing. Oh my goodness, I hadn't even thought about that part. "Clark, please, focus." I teased, pulling my clothes on not facing him.

He laughed as he put on his own clothes. "Oh my sweet Charlotte. Trust me, I have been trying to focus since I met you. It is not easy. My thoughts drift to very intimate places, I can't help it."

I tidied my side of the bed and pulled my hair up into a bun. I smiled at him, no longer embarrassed. Now I wanted to tease him, I realized I had a great deal of sway over this big handsome Beta, "Those intimate places will have to wait until we get to Black Lake. However, I do promise they are coming."

Clark's eyes went wide and his mouth dropped open at my words. I laughed at the look on his face, it was priceless. He crossed the room and pulled me into a hug, a small growl moved through his throat, "Oh my god, you can be a sexy goddess can't you?"

I laughed and kissed his lips slowly, pulling away only slightly and whispering directly in his ear, "Only for you, baby."

He groaned and kissed me passionately, I kissed him back. I could smell his desire for me, it filled the room. Clark's hands ran down my back and over my butt, he squeezed my cheeks tightly as he kissed me.

I pulled back slightly, nibbling on his bottom lip, "Down boy, save it for Black Lake." His eyes were black with desire. I took his hand and lead him from the room. "My god woman, I am at your mercy." He whined. I giggled.

We made our way to my parent's room and knocked on the door. To my surprise Samuel answered and opened it up for us. As we stepped inside I could see my parents were sitting together in the chairs, Clark's mother was standing by the window. As Samuel closed the door behind us, I noticed Marie wasn't in the room with them. I let go of Clark's hand and walked to the adjoining door between our rooms, calling her name over and over again. She wasn't there.

"She's not here, Charlotte." My father finally said.

"Why not, where did she go now?" I demanded. As I came back to my parent's room I sought my mother's face, she looked completely exhausted. I turned to my father, he looked defeated. I could feel something terrible had happened.

"Sit down my dearest, and we will talk about it." My father requested. I sat on the floor immediately. Clark walked up beside me and sat down next to me, taking my hand in a supportive gesture. My father smiled weakly at him and nodded to Clark.

"Well, as I had been saying to the Duffey's thank you for bringing my daughter back to us. Unfortunately, it was already too late. Anthony had marked her, claiming her while she was with him. He took her to a cave and did what he desired to her. Marie says she went willing with him and surrendered to him. So there is no recourse for us to proceed with." My father spoke with immense pain in his voice.

"James don't lie to the girl. Marie didn't have a choice to surrender to him. He took what he wanted, that animal took from our daughter, she gave nothing!" my mother cried out, she stood and fled to the bathroom in tears again. Cheryl followed her, giving my father a knowing look as she passed.

"Dad, did he… force her?" my voice came out as though I were a child again. Clark squeezed my hand. My eyes searched my father's, he broke the stare and shook his head.

"I don't know, she said he didn't. When we asked, she defended him completely but she had so many bruises on her neck and chest. I am not sure." My father's voice shook, "But there is nothing I can do now. She renounced our pack and said she was leaving tomorrow with the Martins to go back to Alberta. They aren't staying any longer, apparently after the 'fuss' we made the exhibition administration has been asking them too many questions and they want to leave as soon as possible."

I looked down at the floor and I felt a horrible ball in the pit of my stomach. I started to sob, Clark pulled me into his lap and held me there. He rocked me back and forth as I cried into his chest. Why hadn't I felt her pain? I was her sister; I should have felt it. Had Anthony hurt her? Had he forced her to be his completely? Had Marie fought back? Had he hit her? Choked her? Pushed her? My mind filled with so many scenarios, they flashed across my closed eyes like nails into my head. I was completely devastated.

Samuel stepped forward and spoke slowly, "James, I know this whole exhibition has been devastating for your family. I am sad to say that not all families are like yours and mine, who command respect and dignity of each other. I would like to suggest that my son stay with Charlotte in her room for the remainder of the exhibition. I can speak to his character as he is my flesh and blood, raised properly. I suggest they attend their classes together and continue to bond while still spending as much time here with you and your wife as possible. At the end of the exhibition we will take Charlotte back to Black Lake with us as is tradition. However, she is free to come to you at Red Rose as often as she likes, with or without Clark."

My father came down to the floor and kneeled in front of me. He pulled my face to look into my eyes. His right hand fell to my shoulder and touched my now healing mark, "My dearest Charlotte, your beautiful moments here have been clouded by our turmoil with your sister." He looked at Clark, who gave him a sad smile. "Clark, my new son. You love my girl?"

"I love and respect her more then anything in this world." Clark told him without a pause. My father nodded, "You will stay with her and comfort her… appropriately until it is time to leave." Clark nodded. He kissed my forehead and continued to rock me as I shook.

Our fathers faced each other and shook hands. "Samuel, I am thankful my daughter is mated to your son. I have complete trust and faith in this young man. He will be an excellent husband." My father told him. Samuel nodded.

I forced words through my throat as I continued to sob, "I want to see her to say goodbye."

My father lowered his head, "The Martins told us she is not to be disturbed by us any longer. Since she resigned from our pack I have no command over it. She begged me not to trouble them any more. They won't let us see her."

"What?!" I cried, "I can't even say goodbye to my sister?" Clark pulled me closer and rocked me harder, I couldn't stop the sobs from pouring out of me. I was hurt and angry all at the same time. My wolf howled in my head. My heart was breaking.

The rest of that terrible day was spent with the Duffey's, their family consoling mine. I had no idea how to process this kind of pain. My mother stopped talking all together and just lay down on the bed, Cheryl sitting with her silently. Samuel took my father out of the room to go and get some drinks. Clark had carried me to my room and we sat on the floor watching various television absentmindedly. He ordered us ice-cream and a huge platter with various sauces and fruits came up. He placed it between us and we ate it, not needing to talk. Clark understood my pain without having to discuss it, he could feel it through our bond. He just stayed with me, holding me when I needed it and giving me space when I needed.

"I love you, you know." I told him suddenly. He smiled and nodded, "I know darling."

His presence helped ease my pain so much. It was still very sharp but I was starting to form a plan in my head. I wasn't going to let Marie leave for Rocky Mountain without saying goodbye to her. I didn't care what the Martins said, I didn't care if they were angry with us. I needed to see her, to tell her I loved her and that no matter what happened I would always be there for her. Forever.

Clark took a large spoon full of ice-cream and searched my face, "So what's the plan darling?"

I giggled and I took my own spoon full, "This bond is getting stronger all the time isn't it?" He nodded, "It will be even stronger after we mate. We will be able to link our minds and talk without words." I shushed him, he looked at me and shrugged, "What, it's the truth."

I smiled and shook my head at him, "You boys and your obsessions with sex."

He smiled seductively and whispered in a husky voice, "It's not an obsession with sex, it's an obsession of sex with you and only you."

"Down boy." I teased, Clark groaned and I lifted a strawberry from the ice-cream and took it into my mouth slowly. "You are giving me chills darling, perhaps you should also behave."

I laughed and nodded. "What if I am really bad at sex?" I asked him seriously. He shrugged and giggled without missing a beat, "Then we will be bad together. I don't know any more then you do about it." I nodded, he made everything so easy. I would never have thought I would be able to have an open conversation like this with anyone. Clark was my other half; it was getting stronger each day. I was enjoying the ease of it. I wasn't expecting the mating bond to be so smooth, no one had told me that. I suspected it wasn't this easy for everyone.

"Plus if we are really bad at it, we have lots of time to practice and get better at it." He suggested. I laughed, "Oh yes, perhaps four or five times a day? Is that sufficient practice?"

Clark took a dab of whipped cream and pressed it to my lips, "Maybe more, it depends on how much stamina you have darling." I paused, he was very alluring at this moment. I licked his finger and pulled it into my mouth, sucking the whipped cream off.

He wasn't expecting me to do that, and he groaned loudly before his entire body shook. Clark's eyes rolled back into his head and his head fell forward. I let go of his fingers, a bit alarmed, "Are you ok?" I asked. Clark raised his eyes to meet mine, they were cloudy and warm. I realized what had happened. My eyes went wide and I moved around and kissed his cheek.

"That was so embarrassing." He muttered, "I completely lost control and I didn't even touch you. My god, Charlotte, you are going to be the death of me."

I giggled, pulling his face to mine and kissing him. "Perhaps we need to work on your stamina and not mine when we get home." Clark groaned and growled a bit into my mouth. He nodded and ran his fingers through my hair. After a while he rose and went to the bathroom to shower, I couldn't help but giggle to myself. This strong Beta was completely at my mercy; to a prowess I didn't even know I possessed. I continued to eat the ice-cream on the floor and watch TV listening to the incoherent mutterings mixing with the sound of running water from the bathroom.

When Clark came out about twenty minutes later he suggested we eat some real food. We got dressed and went down to the restaurant on the main level of the hotel and had dinner just the two of us. I looked around to see a lot of other young wolves doing the same thing with their mates. There was a mixture of excitement, dread and sadness in the room. I was grateful that my experience was happiness when I looked at my mate.

Clark and I talked freely about our plans for the rest of the exhibition. Our parents had already announced it to the administration that we were mates, so our time together was not called into question by the chaperones. We still had two days of classes to attend, so we talked about that.

"Do you think we will learn anything at these classes?" I asked him.

Clark shrugged, "I am not sure. A lot of them are about etiquette based on what my brother told me. He has attended three times but didn't find his mate."

I nodded, "So things we already know." He nodded with me, "Apparently a lot of young wolves aren't taught about the traditions they way we are. Some just try to run off and start fucking in the bushes like animals."

I laughed, I had never heard him swear before. He blushed, realizing what he had said.

"There is also a class about our roles in our packs. Alphas, Betas, Deltas, Gammas, Warriors, Scouts, Omegas, etc." Clark went on. I nodded, "So you will be a Beta yes?"

"Yes. My brother, Heath is to be Alpha of our pack. No Luna yet though, he hasn't been lucky. Heath had hoped he would find her at the exhibition but it didn't happen. Each time he went he came back more depressed, it was hard to watch him go through that. Heath has thought about taking a chosen mate, but that tradition isn't very appealing to him." Clark told me.

"Betas and Deltas are similar in my experience based on their rolls." I offered. Clark smiled, "Yes, very similar. My brother has asked me to be his Beta because he trusts me completely. His Delta is our cousin Timothy, he is already mated and a very steady guy. Heath doesn't have a Gamma selected yet but I am sure by the time our Alpha steps down he will."

"So what do you do at your pack house?" I asked him. "I am one of the top training warriors there. Myself and Timothy are very fast and strong. I am the head of our warrior division so I organize the exercises, drills, new recruits and training. I like it because it allows me to be outside a lot moving around instead of inside in an office doing the paperwork." He told me.

"That sounds great. I am glad you like your role." I smiled at him.

"I know you don't like Alphas very much. I know their aura makes you uncomfortable, but I assure you our Alphas are not that typical. One can lead without becoming a dictator or a monster." Clark reminded me.

"I know. I understand that. I am just happy you are not an Alpha. I am not sure how I would have handled it if I were mated to one. I never wanted to be a Luna, I didn't want to be confined to an office and tied to a mate who has too much power over too many people. It makes me uncomfortable to even think about it." I admitted. Clark's eyes rose and searched mine, "Would you have rejected me if I were an Alpha?"

I couldn't lie to him, "I don't know. Honestly I might have." His eyes filled with pain, he cleared his throat and adjusted in his chair. I reached across the table and took his hand, squeezing tightly. "That isn't the case though. You are Beta, I love you and I will be by your side until the end of time. We are fated to be together, and I am happy to face this life at your side and into the next one."

He smiled at me and raised his eyebrows, "It's funny you know, girls always chase the Alphas. They long for that power, control and status. I see my brother have to cast them off at our pack house all the time. Heath hates the obsession with his station. Alphas always get the girls, and here you are, my perfect mate, who could not run fast enough from an Alpha. You were made for me, it's as simple as that."

"Gross, Alphas. Mmm, sexy Betas." I teased, Clark laughed out loud. He kissed my hand lightly as we rose from our table and headed back to my room. As we crossed the foyer I looked around to see so many paired wolves. The hormones were in the air all around us. I could smell it, I'm sure Clark could as well. I knew he wanted to kiss me, but I made him wait until we were back to my room. I didn't think the whole hotel needed a view of us in an intimate moment.

As the door closed behind us, he locked it and pulled me towards the bed, I could smell his arousal. He sat down and pulled me between his legs, kissing my lips deeply. I returned his kisses slowly, making them last longer and soothing his urgency. Clark moaned into my mouth, letting his hands wrap around my waist and pulling me as close as possible. He broke our kiss after many minutes and looked up at me with a wink, "So my darling, what is your plan with Marie? I know you have one and I want to be a part of it."

I looked down at him with a smile on my lips and rested my forehead against his. "Well I know what my father said, that she has renounced us and we are no longer her pack. I know the Martins don't want us to try and go to her, but I figure if I run into her by accident I could get to say goodbye to her at the front desk if we both just happen to be there at the same time."

Clark nodded, "That could work. You will have to be down there impossibly early though. We have no idea what time they will want to get out of here." "I agree, so I figured I would head downstairs at 4am tomorrow morning just in case they try to sneak her out of here before dawn. I'll just camp out down there on the sofa until she appears." I told him.

We both gazed at the clock, it was 10:04pm. "If we are getting up at 4am, we had better get some shut eye then darling." Clark suggested, he placed his hands on either side of my hips lightly. I leaned down and captured his mouth with mine. I tickled his lips with my tongue, tasting him thoroughly. I let my kisses trail down his throat to his marking spot and nibbled on it softly. I drew my fingers through his hair tenderly and returned my mouth to his as quickly as I had left it. "Mine." I whispered breathlessly. Clark groaned helplessly beneath my kiss, his whole body started to shake again and he pulled me closer.

"Charlotte, this isn't fair!" he cried out, a look of ecstasy on his face, "you have complete control over me and I can't even touch you without breaking the rules."

"Good things come to those who wait my love." I teased him, nibbling on his ear lobe, "Now go clean yourself up and come to bed with me."

All Clark could do was agree. He rose from the bed, adjusted himself and shuffled to the bathroom. I heard the water turn on in the shower and giggled to myself. The familiar mutterings followed suit. I had never considered myself a particularly sexy girl. I mean, I wasn't bad looking or anything but I had red hair, green eyes and freckles all over my face. I didn't have big pouty lips, large breasts or a stunning figure. The males at Red Rose never really turned their heads as I walked past. I didn't have lines of admires, but I never wanted them anyway. I felt as though Clark had awoken something inside me that was primal. I was kissing him in ways I never imagined I would kiss anyone, not even a mate. It was all so new to me, yet it felt being with him was more natural then breathing.

I changed into pajamas and went to bed. Clark joined me after about twenty minutes, cuddling in behind me, forming a protective shield around me again.

"What do you mutter to yourself in the shower?" I asked him. He pulled me closer to his chest and exhaled into my neck.

"I was talking to my wolf about what we are going to do to you when we get you home." He whispered in a low voice, he kissed my mark and shots of ecstasy coursed through my body, I let out a moan. He licked it over and over and the shots fired again, getting stronger each time. Finally, he bit down on my mark and I felt my body release a powerful force. I moaned into the pillow, I was worried my parents would hear us. I had never experienced anything as intense as that by myself.

Clark stroked my stomach and kissed my neck affectionately. He chuckled to himself, "Now we are even my darling. Don't start something you can't finish."

I leaned back and kissed him tenderly. "You are incredible." I whispered. Clark rubbed his nose against mine, "Sleep my darling, we have to be up in five hours."

I turned back and let my body fall asleep in his arms, so safe and content.

# Chapter 6

When the alarm went off at 4am I sat up with a start in bed. Clark hit the snooze button, annoyed and still half asleep. I must be out of my mind to be getting up at this hour, in a way I was, I needed to see her go. Marie and I had never been apart, our entire lives were spent with each other. I couldn't let her go without saying goodbye.

I scooted out of bed and into the bathroom to wash and get ready. The hot water did wonders that early in the morning. When I was done and ready I came out to see Clark was still in bed, moaning slightly. "You can stay here and sleep if you need to. I understand." I told him, getting fresh clothes from my suitcase. When I said that, Clark sat up at attention and forced his eyes open. He swung his legs over the edge of the bed and stood up, "No Charlotte, I will be there with you every minute. This is important to you so it is important to me."

I loved him so much, more each day. I smiled as my half asleep mate moved about our room, bumping into the furniture trying to get to the clothes in his suitcase. Clark dropped his boxer shorts to the floor and began to dig through his bag looking for clothes. His butt was very chiselled and defined. I started to wish he would turn around so I could get a look at his other side. He must have sensed it because he turned to meet my eyes and said, "Hey stop objectifying me, my eyes are up here."

I laughed out loud and pretended to try and take a look around him at the front, "But there is so much I see that I like."

Clark blushed and pulled clean boxer shorts on quickly. I laughed again, I had no shame when it came to him. I enjoyed playing with him, it was so easy. He pulled on some clothes and slipped his shoes on. "Coffee?" we both said at the same time, smiling at each other we snuck out the door and headed down to the lobby where they had a guest service coffee station open 24 hours.

We fixed ourselves on the sofa by the front desk with our coffees and waited. Hours past, the sun started to peek outside the large windows. Clark ended up falling asleep next to me leaning back on the sofa. He was such a kind person, I looked him as he gently snored next to me. I looked down at my third black coffee of the morning, it was 8:39am when I heard the elevator ding open. The Martins strode out like they owned the entire hotel.

My entire body went ridged, Clark woke up next to me and stood up. The entire family stared at me, the father and son glaring. Anthony let out a low growl, "We told your family not to bother us anymore. She is mine now; she is coming with me."

I stood up and let my eyes fall to Marie. She was standing behind Anthony; he had pushed her there. I could see she was torn by the look in her eyes. "I am not going to try to convince her to stay. All I want to do is say goodbye to my twin sister. She and I have never been apart before. We share a bond only twins can understand. Please let us say goodbye to each other. Please, Anthony." I begged him. I heard Marie whimper as I spoke. He looked at her, visibly annoyed by her sound. I could see his mother whisper something to him that I could not hear. Anthony looked back at me and Clark.

"Fine, but she doesn't leave this lobby and only for a few minutes." He shot at me. I immediately ran to Marie who took cautious steps towards me past Anthony. He growled at her slightly. We met in between, I pulled her very close and buried my face in her hair. She smelled different, not worse or better, just different. Clark approached us by a few steps but hung back so as not to agitate Anthony.

I pulled away just so I could see her face. She was scared. Her neck was still badly bruised; she was also shaking. "Marie, I love you so much. I am going to be going to Black Lake territory with Clark after the exhibition. I will write to you every week once I arrive." I told her. Marie nodded at me. She pulled me closer and whispered in my ear, "Have you mated yet?" I shook my head. "Be careful. My first time with Anthony was very rough. I bled a lot and I passed out. When I came to he was on me again and again. It was very scary." She told me.

I searched her face, "Marie that is not ok. You know that." She shrugged and looked at her shoes, breaking eye contact, "He's an Alpha, it's his right, he says. He says I will get used to it, I hope so because it isn't getting better."

I pulled her closer, "I love you Marie, please don't stop communicating with me. I will write to you every week. Write me back, and never forget that we all love you so much." I could feel her holding on to me for dear life, as though I would never see her again.

Anthony cleared his throat, "Marie, here now." Her body went ridged and she stepped away immediately. Her shaky voice managed a few words, "Goodbye my dearest sister. I will write to you, I promise." As she pulled her fingers from mine, I felt as though a small part of me was being ripped away. Anthony slung his arm around her shoulders and dragged her past me out the front door. None of them looked back. Clark pulled me close to his chest as I began to sob, I had held it in for our entire goodbye. I cried so hard I had to fight to breathe. He picked me up and carried me to my room, putting me in the bed and curling around behind me. He let me sob for hours, just rubbing my stomach and kissing my hair. We didn't talk, he didn't try to make it better he just held me as I was in more pain then I had ever been in my life.

"He is raping her." I whispered. Clark nodded, somehow he knew. I had assumed as much, based on what his father had said about the caves of cities. "What if he kills her?"

"He won't kill her darling. She is still his mate. Anthony loves power and control, but if he killed her he would be lost. That is how it works, once we find our mates we need them to function. Especially Alphas, if they don't have a Luna they are a complete mess. It is different if we never find them in the first place, but once they are lost, we become lost." Clark explained to me. I nodded, trying to control my breathing.

I finally turned around to face him, I stared into his eyes and I asked, "What if our first time hurts?" "Then we will go slow or stop if you want to." He said softly. "What if it hurts me so much and you don't want to stop." I shivered. He pulled me close to his chest and kissed me hard, "I will never, ever hurt you Charlotte. Never, I don't care if I am lost in the moment and I don't want to stop, if you are hurting we will stop. Nothing is more important then you." He told me firmly.

I searched his face, I believed him. I trusted him. I wanted him, right now. I pulled my shirt off and my pants down under the covers and un-did my bra quickly. Clark looked at me dumbfounded, "What are you doing?"

I motioned for him to sit up and I took off his shirt and started to undo his jeans, "I want you, right now." He stopped my hands and touched my face, "Are you sure Charlotte, it's against the rules."

"I don't care, I want you, all of you, slowly." I hissed at him, he let me undo his pants and pull them off. I pulled his boxers down too and tried not to look. We lay back down under the covers, kissing softly and touching each other. Clark moved over top of me and let his hands explore, I felt him and it was energizing. We spent some time becoming more comfortable with each other's bodies before he held my hands and rested himself between my legs, "Char, this will hurt and it probably won't last very long. I will go slow ok." I nodded, "I know, I trust you Clark."

He kissed me again and moved forward, I clenched. I tried to breathe, he stopped. Clark moved forward again, I felt a sharp pain, I cried out and pulled him closer. He exhaled and moaned at the same time. We were slow and timid, but we were together in the moments. Our first time was not magical or amazing but we were one. He kissed me, I moaned his name, he didn't last very long. I didn't feel a lot of pleasure, but when it was over we held on for dear life. I knew it would get better with time. "Are you alright darling?" he asked me, worry on his face. "I am fine. It wasn't that painful actually, I thought it would hurt a lot more." I confessed.

"It helps if you are aroused." He told me, and I nodded. "I'm sorry I didn't last very long." I giggled and nibbled on his bottom lip, "We will just need to practice right?"

He laughed and kissed me, pulling me on top of him for another go. We were not flawless lovers but we were madly in love with each other and our sex reflected that.

# Chapter 7

If our parents knew we had mated they didn't let on. Clark and I attended the remainder of the exhibition together. There were sexual education classes, parenting classes, politics classes, pack relations classes and several guest speakers. His parents and my parents became friends over the course of the exhibition. It was a sharp contrast to the Martins. As the exhibition drew to a close I became painfully aware that I was not going back to Red Rose. I started to think about all the things I was going to miss about our territory.

I had asked Clark to let me have our final night at the exhibition with my parents alone. He wasn't thrilled at being apart but he understood. That afternoon, after the final guest speaker Clark held me close in front of my hotel room door. His hands on my hips, slowly edging lower once in a while. He kissed me gently, smelling my hair as he buried his face in my neck. I breathed him in too. "What do I smell like to you?" I asked, "Eucalyptus. It's the cleanest, purest smell in the world. I can't get enough of you." He murmured, inhaling deeply again. I giggled, "You smell like apple pie to me, only you are twice as delicious." A very low moan came from Clark's mouth. Almost a growl. I needed to slow him down or I wouldn't be able to convince him to leave me for the night.

"Clark," I whispered against his ear, "I need to go and spend some time with my parents. I probably won't see them for a long time." Clark nodded, "I will take you there anytime you want to go. I promise." I knew he would, he loved me so much. I knew I had Clark Duffey wrapped around my finger and he would do anything to make me happy. I could have abused it, but I could never do that to him. I loved him fiercely, with every fibre of my being.

"I am more in love with you each day." I moaned into his ear. He squeezed me one last time, then exhaled slowly and looked into my face, "Me too my darling. Have a good night with your parents. I will come to you in the morning, if I can stay away that long." I smiled up at him, kissed his cheek and let myself into my room. I closed the door slowly behind myself, watching him missing me already.

I went into our adjoining room where my parents were sitting waiting for me. I hugged them one at a time, I wanted to commit each moment of tonight to my memory. We went out to dinner and had a wonderful time. When we got back to the hotel my father suggested that he take a walk so my mother and I could have some quiet time together. It was a wonderful gesture.

"Charlotte, I am so sorry your exhibition was clouded by everything that happened with your sister." She said as we entered the room. I sighed and closed the door behind us. "It's ok mom, I am not hurt by that. I am very happy with Clark."

"I know my sweet girl. I hope you will forgive me but I think we should have a talk about mating and heat. I know you haven't had your first one yet and it is important to know what to do. Your grandma

Daisy explained it to me, and her mother to her. I didn't get the chance to explain it to Marie, I worry what she will do when it happens." My mother took my hand and sat down with me at the edge of the bed. I blushed slightly and couldn't make eye contact with her.

"Ok." I pushed through a throat full of fog. She smiled at me knowingly, "I know you must feel the pull by now of the mate bond. When you have your first heat, which will happen after your nineteenth birthday, you will become ultra fertile during this time. Pregnancy can occur at any time like a normal human, but heat is the easiest time to conceive. I realize you are only eighteen so you have a year before it will happen but it is important to be prepared."

I listened intently. There was a lecture about heats during the exhibition but only explaining the hormonal mechanics of it, not the actual effect it had on us as werewolves.

"Now, my dear, when you go into heat you will know it is coming on. Your insides will become uncomfortable, you won't be able to keep any food down and your skin will feel as though it is crawling. Your temperature will spike and you will not be able to sleep. Your mate, Clark will ease all of these sensations by making love to you. Once you have completed the mating the symptoms will temporarily subside, but they will return. Heats can last anywhere from two to five days, depending on the wolf." My mother explained to me, I nodded. "There are herbs you can eat to lessen the symptoms, which your grandma Daisy told me about. I had to take them once or twice when my heat was particularly long, and it helped a great deal. If you mix chamomile, ginger, tea tree and a single stem of primrose in hot water it will ease the heat away. I will write the recipe down for you before you go tomorrow."

She took my hand and rubbed it gently. "Now, you understand the mechanics of sex right?"

I looked into her eyes and I took in a deep breath, "Mom, I think I understand how sex works." My mother searched my face, she opened her eyes a little bit and smiled, pushing my hair behind my ears, "Well, let's keep that little tidbit between us. I don't really think your father needs to know."

I smiled and nodded. "It's nice with Clark, mom. He is sweet and gentle. I like it with him." I told her. My mother smiled back at me, "It should be nice and gentle my dear one. Especially at first."

I thought of Marie. My thoughts drifted to her and what she had told me about her and Anthony. I thought about what she had told me, about how it had hurt. My experience wasn't like that, and I was grateful for it. I was relieved actually.

"I know what you are thinking Charlotte, a mother knows her children. I felt when he hurt her, each time. I know all about it Charlotte." She told me, "and someday, when you have children you will feel their pain too." I pulled my mother close and held her, I felt some tears fall on my shoulder. I didn't realize how she knew; she said she had known before Marie had told me. No wonder the pain was so hard for our mother the morning after Marie had disappeared. She knew exactly what had happened because she could feel it.

"I'm so sorry mom, I didn't know." I whispered. She shook her head into my shoulder, "No darling you have nothing to be sorry for. I love you and we are so happy for you and Clark. You deserve this. You deserve someone who will treat you like he does."

"I love you mom." I told her. "I love you too my dearest." She held on to me tightly.

We talked for a while about the move to Black Lake. My mother said she would have my clothes, books and other stuff sent via air mail to me. I told her how sad I was about not going home to Red Rose. She told me she had felt the same way when she went with my father after their exhibition, but she reminded me that it does get easier with time. I would miss my brothers so much, especially Michael. I hoped they would visit us later in the summer. I was happy to have tonight with my parents.

By the time my father came back my mother and I we alternating between laughing and crying together. He smiled when he saw us together, "Ah my lovely ladies as it should be." I got up and hugged him tight. "Thank you daddy, for everything." I said.

"You are welcome my dear girl. I am happy for you. The Duffey's are wonderful people and I am thrilled to be welcoming them into our family." He told me.

My parents and I talked into the night. It was easily past midnight when I went to my room. I sat in the dark, looking out the window. I whispered in my mind that I wished Clark was there with me. I was almost asleep when I heard a knock at the door. I got up and looked through the hole, it was Clark. I opened the door.

I smiled at him, I had mind linked with him and didn't even realize it. He looked back at me, half asleep, in his pajamas, no shoes. I pulled him by the arm into my room and into my bed. I climbed against his chest and held him close. Clark fell back to sleep in a matter of moments, snoring lightly. I kissed his cheek and found my own sleep. I never slept better then when he was with me. He was quickly becoming the one thing I could not live without.

The next morning, I awoke to find him still sound asleep, sprawled out on his side of the bed. Clark was a heavy sleeper I was learning. I rolled over and lay my head on his chest. His heartbeat was steady and strong. I suddenly felt a little bold and decided to start kissing up his arm and move up to his face. I felt him stir, as he opened his eyes I kissed him awake. I pulled him on top of me and ran my finger nails down his back, Clark growled at my touch. "God Char, you are so sexy I can't even stand it. I have to have you now." He purred into my mouth.

"Good, because I don't like being kept waiting." I whispered hastily.

Our pajamas became distant memories on the floor as our passion heated up the room. Afterward, Clark stayed on top of me heaving his breath. I kissed the top of his head while running my fingers through his hair. I loved his hair, so lovely and dark. He was a handsome guy, my mate. "You are a Goddess, my darling." He murmured into my breasts. I laughed, his breath tickled. He lifted his head to look at me, his dark eyes were so tender. I placed my hand against Clark's face and stared into this eyes, I wanted to get lost in this moment. We stared at each other for a while.

"Char, can I tell you something?" he asked, sitting back on his knees. I nodded, sitting up as well. "I was so nervous to come here and meet my mate. I wasn't sure you would want me when you saw me. When I caught your scent by the buffet table I felt my heart stop. I was afraid you wouldn't be impressed with someone who was from the North, from a smaller pack who wasn't a powerful Alpha. I wasn't sure I would be able to be enough for you."

I cocked my head to the side and pulled my hair behind my ears. Clark continued to talk, "When I walked up to you and I saw your face everything melted away. You are so perfect. When we talked that first night I realized I didn't need to be anyone else because you were made for me." I kissed him sweetly to stop his rambling.

"Clark, my love, you are so sweet. I felt the same way honestly, word for word." I told him.

"Are you sure you want to come with me to Black Lake? I know you would rather be in Red Rose with your family." He offered, uncertain. I stared at him.

"Are you serious?" I asked him, suddenly annoyed. I pulled the sheet with me as I got out of bed and put my glasses on. "We just made love, you told me I was your everything and then say I don't need to come with you to Black Lake? If you are trying to be chivalrous don't bother. I know you love me; you know I love you. I want to be with you, I choose to come with you to Black Lake and make a life with you there. You can recite poetry all you want, but never ever suggest that I leave you again. I will not, I can not. There is no other for me, so no more of this nonsense."

Clark smiled at me, rose from the bed and picked me up off the ground. He kissed me all over my face. "Let's get you packed up darling. I can't wait to show you our home."

Our flight was at 1:20pm so we had to be at the airport by noon. We said our goodbyes to my parents at the hotel. Mother and father cried with me as we walked to the car. "I will call you when we arrive at the pack house, and I'll let you know how everything is." I told them. The Duffey's helped me with my bags. I hugged my parents one last time, knowing it wouldn't be the last time I saw them. I got in the rental car and we were off to the airport. When it was time to board, Clark took my hand and we boarded. I had flown in planes before, but this one was very small. It fit about eight people. Clark held on to my hand as we boarded. I was very nervous but the take off was uneventful. The flight to Black Lake was about three hours, Clark spent the majority of it pointing at different landmarks out the window below us.

"Darling, look, we are almost there." He said, motioning for me to look down. I saw a huge mass of forest, it stretched as far as they eye could see. There was snow topped mountains in the distance and a large body of water in the centre of the forest. It was breathtaking. I had never seen so many trees in my life. I squeezed Clark's hand, "Oh my god, it's so beautiful."

He smiled at me and kissed my temple. "I'm so glad you like it Charlotte." His parents smiled at us. "The humans call it Clive Lake. It is close to the centre of the territory, no human settlements around us. We are essentially isolated from the outside world. The next closest pack is at Slave Lake, with more then triple our number of wolves but we have a treaty with them. We combine forces to deal with rogue problems, though because we are so far north we only get two or three of those a year." Clark explained to me as we descended towards the lake.

Once we landed Clark helped me out of the plane and lead me to a Jeep. Once I was inside the warm heated vehicle he loaded our bags into the back and drove us from the makeshift airport down a snowy dirt road into the trees. I was astonished by the forest. In Saskatchewan we didn't have a lot of trees and forests. Red Rose was nestled in the one area of forest in the province, and even our forest didn't feel nearly as dense and rich as this one. There was still a great deal of snow on the ground here, being so far north I would have to adjust to the longer cold weather. Also, there will be less daylight throughout the year up here. I was in awe of my surroundings, I wanted to explore these forests with Clark. I wanted to track and hunt, shift into my wolf and run wild for a bit.

Clark reached over and stroked my hand before he shifted gears, attempting to bring me back to him. "What do you think of the forest darling?" he asked, not taking his eyes off the path in front of us. I felt a huge smile spread across my lips. "I can't wait to get out and go exploring!" I cried out. I was overjoyed with the natural beauty around me. Clark smiled, "I will take you out tomorrow. We are about twenty minutes from the pack house and we will get you settled in. You will need to meet the Alpha and Heath first of course."

"Yes. Right, your Alpha. Tell me a bit about him. What is he like?" I asked.

Clark shifted gears in the Jeep, it shook slightly on the uneven path, "Alpha David is a very wise and just man. He doesn't like dishonestly, laziness or apathy. He has been running our pack for over forty years, many of our members don't remember a time when he wasn't the Alpha. David is like a second father to me and Heath, he has been at every game, birthday party, holiday. He is a wonderful, dedicated leader."

I smiled and listened intently, "However, he is getting older and he has told us all his time as Alpha is coming to and end. David has no Luna; he never did find his mate. He thought about taking a chosen mate but we wolves often disregard that if we don't experience the pull. David decided not to bother, he has dedicated his entire life to our pack. He is not what you have experienced as a typical Alpha, you will see what I mean when you meet him."

"I hope he likes me." I confessed. Clark laughed and touched my knee with his hand, "I love you, so he will like you darling, trust me."

"And your brother?" I asked. Clark sighed with a smile on his face, "Oh my dear big brother. He is funny, smart, loyal, dedicated. Heath is a character; he has a mind for strategy. Sometimes I think he is a bit stubborn and doesn't like to back down from a fight, but he has good intentions."

"Are the two of you alike?" I was curious, even though I would be meeting him in a few minutes. "Sure, a bit. We look alike for sure." He told me. I nodded. We took a small dip down into a ditch and up a hillside. Once we came down the other side I saw the pack house. It was not a huge place. It had a rugged log cabin exterior with a red tin roof. It looked at though there were about three levels to the place, it was definitely smaller then Red Rose but I was sure I would like it. I already felt like I was where I was supposed to be.

We parked the Jeep and two men came out of the pack house front doors. Clarks parents rolled in behind us as we exited the vehicle. Clark took my hand, his parents hurried out of their Jeep over to us and we all walked up to the two men together. "Alpha David Watkins, this is my mate, Charlotte Gillies of Red Rose Territory in Saskatchewan." Clark introduced me. David smiled at me sternly and extended his hand to me, I took it and he kissed the back. "Charlotte, it is a pleasure to meet you. Congratulations to both you and Clark." He said with sincere warmth in his voice.

"It is a privilege to be here Alpha Watkins, I am very excited to join the Black Lake pack and the Duffey family." I managed to say through my throat of fog. I was nervous.

"Your name is Gillies? Is that any relation to James?" the Alpha asked. I nodded, "He is my father."

David clapped his hands together and smiled a real smile at me, he patted Clark on the back, "Your father and I have known each other for over twenty years. We have attended various conferences together; he is an excellent man. I hope your family will visit us soon, I would love to have a brew with him and catch up." I smiled broadly, I was relieved this was going well.

"Charlotte, this is my brother Heath, the future Alpha of our pack." Clark gestured towards the man standing next to David. Heath looked similar to Clark is every way, except he had brown eyes. He was a bit shorted then Clark, but even more muscular. Heath reached out and pulled me in to a hug, "Welcome to Black Rose Charlotte. I am very happy my brother found you, I am sure you will make him very happy." I wasn't expecting such a warm welcome, but I let him pull me in. I heard a low growl behind me, Heath broke away from me and scoffed.

"Easy little brother, you have nothing to fear." He said, separating from me and shaking Clark's hand. Clark was slightly embarrassed by his primal reaction to his brother hugging me, he looked at me sheepishly. I rolled my eyes at him and shivered slightly, "Come on you big bad Beta, take me inside before I catch my death out here."

"Oh right, Charlotte is a prairie wolf, our winters will be a very tough adjustment for her." David chuckled as we all started towards the pack house. When we walked through the doors, I was shocked to find the foyer filled with about one hundred people. They all remained silent our party shuffled into the front of the room. I looked up at Clark, curious what was happening.

"I'm sorry my love, I was hoping they would make the announcement after we had time to get settled but it appears the Alpha is anxious to make introductions." He linked with me. I sighed and forced a smiled, though I was sure I looked terrified.

"Good Afternoon Black Lake Pack. Our Beta Samuel and his wife, Cheryl are thrilled to announce that their son, Clark Duffey has found his mate at this year's exhibition. Please join me in welcoming Charlotte Gillies from Red Rose Pack in Saskatchewan. I am sure, as your future Beta female you will all show her the utmost respect and welcome her into our family." David let his voice boom around the room, he had a commanding presence. The pack erupted in cheers and I was mobbed by so many people I couldn't even begin to remember names or faces.

The introductions took about an hour; I was completely exhausted after all of that. I wasn't exactly a social butterfly so meeting so many new people in such a short period of time took a lot out of me. Cheryl lead me up some back stairs through the kitchen to the Beta suites. Clark's and my rooms on one half of the hallway, his parent's on the other. She opened the door to our room, it was very warm and homey. All I saw was a big king size bed, I needed to lay down.

"Have a rest before dinner my dear. This has been a very big day." Cheryl told me, ushering me into the room. I thanked her, she shut the door behind me. The room had red wallpaper and carpet, it was definitely Clark's room. There were hunter green curtains and a beautiful matching bedspread. There were two large oak wardrobes, a closet and an adjoining bathroom. I looked around a bit before I laid down on the bed. It smelled like apple pie in here. I must have dozed off, the next thing I remember there was a pair of lips on my ear. I smiled with my eyes closed, Clark was so smooth I was learning.

"Charlotte, would you like to come down for supper or would you like me to bring you some food here instead?" he whispered, tickling my ear. I gigged and buried my face into the pillow that smelled like him. Clark swept my hair off my neck and across the pillow, he started to kiss my ear and down my neck slowly to my collarbone. I sighed heavily and reached up to touch his face. He had shaved, his chin wans cheeks were baby soft and smooth.

I opened my eyes slowly, the digital clock read 5:15pm. It was supper time; I wasn't particularly hungry but I knew if I didn't get now I would be famished later. I rolled on my back and faced him, Clark kissed my forehead gently, "Hello darling.". I smiled up at him, "I could eat."

We went downstairs to the dining hall. There were about one hundred people already seated and eating. Some of the wolves looked at us as we gathered our food, waving and smiling. Others just went about their business. Clark lead me to a table where his brother was already seated. "May we join you?" he asked Heath. Heath gestured to the empty seats around him, "Please."

Heath smiled at his brother as we sat down. He took a long drink of beer, "Well brother, I am very happy for you. I wish I could have been so lucky as to meet my mate when I was at the exhibition."

"Thanks Heath. It was a pretty wonderful experience." Clark said smiling from ear to ear. I started eating my food, the roast was so juicy and tender. I couldn't put my finger on what it was, but it wasn't beef.

"It's moose darling." Clark told me. I looked at him and smiled. It was much more tender then our moose back home, not as gamey. It was so much leaner then beef.

Heath studied us for a moment, then set his cutlery down, "You sly dog, you two have already mated!"

I dropped my fork, the telepathic communication only happened after the mating and marking, I had forgotten. Heath started laughing, apparently my face was priceless.

"Stop it Heath, you are embarrassing Charlotte." Clark hissed at his brother, which only made Heath laugh louder, people were looking around at us at this point.

"I'm sorry, I just wasn't expecting a goody goody like Clark to act so... primal so soon. I'm sorry Charlotte, I didn't mean to make you uncomfortable... I only meant to make Clark uncomfortable." Heath continued.

Clark smacked his brother playfully on the head, "I'm telling mom and dad!" Heath teased. At this point I was laughing as well. There was a genuine affection between Clark and Heath. It wasn't forced or uncomfortable. I enjoyed seeing this side of Clark with his sibling.

"Clark, I never thought I would say this, but I am jealous of you." Heath said with a sigh. "I would give anything to find a woman to look at me the way Charlotte looks at you. You are so lucky to have found her." Heath went on, "Congratulations you guys, I really mean that."

I smiled and gave Heath a hug, he seemed surprised I did that. "Thank you." I whispered.

Heath rose and patted my back again, "Welcome to the family, sister."

After dinner we strode back to our room. "This is a beautiful house." I said, running my hands along the corridor.

"We built it as a pack seventy years ago. The old one was more then two hundred years old, so it was time." Clark told me. I nodded. Black Lake was smaller then Red Rose, but it was very homey. I felt that I could be happy here.

Once we were in our room Clark pulled me close to his chest from behind. He breathed in my scent from my hair deeply. I could feel his hands rubbing my stomach slowly. I sighed and leaned back into his chest. I reached up and ran my fingers through his hair. He felt so good.

"Are you looking forward to the mating ceremony darling?" he asked me.

I turned around and nodded into his chest, breathing his scent in heavily.

"I am so thankful your family is the way they are. They have welcomed me in with open arms. I am excited for us to have our ceremony and to become an official member of the Black Lake pack." I whispered in his ear.

Clark kissed me with more urgency, his hand moved down my back and over my butt. He lifted me up and carried me over to the bed. I wrapped my arms around his neck to pull his kisses closer and harder. I wanted him, I craved him.

He lay me down, we undressed in record time. Clark moved on top of me, kissing my face, neck, chest stomach. "I have wanted to make love to you in this bed since the moment we met." He breathed into my ear. I moaned and shivered at his words. "I love you, so much. Come here." I pulled him to me.

Our love making had gotten better since our first time. Clark lasted a lot longer now, we had learned more about each other's bodies, what we like and don't like. All the pain I had felt in the beginning was now replaced with pleasure. I felt so close to him when we made love. The sparks running through my body when we were intimate made me believe in magic. Clark was very considerate, he took great care to make sure I was satisfied and enjoying myself.

Afterward, we stared into each other's eyes and tried to catch our breath. I touched his face gently, "What time do you have drills?" He sighed and kissed my forehead, "6am. Once we are done I will come back and give you a proper tour of the place. We usually finish around 9am."

"Can we go for a run tomorrow?" I asked, "I think it's time for our wolves had some quality time together."

Clark smiled at me and wiggled his eyebrows, "If you want we can have another round right now." I laughed and kissed his lips, "No, no it's their turn, Clark." He nodded and pulled me closer onto his shoulder. I was falling asleep in the bed I was going to sleep in for the rest of my life, next to the man I would love for the rest of my life. I listened to his steady heartbeat, it was so soothing. It lulled me to sleep softly.

# Chapter 8

When I awoke the next morning I was alone in the bed and the room. I didn't think I could ever get sick of the smell of apple pie. I went to the bathroom to take a hot shower; it was very nice. I climbed into the shower and let it wash over my body, I felt so wonderful. I got dressed and went downstairs to the kitchen. I must have missed breakfast, there was no one in the dining hall so I took some fruit and sat down at one of the tables. I ate absentmindedly and looked around, there was not a soul here, you could hear a pin drop.

I walked through the house. It was so beautiful. There were intricate wood carvings into the walls of flowers, animals, plants and shapes. There were no paintings at all on the walls, just carvings and tapestries. I had never seen anything like it. As I walked down the halls I finally started to hear some voices. Three women around my age came out of a room chatting. They all turned and smiled at me, walking over.

"Good morning Charlotte. Are you finding everything alright? Can we help you?" one of them asked me.

I smiled, "I'm just examining these beautiful carvings. I have never seen anything like it before."

"Yes, wood carving is an excellent medium. Many of us do it in various ways. The best of us end up carving on the walls." A different girl told me.

"Sorry, we should introduce ourselves. I'm Tabitha, this is Amy and Melanie. We are Omegas here." Tabitha told me.

"It's lovely to meet you all." I said, shaking hands all around.

The girls invited me to join them in the library, so we all walked there together. I had never seen so many books in all my life. It was easily two levels of shelves full of books. There were ladders going up all the way to the ceiling. There were three computer stations as well. Two big bay windows looked outside over the training grounds, I looked but I couldn't see Clark.

"This is an amazing library," I said, running my hands over the books along a shelf, "I am in love."

Amy smiled and said, "There isn't a lot to do around here for extra entertainment. We don't have Wi-Fi so reading is an excellent escape. These are the only computers in the place, so we all share."

I nodded, "Do we check books out or do we just read them here?"

"You can take them out, but watch out for Mary. She keeps very strict records, if you don't return a book on time she will hunt you down." Amy told me with a giggle.

Tabitha pointed to a woman I assume was Mary putting some books away up high on the ladder. I looked at the clock in the library and it read 9:15am. I gasped, "Oh shoot I am late to meet Clark. Thanks for showing me around, I'll see you all later."

The girls all waved goodbye to me as I hurried out the door and back to our room. They seemed very nice and friendly. It was good to know I could make friends here. I got to the room and went inside, I didn't see Clark but I heard the shower running in the bathroom. I was overcome with an urge to be brave, so I stripped down to my skin and tiptoed into the bathroom. Clark had his back to the door so he didn't notice I came in. This was the first time I got to look at his entire body naked. He was impossibly fit and toned. His muscles were very defined, his skin had a natural tan. As the water washed across my Clark's body, I noticed I was licking my lips longingly. I tied my hair up in a bun and walked up to the shower, I pulled the door back and stepped inside.

"Hello there handsome." I whispered gently and ran my fingers along his shoulder blades. Clark shuttered and spun around to face me, he looked me up and down. His eyes filled with lust and I saw his excitement in his lower body. Clark pulled me to his wet chest and smelled my hair deeply, "Char, oh my god, what are you doing to me."

I ran my fingers over his pecks and kissed his chest and neck slowly. He moaned into my hair and wrapped his arms around my waist. "I missed you." I whispered.

I let my hand drift down his chest, his stomach going lower and lower. I took Clark's member in my hand and started to rub it slowly. A loud gasp escaped his lips and his eyes slammed shut. He started shaking as I increased pressure. "Ooohhhh, darling oh my god." He mumbled. I sucked and licked his mark, making him quiver in my hand.

"Does that feel good?" I asked him shyly. Clark opened his eyes, they were pained with pleasure. He buried his face in my hair again and groaned, "Yes, impossibly good. You make me feel so good, Char. Oh god."

"Do you want more?" I giggled into his ear, removing my hand from his manhood. Clark hissed as I broke the contact, he kissed my neck and licked my mark, making me tremble, "Yes, please Charlotte."

I stepped out of the shower and moved towards the door, still dripping wet, "Then you better come and get me."

I went to the bedroom and sat at the edge of the bed. Clark was right behind me, also soaking wet. He grabbed me and pulled me down on the bed, we erupted in hot kisses and deep embraces. We made love several times that morning, I couldn't get enough of his touch.

"Charlotte, you are quite the naughty little vixen." He whispered into my ear, "I didn't realize how sensual you were when I first met you."

I smiled at him and I had to confess, "I honestly am not like this normally. I am very shy and I have absolutely no experience with men or sex. Everything I do, it's because I feel it with you. I didn't want to do anything until I met you. It's almost as though you awakened my sexuality."

Clark smiled at me and kissed me slowly. He explored my mouth with his tongue and I sucked on it slowly. He moaned and entered me again, "I never thought I would love someone as much as I love you. I want to make love to you all the time, nonstop. Is this normal?"

I squirmed, encouraging him to move, Clark moved his hips lazily, "I feel like when I am inside you I am complete. We become one body, soul, heart. I never thought this was possible." I kissed his lips and moved my hips against him, making us both moan.

"I don't know what is normal. All I know is I feel the same as you do. "I whispered in his ear, nibbling on the lobe. We made love one final time before getting up and taking on the day.

Clark took me to the TV room, the library again, the kitchen, the medical centre, the training ground and the greenhouse. There was a lot to see, I was amazed at how much they had for a small pack. We ended up back in the library where Clark showed the computers and the vast collections of books. "We don't have Wi-Fi up here so the online stuff for the whole pack is done here. Sorry darling, I know it will be inconvenient for you." He said, sitting down at one of the computers.

I smiled and ran my fingers through his hair, "It's alright, I'll adjust. I will just have to write my letters here instead of on my phone. No big deal. This library is incredible. I can't wait to dive in."

He smiled and took my hand, guiding me over to the large windows, "When you told me you liked to read I knew this would be your hide away. I am so happy you like it." We kissed and looked down at the training area. There was a new group out there now running drills. I turned back to Clark and smiled, "Shall we run our wolves?"

He beamed at me, I could tell he was thrilled to run with me. It is a very special thing for mates to run their wolves together. Clark ran his fingertips up my arms and stroked my face, he took my glasses off. "Let's go Char, I can't wait to see what you look like."

We dashed outside, Clark took my hand and I followed him into the woods. We stripped down and I shifted first. He looked at me with loving eyes, stroking my fur. I ran my muzzle over his face and licked him. "I somehow knew you would be grey," he whispered, "Just like me."

Clark shifted and he was indeed grey, but a very dark grey, almost black. Mates don't always match in colours but sometimes they do. His wolf was huge, three times the size of mine. He rubbed up against me and we nuzzled each other. Clark lead and I followed deeper into the woods. We ran, jumped and played together for hours. It was amazing. These woods were so vast; I was sure I would get lost without him with me. It would take me a long time to get used to them. I looked forward to it though. By the time we went back to the pack house it was sunset. We got in just in time to see people gathering to eat. We got in line and took our food to a table where Heath was sitting with another man.

"Charlotte, it is nice to meet you. I am Timothy, future Gamma." He introduced himself, shaking my hand. I smiled at him, I was wondering when I would get to meet him. "I apologize for not being here yesterday when you were introduced, I was on a patrol of our boarders."

"It's a pleasure to meet you Tim. I have heard good things about you." I said, sitting down with Clark. Melanie came up next to Timothy and sat down with him, she smiled at me shyly, "Hello Charlotte, how are you?"

I smiled widely, "Melanie, hello!" Timothy rubbed Melanie's back, "I see you have met my mate, Melanie."

We both nodded, "This morning, she, Tabitha and Amy showed me around a bit while Clark was at drills." Melanie and I exchanged smiles, she hadn't introduced herself as the Gamma female, I realized she was probably waiting for Timothy.

"It's good to see you are making friends already." Clark whispered to me, running his hand up my back to my shoulder blade. "Everyone is very kind here," I told him, "I feel very welcomed."

"You should," Heath said curtly, "this is your home now Charlotte. You will be the Beta female. Which means without a Luna, you will end up shouldering a lot of those duties so this pack should welcome you with open arms."

I was taken aback by his abrupt tone. Heath made eye contact with me and sighed, he realized he sounded harsher then he intended. "I mean; it is important for everyone to take care of you here. We all take care of each other. It's important to us." He rephrased. I nodded. Clark shuffled in his seat beside me a bit, "She's not taking on all the Luna duties."

The brothers made eye contact and our table was very silent. Heath realized what Clark was suggesting and laughed whole heartedly, "Oh brother, no I didn't mean THAT! Give me a little credit here Clark."

Clark exhaled with a low growl, and smiled. I wasn't really sure what that exchange was about but I was kind of glad I missed the point. We continued to eat with pleasant conversation. It was nice to visit with another couple. I was sure Heath was feeling like the fifth wheel though. He looked board but he was too polite to leave the table. I smiled kindly at him, he returned it. I could understand his loneliness; I am sure as a future Alpha he wanted his Luna so badly. He would crave the bond, having a Luna made things easier I understood, Alphas have a hard time without a Luna. They keep the Alphas grounded and humane, according to what I had heard.

Cheryl approached our table long after we had finished eating, "Charlotte, I am so pleased to see you all smiles. I take it you are settling in fine?"

"Yes Mrs. Duffey, everyone has been very kind and welcoming." I told her. She placed a hand on my shoulder, "Please dear, call me Cheryl or if you would like someday mom." I caught my breath, I wasn't ready for that but it was nice to know I could when I was. Clark squeezed my hand, he felt what I felt.

Cheryl sat down next to us, "I wanted to talk to you about your mating ceremony. David would like you two to set a date so we can get it planned out for later this month. I know it seems soon considering you just got here, but we should get the event in motion to make it official to our pack." I turned to Clark, he smiled at me and stroked my hand with his thumb.

"Well, we could do it on May 3rd. That gives us a two weeks to plan and it should give us enough time for my things to arrive from Red Rose." I suggested, Clark nodded, following my lead.

"Excellent. I will tell the Alpha. He will be pleased." Cheryl beamed, "Melanie, it is good to see you and Charlotte getting off on the right foot. Perhaps you and your friends can help her with some of the arrangements?"

"It would be a pleasure." Melanie said, wholeheartedly. I smiled at her and mouthed, Thank you. Cheryl clapped and stood up in one motion, "It is settled. Charlotte I will come and get you tomorrow at 8am, Melanie can be ready at that time as well. Tomorrow we start planning a fabulous event!" With that, their mother was off, she was so excited I could tell she had wanted to plan an event like this for a while. My heart skipped a beat as I realized our mating ceremony was going to be a fancy affair where everyone would be looking at us. Clark could sense me, he pulled me closer to his side and kissed my head, breathing me in.

"Don't worry darling, we will do our best to keep her from going overboard." He whispered into my hair. I giggled. I glanced at Heath, he produced a smile but his eyes betrayed his pain. I felt a sharp stab in my stomach for him. He was so lonely; it must have been terrible for him to see his brother so happy.

After dinner Clark, Heath and Timothy stayed in the dinning hall to discuss drills and scouting. I wandered upstairs and found myself in the library again. I sat down at one of the computers and started to send emails to my parents, my brothers and to Marie. Each email was easy to write until I came to Marie's. I took more then thirty minutes to write to her. I told her about Black Lake, the pack house, how wonderful it was. How perfect Clark was. I told her about our mating ceremony. I tried to keep it as positive as I could, knowing that Anthony would probably read it over her shoulder and I didn't want to cause any conflict there. At the end I asked her how she was, how she was settling in and when her mating ceremony was. When I sent it, a box popped up on the computer asking me if I wanted the option to know if this email had been opened by the intended recipient or not. I selected yes. I wanted to know that if Marie wasn't the one reading it, that at least someone was. I sat back at the computer and looked out the windows at the dark night. The stars shone like diamonds in the sky, it was so beautiful. I enjoyed the silence for a few minutes before returning to our room. I fell asleep quickly with my senses full of apple pie.

The next two weeks were full of daily planning and organizing for the mating ceremony. Cheryl and Melanie were like machines. I elected to wear my green dress I had bought for the exhibition. I already loved it and I hadn't got to wear it very long before the unhappy confrontation between my father and Alpha Martins. Tabitha offered to do my hair for me, which was a welcome since my mother wouldn't be able to do it. The mating ceremony was in two days when I arrived in the kitchen one morning to see a very stressed Cheryl.

"What's wrong Cheryl?" I asked sitting across from her at the island. She huffed and forced a smile, "Nothing serious, just the menu. Our hunters are having trouble getting a caribou for the dinner. It is tradition to have one at mating ceremonies. They are rare, so our hunters have been trying hard. Clark even went out with them all week to try and track one but still no luck."

I smiled at her and took her hand, "You know, mom, I am fine without it. I know it is tradition but the stress it not worth it. We can have moose instead."

Cheryl's eyes filled with tears. She hurried around the island and engulfed me in her arms, "Oh my sweet girl. You are so thoughtful. Thank you. I will link the hunters and tell them to relax. We already have moose so they can come home." I nodded into her shoulder, she was holding on for dear life.

Melanie came in with Amy, they each took a cup of coffee and sat with us, "So, what's on the agenda for today?" Amy asked, giving me a wink.

Cheryl pulled away from me, still smiling, "Well the menu isn't going to be perfect but my daughter in law is so that makes up for it. We can cancel the caribou and replacing it with moose. That was honestly the last hitch."

"Oh caribou, they are hard to get," Melanie nodded, "We finally got one the morning of our ceremony. It was a huge deal to have it ready on time for everyone to eat. My mother actually missed most of the ceremony preparing it. She still mentions it when she is sad." Amy nodded. I went to get myself a cup of coffee as well, "It's alright. I don't mind at all. Moose is delicious. I love all the wild meat up here. Our prairie moose are not nearly as delicious as the moose up here."

Amy piped in, "Just wait until summer time when we have bison." I giggled, I liked bison, we had it often back at Red Rose, but I was sure the ones up here were also mouth watering.

Tabitha came in with a small assortment of flowers, she set them on the counter, "So Charlotte, I was thinking these would go in your head wreath for the ceremony. Do you like?"

I ran my fingers through the flowers, there were hints of purple, pale pink and white against greens. I was sure it would be beautiful, "I trust you completely, Tabitha. Thank you for making this for our special day." Tabitha smiled and gave me an unexpected hug, "I am glad you like them. I tried to pick nicest ones but it is still early spring so a lot of our flowers are not in bloom just yet."

I was grateful that all these women were taking our ceremony with as much care as if it were their own. I was thankful to have a wonderful family here, I wasn't expecting it to be as easy of a transition as it was. When I realized I was moving to Black Lake to be with Clark I was terrified. I thought I would hate it here but this place was starting to feel like home to me. I knew the bond between my mate and I helped with the uneasy feelings of new surroundings. I did miss my family desperately though, my mom and especially Marie. I hadn't heard from her since we said goodbye to each other at the exhibition. I had sent an email each week. Each week I got a notification that the email was open but she never replied back. I wanted to talk with her. I had spoken to all the other member of my family, but none of them had heard from Marie either. I wasn't even sure she was the one reading my emails. It could have been Anthony.

"I really like the dress you are wearing, Charlotte. It's perfect for you." Amy mentioned. I shook my head and brought my mind back to them. Of course, yes, the dress. "Thanks, my mom helped me pick it out. I love it." We sat around the island finishing our coffee and discussing the various tasks still to be completed.

The day passed by quickly, it was almost supper time when I realized I hadn't seen Clark all day. I tried to mind link with him but he must have been out of range because I got no answer. I went to the Alpha's office finally when I had looked everywhere for him. I knocked and went inside, David and Heath were sitting on either side of the desk, they turned when I entered and both stood up.

"Hello Charlotte. Can we help you with something?" Heath asked kindly.

"I apologize for disturbing you both, but I was wondering if you had seen Clark? I haven't seen him all day. I have looked everywhere and I tried to link with him but I haven't been able to reach him." I asked.

David turned to Heath, "What time is it?" Heath looked at his watch, "Almost 5." They exchanged a smile and walked towards me, "Well I guess there is no harm in telling you now." David said.

I starred at them confused. Heath laughed out loud, "My brother went to get you a very special mating ceremony gift, he should be arriving back any moment now. He had to fly out early this morning to get it."

"What? He didn't tell me." I cried, a bit confused. "Trust us Charlotte, you will love this surprise." The Alpha told me. I nodded. I thanked them both and left the office, confused. What would he have to go and get? Two days before the ceremony, it was cutting it pretty close. I wasn't unhappy he got me a surprise but to fly out and back in one day, it had better be important.

I was in the dining hall with Heath, Timothy and Melanie when the pack house door opened and I heard Clark's voice. I looked up to see him ushering in my parents and brothers. I stood up and let out a loud whimper, my eyes filled with tears and I couldn't stop myself from running to them and leaping on top of them all. Clark had brought my family to me for our mating ceremony. I couldn't believe it. My heart was racing; I was never so excited in all my life. We all exchanged hugs, loving words, deep glances and hearty handshakes. My heart was ready to burst with happiness.

I sat with my family as they ate dinner. They told me about the flight, how Clark had arranged all of this from the moment we set the date. My brothers were so happy to see me, Michael kept himself next to me as though his life depended on it. Byron told me how Clark was going to do some training with him tomorrow and show him some new tactical moves. I laughed out loud. My parents watched me with loving eyes, I was happy they were able to be here. It wasn't always tradition for the families of the females to come to the mating ceremonies.

Often they didn't visit their daughter's new packs at all. I knew Black Lake was not like that, but I wasn't expecting this.

We stayed in the dining hall well after midnight, finally Samuel ushered my family upstairs to their rooms so they could get some rest. Clark picked me up and carried me to our room. I locked the door behind us and I ravaged him on our bedroom floor. His eyes were full of exhaustion and ecstasy before I was finished with him.

"I can't believe you did this for me." I said, crawling into our bed. He pulled me close and kissed me tenderly, "How could I do anything else. They are my family too; they need to be here for our ceremony. It is important."

I let the gentle tears fall down my face, "I love how you are so considerate and accepting of my family. I adore how we have the same values and beliefs. I did not think it was possible for me to love you more then I did yesterday, yet I do." Clark kissed my tears away and breathed in my scent.

"I adore you my darling, with every cell in my body. You were made especially for me; I will never take that for granted." He whispered. I nodded, "Me neither."

We held each other as we fell asleep. It was going to be a wonderful event, our mating ceremony. The joining of our families officially.

The next morning, I woke before Clark for once. I showered, dressed and kissed him goodbye before slipping out of our room. I went to the kitchen, to my surprise my mother and Cheryl were already up. They appeared to be cooking something that smelled so much like home it made my heart ache.

"Good morning sweetheart. Did you sleep well?" my mom asked, giving me a cup of coffee. I sat at the island and watched them. I noticed large plastic containers full of berries, and my eyes went wide. I pointed to them, "Are those what I think they are?"

My mother nodded and I squealed very loudly, I was sure I would wake the whole pack house. Cheryl laughed out loud and stirred the large pot that was bubbling on the stove.

"We couldn't very well come all this way and not bring a bit of Red Rose with us now could we?" my mother asked with a knowing smile.

"Oh Cheryl, just wait until you taste my mother's Saskatoon Berry crisp. It is unmatched." I stated, my mother blushed slightly, "It's grandma Daisy's recipe. I just follow what my mother told me to."

"This will be the dessert of the ceremony. A little bit of your home coming to ours." Cheryl smiled. I went over to her and gave her a hug from behind, "I love you mom. Thank you." She leaned back against me and sighed. I could honestly say I adored my mother in law.

I sat with the mothers for the majority of the early morning before the Omegas came in to prepare breakfast for the pack. Tabitha and Amy were among them, they both started to lick their lips when they smelled the hot Saskatoon Berry mixture on the stove. "What is that delicious smell?" Amy asked.

"That is my grandmother's Saskatoon Berry crisp recipe. It's the dessert tomorrow night." I told her. Tabitha and Amy nodded, both wanted to eat it now I was sure. I didn't go out for breakfast with the pack, I stayed in the kitchen and ate there. I wanted to spend as much time with my mother as possible.

"Have you talked to Marie?" I asked her. She shook her head, I saw her body tense up and she hurried herself around the kitchen to try and hide it. "I have been writing to her, but she doesn't reply."

"We called everyday after we got back home. The Alpha wouldn't let us talk to her. Finally, your father asked ours to call Antonio but that didn't get us any further. I have tried to call the Luna as well but she won't take my calls. We have emailed her as well but nothing is coming back." She finally confessed. I nibbled at the apple I was eating, trying to remember to chew as I focused on my mother's words.

She went on, "All they have told us is she is fine, they haven't had the ceremony yet and Marie is getting settled into her life at Rocky Mountain. We have tried to call her cell phone directly but it has been cut off. I don't know if she has a new one, when we ask they won't say. It seems they are determined to keep her from us. I have had to stop your father from going there several times, I am not sure what Antonio would do to him in his own pack territory. I was afraid I would never see him again."

I stood up and hugged my mother. She let a few tears fall, but I could tell this wasn't new pain for her. She had been trying to get in touch with Marie for almost a month with no word. She had probably cried herself to sleep many nights, my father as well. I just held on to her, I didn't need to say anything. I was there, she hadn't lost me. The Duffey's would make sure that never happened. I would make sure that never happened.

"I am sorry Charlotte, we should not talk about such sad things on the eve of your ceremony," she apologized, "this is a happy time for you and Clark. All of us actually."

"Don't apologize Dorothy," Cheryl said, still stirring her large pot, "I can't imagine how I would feel if I was in your shoes. We are all family now, your fears and joys are ours as well." My mother nodded to her, she was right.

My brother Michael came in and joined us in the kitchen. He looked run down, I touched his shoulder with concern, "What's up Michael?"

"I just talked to Stella, she won't be back home when I return. She's been with her parents now for over a month." He muttered. My mother sighed and gave him a sad glance, "Give her time Mike, she has a lot to adjust to."

"I've given her lots of time, mother. I'm sick of giving her time. It's been over a year now; she has spent almost half of that time away from me. How much more time could she possibly need?" he growled, anger was coming to the surface.

I linked my arm with his and pulled Michael towards the door, "Come big brother, I'll show you the library. It puts ours back home to shame." Michael came with me and we went to the library alone. He was amazed at the number of books. I lit a fire in the hearth and invited him to sit on the sofa with me to talk about what was going on with Stella.

Michael ran his hands through his red locks, he was so frustrated, filled with sorrow. He let it all fall out, "She doesn't want to be with me Charlotte. I can't explain it; our mate bond is so weak. It's not sup-posed to be this way. I thought when she first came back to Red Rose with me that it was just nerves so I gave her lots of space and time. I thought she would come around. It has never happened; Stella doesn't love me. When we are together, I feel her pulling away more and more each time."

I pulled a blanket from the back of the sofa and spread it across our laps. I nodded, encouraging him to continue. He exhaled loudly, "She is always so happy before she returns to her family and so unhappy when she returns to me. She won't let me kiss her anymore, not even a peck. When we have sex, it's actually awkward. It isn't fun, it never was. She doesn't finish and I can't do anything to make her happy. I don't know what to do." Michael began to cry; he was in pain. I knew their rela-tionship was never very easy but I didn't realize it was this bad. I knew Stella had trouble adjusting to life at Red Rose. She had told me that. She was a kind person but she wasn't happy there. It had gotten worse since I moved to Black Lake I guess. She had been gone from Red Rose for a week when we left for the exhibition, so that meant she had been with her family for over a month. I could feel Michael's anguish. He was desperately unhappy.

"Have you thought about going with her? Maybe you two should be with her family instead of ours." I suggested.

He sighed and cried harder, running his hands through his hair, "I offered her that six months ago. She refused, she said she just needs to be alone with her family sometimes and I need to be patient. I don't know what else to do. I offered to move back there, but she doesn't want me with her. Stella doesn't want to be with me at Red Rose and I can't be with her with her family either. She may as well reject me."

I let the room go silent. Michael looked at me with shock. I could tell he had never said that out loud before. I looked at him with calm, quiet eyes, "Perhaps you should let her go, Michael."

He searched my face before burying his in his hands. I pulled my brother close and let him cry into my chest and lap. Michael was beside himself at the thought. I rocked my body to sooth him as much as possible and we stayed like that for a long time. He cried and I held him tight. I mind linked with Clark, asking him to keep my family away from the library so Michael wouldn't have to explain everything again to them if they found us. He said he would.

Michael finally calmed down after about an hour. He stood up and looked out the windows down at the warriors doing training. I followed him and stood shoulder to shoulder, "I have been thinking about it. I don't want to but she is not happy. Stella won't give me a chance to make her happy. I have done everything in my power right?" he asked helplessly, I nodded. "I am glad you won't have to feel this pain. Loving someone so much knowing they don't love you the same is excruciating."

"I'm sorry Michael." I whispered, he nodded, "I will call her now. It's better to just get it over with. Stay with me, Charlotte, I may be in pain after." I sat down on the sofa as he sat at the library phone and dialed.

"Hello Stella," he said into the phone, his back to me, "I know I already called you this morning but I needed to speak with you, it is urgent. Are you sitting down?"

Michael took a very deep breath and pushed the words out of his mouth with a shaky voice, "I Michael Gillies of Red Rose Pack reject you, Stella Meredith of True Dawn Pack as my mate."

I heard Stella's muffled voice at the other end of the phone. It was brief. Michael nodded, "Ok, I'll let them know. Take care." He hung up the phone.

I went to my brother as he fell to his knees, "She accepted and thanked me. She actually thanked me for letting her go." I held on to him for dear life. Michael wept openly, without even trying to hold back. I cradled him like a child lost. You could feel his heart breaking, a roar ripped through his chest like I had never heard from him before. The pain was excruciating. I knew if I could feel it, mother and father would feel it too. "What do I do now?" he cried out. I rocked back and forth, back and forth. "You just feel it and let yourself heal when it is time." I whispered. Michael couldn't say anything else, he just lay in my arms on the floor, unable to control his sobs.

My father came to the library a short time later. He knew what was wrong, like I had felt it so had he. He knelt down next to Michael and took his face between his palms, "You did what was right my son, you did the bravest thing today. Come, let me take you to your room, Charlotte will help your mother with some tea."

Michael nodded and we helped him to his feet. My father led him down the hallway and I ran to the kitchen. I found my mother there with a collection of herbs from home. She asked me to help her make some mushroom camomile tea for my brother, "It will heal his heartache from within. Once that has begun his spirit will be able to search for his second chance mate. I pray he gets one, he did everything right. It's not his fault the bond didn't take. Michael deserves a second chance." My mother told me. I nodded. I watched as her steady hands slowly selected the perfect bunches of herbs for the tea. I heated up water and brought it to her. We mixed everything together and brought it up to Michael's room he was sharing with Byron. We forced him to drink it, lots of it. "Mother says this will heal your heart and help you to love again." I told him.

Michael glared at me, "Love again? Why would I want to go through this again?" He growled, drinking the tea, his eyes were red with the pain. "Someday," I said, "you will find her. She will be your second chance at life." He huffed, drinking down his third cup of tea. I left Michael when he fell asleep, crying takes a great deal out of anyone. I ran into Tabitha in the hallway, she had brought me a few more flowers to see. We walked back down to the kitchen discussing the wreath for my head. It was coming together nicely.

Byron and Clark came in after their training session. Byron was talking nonstop about all the new ways Clark had showed him how to defend himself from attacks. I was impressed that the two of them had bonded so quickly. Clark wrapped his arms around me and I breathed him in deeply. We were to have our ceremony tomorrow, I couldn't wait. I looked up into his blue eyes, he kissed my hair. "You two need to get a good night's sleep tonight. Tomorrow is a very big day." Cheryl told us, my mother nodded in agreement.

We went to bed that night full of excitement. I went to check on Michael before I went to our room, he was alright. Still in a great deal of emotional turmoil but my father told me to go and get some rest, he would take care of Michael. I returned to our bedroom to find Clark sitting up on our bed waiting for me. He smiled when he saw I locked the door.

I crossed the room and climbed into his lap. I pulled him as close as possible, even that wasn't close enough. He chuckled at me, "What's going on Char? Are you alright?"

"Michael had to reject Stella today. Neither of them were happy, he let her go. I spent the entire afternoon with him sobbing. He is completely devastated." I told him, Clark nodded. "I know; I can feel how you feel remember. I know how much you care about your brother." He whispered.

"It doesn't make any sense to me," I told him, "Why would the moon Goddess pair two people who can not make each other happy? Why would she be so cruel to cause anyone the pain of having to reject a mate?" I nestled close to him.

Clark sighed and buried his face into my hair, he pulled my glasses off and set them on his night stand. "My father used to say that not all mating bonds take. That some are a lot of work for both wolves to make the bond stick. Others are never the right fit and one or both are unhappy which is where the rejections happen. Still others are even worse, when one is unhappy but the other will not let them go and then it leads to a lifetime of heartache and pain." He explained. I shook my head, "Michael does not deserve this."

"It's not about deserving darling. Some of us don't get lucky. Honestly, the moon Goddess might just pair us off at random and hope that it sticks." Clark said with a laugh. I didn't laugh, it wasn't funny to me. The idea of being paired with someone who didn't make me happy was horrible. It was my greatest fear. I had been so scared before Clark that I would be mated to someone who wouldn't make me happy. Once I found him, I never looked back.

He lifted my chin up with his hand slowly to look into my face, "We got lucky my darling. Honestly I don't know if it was fate or not but I wasn't expecting to find you and love you as much as I do. I knew my parents had a wonderful bond, but after seeing Heath struggle I wasn't as optimistic. I am grateful that we will have a romantic love story. We are blessed because of it."

I smiled at him, "I wish others we love were as blessed as we are." Clark kissed my lips tenderly, "They will get their chance hopefully." I nodded. We lay down together and fell asleep wrapped up in each other's arms, as though we were one. I hoped one day my brothers would find this kind of peace.

The next morning, I was awake before my eyes opened. I could hear Clark rumbling next to me, waking up himself. The smell of our room was so soothing, apple pie and heat. I loved it, I never tired of that aroma. "What time is it?" I asked him, just above a whisper. I heard a growl of longing and a small grunt, I giggled at his morning noises.

"Almost 7am." He murmured, rolling over and pulling me to him. His face was buried in my hair again, his favorite spot. "We should get up and eat. We will need fuel to get through today," I suggested. Clark huffed and started to kiss my neck, which moved to licking and nibbling. Soon he was on top of me between my legs kissing my lips with hunger. I laughed and caught his face between my hands, "Easy boy, we need to save that heat for tonight."

Clark groaned sadly and collapsed on top of me, almost protesting. I tapped his shoulders, "Come on baby, lets get up and eat. We have a big day today." Reluctantly he nodded and rolled off me, and sat up at the edge of the bed.

"You drive me crazy, Char." He said, stretching his shoulders over his head. "I know." I whispered, smirking. Clark spun around and lifted his eyebrows as he smiled at me. "Oh you vixen, I'm going to have a lot of fun with you tonight." I went to the bathroom to take my shower, turning back to him with a sexy wink, "You better, now go and run some of that sexual energy off."

I closed the door and heard him groan loudly before turning the shower on. I washed away the sleep from my body and let the water flow through my hair. After brushing my teeth, I pulled on some jeans and t-shirt and ran downstairs to have a bite to eat. The dining hall was full, I grabbed a plate and found my family to join them. The Duffey's were sitting with them between two tables. Everyone cheered when I sat down, various congratulations were spoken all around before my mother and Cheryl started listing off the list of the day. I was listening as they told me I had to be in hair and make-up in about two hours. I was ready, I knew today was going to be full but I had one thing I had to do before I was swept away.

"I'll be back down in a bit, I need to send an email before we get started." I told everyone, rising from my seat. My mother nodded at me knowingly. I dropped my plate off and jogged to the library. I checked my emails, still nothing from Marie. I sighed, I had hoped she would send me something today. I wrote her a note about how exciting today was going to be, how I wished she was there. I asked when she was having hers and how she was. I told her I missed her terribly and that I would love her forever. I sent it. As I stood up I heard the computer beep, I looked and there was a reply in my inbox from Marie. I opened it. It read;

"Hello Charlotte, I miss you too. I am happy for you, thanks for sending me messages. Congratulations. Good bye."

I read it aloud, I was confused. The message didn't sound like Marie had wrote it. In fact, I was fairly certain she didn't. I closed my email and took a deep breath. I was fuming, I knew Marie hadn't responded to my message, was she even getting my messages? I went to the land-line phone and called the Rocky Mountain pack house. I asked to speak to Antonio.

"Hello, Alpha Martins here." He said, a small growl came over the phone as I am sure I was interrupting something.

"H-hello Alpha, this is Charlotte Gillies, Marie's sister. I was wondering if I would be able to speak to her? I would normally just email her but today is my mating ceremony to Clark Duffey and I would really like to speak with her." I said quickly, not giving him a chance to cut in. I heard nothing on the other end of the phone, only silence. I waited, still silence. Clark came into the library; he was still in his workout clothes. He must have sensed my anger and come to find me. He saw I was on the phone so he sat down on the sofa and waited with me.

"Hello Charlotte. I am going to pass you to Anthony now." Antonio said coldly, before I heard a muffling and then I could sense Anthony was on the phone. There was a quick growl, "Hi Charlotte. Can I help you?"

"Hello Anthony. Would I be able to speak to Marie please?" I asked, my voice shaking. Clark stood up when he heard who I was on the phone with. He walked behind me and wrapped his arms around my waist.

"She is unavailable right now, she told me she sent you a message today. Congratulations, by the way." Anthony told me, I could hear he was annoyed he had to talk to me.

"Yes I did receive the message. I was just hoping to hear her voice today. I miss her terribly you know." I told him, my voice cracked as I said I missed her.

Anthony went silent. I heard muffled sounds before he sighed into the receiver, "Sorry Charlotte, today isn't good. I'll be sure to tell her you called. Maybe she will make some time to call you another day. Goodbye." He hung up. I put the phone down and I was shaking. Clark turned me around quickly and pulled me impossibly close to him. I didn't cry like I thought I would. I was angry. Anthony was keeping Marie from me, from all of us. He was isolating her to control her. I knew he was probably abusing her. I was furious.

Clark picked me up silently and carried me to our room. We had a bit of time before I would be overtaken by our mothers to begin getting ready for the ceremony. He rubbed my back, neck and legs. He was trying to ease my tension. I let him. As he rubbed, my body became let go more and more. "Thank you." I murmured into the mattress. He laughed a little and kissed my ear. "I love you Char. So much." He told me, "I'm going to take a shower darling, then I'll be out of your hair to get ready."

I rolled over and smiled as I watched him go into the bathroom. I pulled myself up from our bed and took out my dress, hanging it up on the wardrobe. I took out my shoes and polished them a little bit before setting them down. I let my hair fall down and started to brush it out. I knew Tabitha hand lots of plans for it but I wanted to make sure she had a clear blank canvas to work with.

When Clark came out he was naked, but he quickly put on sweats and a shirt. He kissed me quickly and ran out the door, "See you in a couple hours darling." I was alone for a total of five minutes before a flurry of women came into my room with bags of various ceremony essentials.

Cheryl spoke loudly so everyone could hear her, "Alright ladies, it is 11: 28am, the ceremony begins at 2pm. We have two and a half hours till then so let's get going. I've asked some of our Omegas to bring us a quick lunch at 1pm. Let's get this show on the road."

My mother held my hands and gave me a kiss on the cheek, "I am so proud of you sweetheart. Your father and I are happy for you and Clark. I was so pleased that Clark took the time to plan for us to come here for this special moment. He will make a wonderful husband, father and leader."

"Thank you mom." I whispered, pulling her close. She whispered in my ear, "Thank you Charlotte, for being so easy and perfect. We are blessed to have you as our daughter." I giggled, I never thought of myself as either of those things, but I suppose under the circumstances I was probably the easiest child they had.

Amy stepped in and asked if she could do my nails while Tabitha started working on my hair. Cheryl took my dress to the bathroom and ran some hot water to steam out any wrinkles before I put it on. My mother took a look at my black flats and tsked, bringing them to our bed and breaking out the shoe polish. Over the next two hours I was pampered and made beautiful by this group of women. When the Omegas arrived with our lunch of sandwiches and hot soup I thanked them. We ate a quick meal and then I got into my dress. I loved that hunter green dress. It flowed beautifully over my small form. My shoes were next, as soon as my mother was satisfied they were shinny enough.

Once my make-up was done, Tabitha asked for the wreath. Amy brought it over to her, it was a masterpiece. I have never seen anything more elegant yet rustic in my life. "What are these flowers?" I asked.

"Well we have some poplar, bearberry, mountain avens, lilacs and of course some crocuses." Tabitha told me with pride. I smiled at her, this wreath was so elegant. I loved it, I couldn't wait to wear it. She told me to face the mirror, I did. Tabitha slowly placed the wreath on my head and pinned it into place. She pulled a few extra mountain avens from her bag and placed them throughout my hair that fell down my back. I could smell the flowers and tree bits on my head, it was heavenly. I looked at myself in the mirror, I thought I had never looked so beautiful. My mother and Cheryl teared up, linking arms. I sighed and stood up.

"One more thing," Tabitha said, touching my arm. She pulled out a small spray bottle and a cloth from her bag, "Better clean those glasses." I laughed out loud and handed them over to her. Tabitha gave me a wink as she sprayed them down. I took the cloth and whipped them off, now I was ready to go.

We started downstairs and took the back way through the kitchen. Once we were on the main floor we crossed the lobby to the back door where my father was waiting for us. Tabitha, Amy and Cheryl went on ahead out to the training grounds. I stood back with my father and mother until it was time. My father took my arm and smiled at me, "Charlotte, you look beautiful. I am so happy for you."

"Thank you father." I whispered. My brother Michael came up to us from outside and motioned that it was time. I pulled my parents close on either side and took the deepest breath of my life. We started moving out the door towards the training grounds.

Samuel and Cheryl did a wonderful job of putting up a large array of twinkle lights and torches. There were chairs set up where all the pack members were sitting, smiling back at us. The faces blended together as I walked towards the people. There was an alter in front of everyone between two torches where Clark, his parents and the Alpha stood. My parents walked me around the pack, while they all made complimentary mutterings about how I looked. We slowly came to the alter, my parents stood with me opposite Clark and his parents, the Alpha between us. I exhaled the breath I had been holding when Clark and I made eye contact. We both smiled.

"Shall we begin?" David asked. I nodded.

"Thank you Black Lake pack for joining us here today and for our special guests from Red Rose pack for making the journey to attend the mating ceremony of future Beta Clark Duffey and Charlotte Gillies. The moon Goddess creates each and every one of us before we come to this world, while at the same time creating a mate for each of us to find in our lifetime. This bond is meant to guide us on the path of our ancestors, to make us all stronger and keep our communities safe. We honor that bond with this ceremony here today." Alpha David spoke to the pack.

He turned to my parents, "Delta and Mrs. Gillies, please wrap your daughter's hand in this red scarf." My father took my right hand and wrapped the scarf around my wrist, tying it off. The Alpha then turned to Clark's parents, "Beta and Mrs. Duffey, please wrap your son's hand in this black scarf." Beta Duffey followed suit. David took both the scarves from our fathers and braided the scarves together. Clark and I held hands and stared into each other's faces.

"Now, you both repeat after me in unison," he requested, "I swear here in front of this pack and the moon Goddess that I will uphold the precious gift of the mating bond each and every day. I vow to protect, love, honor and cherish this mate until I last draw breath. I promise to honor this pack, making them my family for the rest of my days."

Clark and I repeated what he said. Our hands held on tighter as we spoke. My heart was pounding, and I could hear his as well. "As the Alpha of Black Lake pack I ask that the moon Goddess bless this union. Congratulations to Clark and Charlotte Duffey on their mating union here today. You may now renew your marks and kiss." Alpha David said with a broad smile.

Clark drew me close and nuzzled into my neck, I followed suit. We remarked each other gently, I moaned. We kissed and the entire pack erupted in cheers. I felt the whole world was in my hands at that moment. I kissed him slowly, exploring his mouth with my tongue. Clark growled and nibbled on my lip. "I love you Char." He murmured against my cheek. "I love you too." I whispered.

We turned towards the crowd and raised our tied hands, symbolizing our bond forever. Clark lead me to a table outside where we found a buffet of various delicious food, including Saskatoon berry crisp. Our guests came to greet us throughout the night, wishing us well. It was a lovely night. Heath came to find us a bit later to offer his congratulations.

"Congratulations again you two." He offered, pulling us in one at a time for a hug. "I am so happy my brother has found his perfect mate."

I pulled Heath in for a second hug, he was surprised I did. Clark looked at me confused. "I know you will find yours. She is out there somewhere." I whispered in Heath's ear. He froze and pulled me to him, hugging me back tightly.

When we let each other go, Heath looked into my face, "I have never had a sister but I hope you can teach me how. Thank you Charlotte, I hope you are right." Heath shook Clark's hand and went off to his rooms.

Clark pulled me close to him, "What was that about?" I shrugged, "He looked like he needed it. I mean, his younger brother just found the love of his life and is blissfully happy. Meanwhile he is a future Alpha without a mate, never even been close and is probably a little blue about it." Clark searched my face before wrapping his arms tightly around my waist and growling under his breath. I met his eyes, I could see they were jealous.

"Did you have to hug him a second time?" he asked. I rolled my eyes and sighed, "Listen here boy, I'm not interested in possession or jealousy and you know that. If that's what's on your mind you can just let it go. I love you, only you, forever. Your brother is not a threat, he's never been in the running, no one but you have ever been. I want him to know I care about him like I care about my biological brothers. So stop that prehistoric growling and kiss me."

Clark smirked and brought his lips to mine. He knew I was right. He knew I adored him and I would never consider another male. It just wasn't a possibility in my mind. "No, take me to bed and make me yours all over again." I whispered in his ear, taking his earlobe in between my teeth and nibbling. Clark moaned into my neck and licked my marking spot. I sucked in a sharp breath. We hurried back to our room, Clark lifted me off the ground and carried me over the threshold of our bedroom. I laughed out loud, he was so cute. He closed the door behind us and locked it.

Clark set me down on my feet and let his hands stroke down my arms, sides and rested on my hips, "I'm going to make love to you slowly my darling, I'm going to make your feel amazing. Let me make you feel good, like you make me feel every time." I took his face in my hands, "You make me feel good every single time, don't you ever doubt that." Clark looked down before taking my hands in his and kissing them. "I'm still coming too soon." He whispered, so quietly I almost didn't hear him.

I pulled his suit jacket off his shoulders, tossing it aside. I lifted his chin with my hand kissed him slowly, parting my mouth so he could slip his tongue inside. Clark moaned and wrapped his hands around my back. "You always make sure I am satisfied, Clark. You never leave me hanging, so when it comes to… that, I am not concerned. We are still new at this; it takes time to master something like sex. The more we do it, the better it gets. I wouldn't trade what we have done together for anything or anyone else." I said proudly, I meant it. Clark slid my zipper down my back and let me dress fall to the ground. He slipped my bra and underwear off. I stepped out of my shoes and moved over to the bed, standing next to it in a sexy pose with my hand on my hip. Clark lost his clothes in record time, running after me and pushing me back onto our bed. He kissed me passionately and moved himself inside me slowly. "I'm going to make you feel so good darling. I want tonight to be special for you." He moaned into my hair. I sucked air into my lungs with a quick gasp, "I love you so much Clark."

That night was unlike any other time with Clark. He held on for a very long time, making me feel ecstasy from my tip toes to my eye lashes. He focused on making me feel as good as possible for as long as he could hold on. The pull between us was electric, I couldn't stop myself as my release coursed through me before he finished. When he finally finished I thought he would pass out on top of me, his moaning was so loud. Clark kissed me gently before he rolled me on to his shoulder and wrapping his arm across me protectively.

"That was phenomenal." I hissed, still coming down from my high. Clark rubbed his nose in my hair, "I am going to spend the rest of my life making you happy." He promised me. I sighed lazily and let my body fall asleep with the man I loved the most.

## Chapter 9

Michael wanted to stay behind at Black Lake for a few extra weeks after my parents went back. He was depressed and didn't want to be reminded of Stella and the loss of their bond all over again. Clark and I were happy to have him with us. We figured the time away from Red Rose and all the memories would be good for him. My mother offered to clear out Stella's things before Michael got back and send them to Regina for him. It was one less thing for him to deal with during his heartache.

Before she left, my mother gave me my grandma Daisy's recipe book. My mother had added her own recipes to it over the years, she said it was my turn now. In it were all kinds of mixtures of various herbs and plants to create different concoctions. Some for healing, medicine, energy, arousal, health, sleep and even power. I had always been interested in herbology but I wasn't expecting to enjoy it as much as I had. My mother gave me a big hug as she left, "Be sure to make Michael the tea everyday. His heart is healing; I can sense it." I nodded.

My parents flew back three days after our mating ceremony. I was still so thrilled they had made it. After they left I took Michael by the arm and walked with him to the library. He and I both selected books and spent the majority of the day reading. Amy brought some sandwiches for lunch, joining us for a while for some conversation. After she took the dishes out of the room, I opened the copy of Jane Eyre I had been reading when Michael took the book out of my hand.

"Thank you for letting me stay here Char. I need it right now." He said sadly. I smiled at him and nodded, "Of course. My home is your home."

"Do you believe in second chance mates?" he asked me.

"Well I wasn't sure I believed in mates in the first place before I met Clark. Now I believe whole heartedly. So yes, I believe in second chance mates." I told him with confidence.

Michael pondered my words and he bit his lip. He glanced back at me, "I wonder why it didn't take with Stella? The mate bond is supposed to be the strongest one in the world, yet mine was so weak it was barely a pull. It wasn't what I had be told my whole life it would be like."

I shrugged and adjusted myself under the blanket, "Clark and I were talking about this a few days ago actually. His father told him that the bond isn't the same for everyone. Some mates have to work a lot harder at their bond then others. Some never bond fully. Sometimes one side would bond and the other never would feel as strongly. He thinks to a certain extent it is just the luck of the draw."

Michael chuckled darkly, "You know, he might be right. My mate bond was very one sided, and it was horrible."

"I still don't understand why the moon Goddess would pair two wolves together if it wasn't going to take. It seems like a lot of heartache for nothing." I muttered. He smiled and gave me back my book, "I'm sure she has her reasons."

"Perhaps Stella wasn't your great love after all," I suggested, "perhaps the one you are supposed to spend your life with is just waiting for your heart to heal."

We didn't speak for a while, both thinking about what I had just said. I eventually picked my book back up and continued to read it. Michael seemed lost in thought, I let him be. Clark linked me asking where I was, I told him. Five minutes later he came in, freshly showered. He had been training warriors for the majority of the day, picking up extra sessions since we had been so busy with the ceremony. Clark came over to me on the sofa, leaned down and kissed my lips tenderly. He went to a shelf and took out a book, came back, lifted up my legs and sat beneath them on the sofa, adjusting the blanket to make sure it covered all three of us. Clark never said a word, he didn't have to, he just knew me and I knew him.

After a while Michael sighed, "See that is what I want."

"Want what?" Clark asked, confused. I giggled, knowing he wasn't a part of our previous conversation.

"I want a mate who just knows me, comes to me and everything is easy and simple. You just came in here, kissed her, curled up with her and no words had to be spoken. You just know each other and it is understood. I want that." Michael told him.

Clark and I looked at each other and smiled. "I don't know what to tell you," I said, "It was like this from the beginning. He brought me ice-cream in my room when I had a panic attack at the ball."

"You never told me that." Michael said concerned. I waved my hand, "It's ok. Alpha Martins and father were having an argument about Marie and Anthony. I got very upset and tried to pull her out of there. It ended with her returning to the party and me having a panic attack. But then Clark came and found me with ice-cream."

Clark tucked my hair behind my ears. "It was always easy, like she said. I loved her the moment I caught her scent, before I even saw her face."

Michael nodded, he opened his book back up and started reading again. I looked at Clark, he leaned over and kissed me. I sighed into his mouth and returned the kiss.

"David and Heath asked me to talk to you about a meeting they want you to attend with us with the leaders of the werebear pack to the west of us. We have been trying to get a treaty in place for the past three years." Clark said, changing the subject.

"I didn't know there were werebears around here, though this far north I'm not really surprised." I added. "When is it?"

"It's at their pack house in two days. We are in neutral standing with them. We are currently the only werewolf pack in the Northwest Territories they are talking to. Usually werebears and werewolves don't cooperate but their Alpha and David have a mutual respect so we are trying to secure a treaty to enable some trade and cooperative protection." Clark told me. I nodded.

"I'd love to attend if you think I would be of help." I offered. He smiled, "You are always helpful my love." I giggled and moved around, resting my head on his lap and opening my book again. We read for another hour before all going down to dinner.

The three of us found Heath in the dining hall, joining him for supper. "Did you ask her?" Heath looked sharply at his brother. Clark nodded, "She will come."

Heath exhaled loudly and smiled at me, "Thank you Charlotte. We need a female presence at these meetings. The werebears haven't agreed to anything with us before because of our lack of mated male leaders. They believe females are the keys to a successful pack. It is very hard for them to trust us when it's only males at the meetings."

I looked at him confused, "We believe that as well though. We have Lunas in our packs. They wouldn't function without females. I'm sure werebears know that."

"They do, but their mating bond is very different from ours. Werebears don't have a pull like we do. Their beliefs don't include a predetermined match made by the Goddess or a higher power. They choose their mates when they come of age, they don't always mate for life either." He explained to me, "So for them, mating is less complicated. When we have had meetings in the past with their leaders they find it very hard to trust us when it is David, our father, Clark and myself considering only our father is mated."

"So now that Clark and I are mated, you believe that will help relations with the werebears?" I asked.

Heath and Clark both nodded, Clark spoke first, "I think the fact that you and I are also young will help them to trust us. Seeing a newly mated couple will enable them to understand our beliefs and values as well. They may want to ask you some questions, I would ask that you answer all the ones you are comfortable with."

Heath snickered and chimed in, "And even the ones you are uncomfortable with."

I laughed, Clark growled at his brother and Michael made a face with his nose, obviously not wishing to imagine his sister and brother in law in a compromised position.

I locked eyes with Heath and said calmly, "I will give them every little dirty detail but I am not sure they will be able to handle the heat."

"CHARLOTTE!" Clark and Michael cried in unison, Heath howled with laughter. The entire dining hall heard them all and looked at us in confusion. I smiled, adjusted my glasses and took a sip of my drink.

"You know, Charlotte, you look like a librarian but my brother has turned you into quite a vixen." Heath chuckled.

I shrugged, "What can I say, he brings out the animal in me." Clark raised his hands, almost pleading, "Alright enough! My mate and our sex life is no longer a topic of discussion at the dinner table or any other table."

"Seconded." Michael agreed. Heath and I both chuckled, I raised my glass to him, he raised his and we clinked together.

Clark rolled his eyes and kissed my head lightly.

# Chapter 10

I spent the next two days learning all I could about werebears in the library. Their history was quite extensive, not as old as wolves but still very ancient. Like Heath had said their mating practices were different from ours but they still believed in the moon Goddess like us. They also believed the northern lights granted special abilities which is why most werebear packs live in northern areas of the country. They hibernate for three months out of each year, shutting down their lives to slumber. This wasn't a choice, the werebears needed to do this in order to function, if they don't their ability to shift is lost for and their bodies weaken extensively. Hibernation has lead to many werebear packs being targeted for extermination, as if they are not concealed well enough they are wiped out. I learned from the history books that it was often werewolves that carried out these exterminations.

Based on that I could understand why werebears were hesitant to trust us. There was a long history of violence between our species, often with the werebears all dying out in the process. I could tell from the stories that werewolves had stronger packs then werebears. However, werebears had the ability to convert body fat for long term storage, so they could eat less then us for long periods of time, making survival in the wilderness much easier. They also had great traditions of healers, who used herbs to work all kinds of miracles. I read that their healers, who they called druids, had a massive amount of herbology knowledge. I was looking forward to meeting some of these druids and learning form them. Apparently their druids were exclusively female, it had something to do with their cycles and ability to give life. The werebears believed that only females should possess such knowledge.

Clark linked me, asking what I was up to. I told him where to find me.

He came to the library, giggling when he saw that I was at a large table behind stacks of books taller then I was. He came behind me, wrapping me in a warm embrace and kissed the top of my head, breathing me in deeply.

"How is your research going darling?" he asked, still nuzzling my hair.

"Werebears are so fascinating. Did you know they gain special abilities from the northern lights? And did you know they have healers, called druids, who can do amazing things with herbs? I am so excited to meet this pack and learn from them." I told him, still engrossed in my research.

Clark moved his mouth down to my marking spot and nibbled slowly, I moaned and tilted my head back into his chest, he had my full attention now.

"I am glad you are looking forward to it, I was worried you might find this part of your duties boring." He admitted. I shook my head, "This is going to be interesting. I am learning so much about werebears, I hope I can help with the treaty."

Clark let his hands explore my sides, my stomach, my chest. He continued to nibble on my mark and lick it gently. I moaned louder, "Take off your pants, now." He obliged me and, I shed mine and we had a quickie on the floor, though luckily for me it wasn't that quick.

We dressed in a hurry, praying no one would catch us. We were in luck; no one came into the library until a while after we were done. He pulled up a chair next to me and wrapped his strong arm around my shoulders, "I never thought sex would be so good," he whispered in my ear, making me groan all over again, "I know our bond is strong, very strong. That must be why."

I locked eyes with him and murmured, "It's because your body and mine were made to fit together perfectly. Every single part of your body fits into mine with ease. That's why it is so good, and it will only get better. The longer we are together the better and stronger everything will get."

Clark shivered at my words, he moaned as I kissed him slowly. He knew I was right, he loved that I was right. Our sex had become so amazing in a short time; it was only getting better the longer we were together. I was grateful for our bond, that it was so strong and growing everyday.

I hadn't realized it was supper time, I had completely missed lunch and now I was starving. We headed down to the hall and grabbed a table. Heath joined us, as was now tradition. Michael ended up sitting with some of the older wolves on the other side of the room. I was happy to see he was making friends with others in our pack. Tabitha came and found us, joining us as well.

She leaned over and whispered in my ear, "What is the story with your brother?"

I smiled at her, knowingly, I filled Tabitha in on why he was here with us. I didn't give her all the details Michael had confided in me but I told her as much as she needed to know. When I finished she nodded slowly and took a bite of her dinner.

"That's too bad, I haven't heard of a bond that didn't take before. I mean, we all know it's a possibility but I have never actually seen one." She said, glancing over in Michael's direction.

"He's healing right now. He's staying with us until he feels well enough to go back home. I am happy that he likes it here." I said, following her gaze. Tabitha seemed satisfied and we changed the subject to other pack house gossip.

"So Charlotte, do you have any questions about this meeting? I'm sure it's a lot to take in, especially if you have never been in the presence of werebears." Heath asked, not looking up from his food.

"Actually I have been studying up the last few days in the library. I've learned so much. I am thrilled to be going to this meeting, I want to learn more from them." I told him eagerly.

Heath looked up at me with awe on his face, he looked to Clark who nodded at him and back to me, "Thank god for you." I laughed. "No seriously, this is just what we need. If you have a genuine interest in them and care about it that will make a big difference. Clark, if you ever let go of this girl I will beat you senseless and then claim her for myself."

Clark went ridged next to me, I could feel panic through our bond. I looked at him, his face gave nothing away but I could feel his heart beating within his chest like a jack hammer. He was freaking out inwardly, without showing it on the outside. He smiled at his brother, looking at him in the eyes, "I never will."

Heath didn't look up from his food, he hadn't registered the strong reaction Clark had been having. I was certain he hadn't meant anything by it. Heath and I had become friends, but he respected the mate bond, he wasn't about to try and stake a claim on me. He respected his brother, he loved his brother. That wasn't who he was. He was happy to see Heath had found a strong mate to be by his side.

The rest of dinner passed easily. Clark was full of anxiety and fear; I could feel everything he felt. He was in a panic. After he finished eating he pulled me by the hand to our room, locking the door and turned to look at me.

His eyes were full of tears now; he was letting them fall when we were alone. I wrapped my arms around his neck and kissed his face slowly, trying to calm him. It wasn't working.

"He can't have you. You are mine. I will die without you. Please Charlotte, please." He cried into my neck, lifting me up to his shoulders. My legs lifted off the ground. I held on to him, rubbing his back and making soothing sounds.

"I know it is silly to feel so afraid." He admitted, "I know you don't want to be with an Alpha. I know you love me, that we are mated and you want me. I can feel how you feel for me, that our bond is so strong it is unbreakable. I know all of that but when he says things like that it fills me with such panic. If Heath wanted to, he could take you from me. He could kill me and take you as his own. I would die without you now. I would die for you."

I continued to make calming sounds and rub his back. Clark was very aware of how I felt about him and how I didn't want his brother. He knew, I didn't need to say it.

"I think you need to tell Heath how you feel when he says things like that. He may think it is funny but I doubt he knows how if effects you." I told him. Clark looked at me, as though he hadn't considered that. "Your brother loves you so much, I think if he actually realized how much turmoil it fills you with, he wouldn't dream of saying a thing like it."

Clark thought about it for a moment. He seemed to be mulling over my words, "Maybe you are right." I nodded. He set me down finally and kissed me quickly. I motioned for him to go.

"Right now?" he asked, I nodded. Clark sighed heavily and turned, leaving me in our room. I smiled as he left. "Silly brothers." I giggled to myself.

I went to find Cheryl after that, I wanted to have a visit with her about werebears. She would also be at the meeting so I thought we should go in as a united front. When I arrived at their room, I could hear giggling and hushed voices. I smiled to myself and thought the better of knocking on their door. I turned to walk away, hoping Clark and I would be just like them when we got to be that age.

I returned to our room, laying down and reading some more of my Jane Eyre book. I could feel Clark's side of the conversation he was having with his brother. There were many emotions; fear, hurt, empathy, love, jealousy, embarrassment. I could tell it was going well. I smiled to myself, taking off my glasses and turning out the light. I went to sleep, figuring Clark would wake me up when he came in.

He did not. I woke the next morning uninterrupted. Clark lay next to me snoring gently. I smiled at him, the conversation with Heath must have gone well if he didn't feel the need to wake me when he got in. I moved out of bed quietly and went to the bathroom to shower. It was going to be a busy day today. Our meeting was tomorrow morning so I had the rest of today to finish my research and have a sit down with Cheryl. First, though, I need to send Marie a letter. I hadn't in a week and it was time for me to keep my promise.

I dressed and went to the dining hall. Amy and Tabitha were up already preparing breakfast for the pack with some of the other women. I greeted them and helped myself to some fruit, I offered to help but Tabitha shooed me away, "We got this lady. Don't you worry." I smiled and left for the library. One thing I really liked about Black Lake was the Alpha would eat with the Omegas and it wasn't considered odd. We were all one, sure there were different ranks but everyone took care of each other. It didn't matter that Amy and Tabitha had a different rank then me, we still spent time together and took care of each other. I liked that very much.

The library was deserted; Mary wasn't even in there muttering to herself about how messy people left it. I drew the curtains back and watched at the sun peeked out, still under the tree line. I sighed heavily, what a beautiful dawn. I pulled the chair behind me to sit and I started my letter to Marie. I told her about Michael and Stella, how he was staying with me here at Black Lake for a while. I suggested she and Anthony visit, though I knew that wasn't going to happen. Honestly I would be lucky if I ever saw her again at this point. I wrote about the recipe book mother had given to me and about my interest in herbology. I asked how she was doing, what was new, how Rocky Mountain was and so on. I sent it. My fruit bowl was tasty, I had eaten almost all of it when the computer dinged at me, letting me know the email had been opened. I knew Anthony read all her emails, especially from me.

Suddenly an email from Marie appeared in my inbox. I sat up straight and opened it with a start. It read;

Char, I miss you so much. I am ok, things here are not great. Anthony and I had our ceremony two weeks ago. He won't let me mark him. I know he is sleeping with some of the Omegas here, I can feel it through the bond, but because I can't mark him I can't tell where he is. He hits me every day, not always in the face but often. He keeps threatening to collar me if I misbehave, but all I want is to understand why he isn't faithful to me. He forces himself on me every day. He wants pups so badly, he told me I have to give him what he wants. I haven't had my heat yet, we are still too young, but I'm sure I will be pregnant before then. I love you Char, I am sorry about Michael. I think you know I can't visit, it's impossible. I will be in trouble for writing you back, I was only able to do so because I could find my email on his phone while he is still asleep. I will have to delete it, so don't reply to this email please. I am alright, Mrs. Martins is helping with my adjustment here, it's pretty rough but I am ok. She says her husband was like this too in the beginning, but it won't last forever. I am not sure whether to trust her or not, but I don't really have a choice. Tell everyone I love them. I'm sorry.

It was actually her; I knew it was her. Tears spilled from my eyes. My heart broke and I wailed. I mind linked Clark, yelling for him to come to the library. He was there in under a minute, I could tell he had been asleep, "What?!"

I pointed to the computer screen, he came over and read it behind my shoulder, wrapping his arms around me. Clark sighed heavily and pulled me as close as he could. I wept, both happy to hear from her and broken because she had confirmed all my greatest fears. Anthony was unfaithful, he was raping her, he was hitting her. What was he thinking? Collaring? Clark took my tear covered glasses from my face and cleaned them off with his shirt. He set them next to the keyboard. I exhaled into his chest, trying to control my breathing.

"If he collars her, she will die." I whispered. Clark shook his head, "No darling, it won't kill her but it will hurt, she will have scars."

I wiped my face and took a deep breath. He was right, she was stronger then that. Marie would survive, she had to survive him.

"Charlotte, I want you to forward that email to me and Heath. Anytime you get an email that is actually from your sister I want you to send it to both of us. We are going to start keeping a record of her abuse. Eventually we may have enough evidence to take her away from him, the elders of their pack will have no choice but to listen if there is an ongoing problem like this. I've seen it done in other packs." Clark told me calmly, I looked up at him. He smiled, "She is my sister now too, this isn't right. Anyone who hurts my family hurts my pack. Blood or not."

"I love you so much." I whispered into his chest. He leaned down and kissed my head, smelling my hair, as always. He growled lowly, I knew he loved me too. I turned and set off the email to Heath and Clark, closed down the computer and cleaned up my bowl of fruit. I needed to get on with the day. I put my glasses back on my face, Clark adjusted them slightly and kissed my forehead. We had a meeting with the werebears tomorrow and it was very important to more then just me but the entire pack and the North West Territories.

## Chapter 11

I met with Cheryl after lunch about the werebears. She had a large folder for me to go over full of werebear lore. I read through it in the library, asking her questions as I went. Tabitha brought us tea and sat down with us, examining the papers as well. I learned that this werebear pack was called the Ice Water pack, home to about four hundred werebears. They were the largest pack in Canada, but only about a dozen werebear packs still exist in the entire country. They are very secretive, not trusting outsiders with much information including other werebear packs. According to one document, there used to be many more werebears but they have been wiped out by werewolves over the years over resources and territory. It seemed like a long a bloody history between our species.

"Based on what these documents say, this pack shouldn't be meeting with us. How is this meeting even happening?" I asked Cheryl.

She smiled at me knowingly, "The Ice Water pack are a very large pack, so they are not as threatened as a smaller pack would be. Also they outnumber us four to one so we are actually the underdogs as it were. Our packs have lived peacefully up here for over two hundred years in close proximity."

I nodded, handing another document to Tabitha to read, "So what are we hoping to get out of this meeting?"

"We are hoping to draft a treaty between our packs, the very first of it's kind between werebears and werewolves. We would like for them to share their medical knowledge with us in exchange for protection and support during their hibernation periods." Cheryl told me.

"That sounds amazing. Do you think they will agree?" I asked.

Cheryl smiled, "I hope so, I know that their Alpha has great respect for ours. We have helped them in the past with food for their pack. Their hunting skills are not excellent, when werebears come out of hibernation they are starving and weak. In the past ten years we have brought them several fresh kills at this time to help sustain their packs."

I continued through the documents, there was so much to learn. I felt a bit overwhelmed with it all. Tabitha poured us all some more tea and seemed engrossed with the information as well.

"There is one more thing that is important to know, the werebears will not train males to be their druids, only females are given that gift. They see it as a connection between the earth and our cycles. Since females can give live, they are also in charge of healing it." Cheryl told me. I looked up at her, my eyes wide. That was indeed interesting.

Cheryl excused herself, telling me she would be happy to help out with anything else if I needed her. I stayed in the library well after supper time going over all the documents multiple times. At some point Tabitha brought me soup and a rabbit kabob, though I can't say what time that was.

Clark mind linked me, asking me where I was, I looked at the clock in the library, it was almost 9pm. I was amazed I had been in there for so long. I told him I was coming to our room as I packed up the folder.

I arrived in our room to find Clark was laying on our bed, reading a book. He looked up and smiled at me, "What have you been up to? I missed you at dinner."

"I was in the library reading about the werebears." I told him, lifting the folder before I set it down on our dresser.

He nodded, "You have been busy my darling, I am sure you are more prepared then Heath or myself at this point."

"Your mother was a very big help. She is amazing, I just love her." I told him. I started to undress. I did it slowly, not really looking at my mate, just taking my clothes off one piece at a time to see if I could get a reaction.

"I am glad you and my mother get along. It certainly makes my life easier." Clark said, laughing. I giggled, undoing my bra and tossing it into the hamper. I let my breasts be bare as I started to unzip my jeans.

Clark started to study me, I heard his book snap shut. I could sense he was paying more attention to my movements.

"I hope I am helpful tomorrow, "I muttered, trying to remain nonchalant, "I have no experience with werebears." I slid my jeans down to the floor and slipped my underwear down, bending all the way over to pick the up and toss them in the hamper as well.

Clark moaned as he lifted himself off the bed. I let my hair fall down my back as I removed my hair tie. He was coming up behind me, "Not having experience doesn't mean you won't be good at it my darling."

I turned around to face him, he was right behind me. Clark caught me in his arms and pulled me into a warm embrace. He kissed my lips with heat, slipping his tongue in my mouth. I wrapped my arms around his neck and pulled him closer. I lifted my leg and wrapped it around his hip bone. Clark moaned into my mouth, sliding his hands down my sides to my hips.

"I just want to do a good job for our pack," I whispered against his lips, "to make you proud."

Clark lifted me up against chest, I wrapped my legs around his waist and nibbled on his lips.

He moaned into my mouth, "I am always proud of you, you are the most amazing woman in the world to me. I am in awe of you every single day."

"MMMM," I groaned, "you are quite the sweet talker Beta Duffey."

Clark giggled against my lips, "I'm only smooth because you make me smooth."

I slid my hands down his back, letting my finger nails trail. He gasped, "Oh god Char, you are making me crazy."

"Good." I teased, licking his mark following up with a small nip. He growled loudly, finally giving in and taking me to the bed. He fell backwards letting me land on top of him, we fell into a deep kiss. After we made love we fell asleep, I could get used to the daily doses of sex and the deep sleeps at Black Lake.

We were up at dawn the next morning, eating breakfast and outside the pack house by 7am. We had to take the side by sides to the meeting since roads were non-existent in our territory. Clark and I were with his parents, Heath took David and Timothy. It was about an hour from our pack house to theirs. When we arrived I was amazed at how huge theirs was. It was built into the side of a rock face. There was no way to tell how actually large it was from the outside because it went into the rocks but I was sure it was very large considering they have more then four hundred pack members. Clark rubbed my shoulders as we stepped out of the vehicle and up the steps to the pack house. He could tell I was nervous.

Three men came out the front of the pack house before we could reach the door. They all towered over us, and the Duffeys were not small men. I had never seen werebears before, but even in human form they were enormous. There were handshakes all around, no real words were spoken, we were led inside to the foyer. The pack house was indeed huge. I could see there were many levels to it, going underground and far back into the rock face. There were warm animal skin rugs all over the floors and florescent torches mounted on the walls. It was definitely a cave.

A woman with black hair strode up to us and greeted David, they embraced, saying words to each other I could not hear. She turned and motioned for us all to follow. We walked down a series of corridors, deeper underground. I was sure I would never be able to find my way out of here on my own. Clark held my hand as we continued to follow the woman. No one seemed concerned so I felt uneasy for nothing. We came to a large oak double door with intricate carvings all over it in she shapes of bears. The woman motioned for us to stop and then moved inside the door, leaving us all outside. No one spoke, we just waited for a few minutes until the doors were opened wide for us.

I followed the others in, there were paintings along the walls appearing like cave drawings only modernized. There was a large conference table in the centre of the room with stools around it. Everything looked to be hand carved. There were four women sitting at the end of the conference table, they all rose as we came into the room. David lead us around the table, walking right up to one of the women and kissing her cheeks as a welcome.

"Good morning Alpha Doris, it is lovely to see you." David said happily. She kissed his cheeks as well, "And you too Alpha David."

That was one thing that wasn't in the folder, werebears had female Alphas. I was so intrigued. I instantly couldn't wait to learn more.

"Welcome to Ice Water pack house. I have asked my Beta Renee and my Gamma Rose to join us." She told us gesturing to the other two women standing. They nodded their heads with respect.

"Of course, you know my Beta and his wife. You also remember future Alpha Heath, who will be taking over the pack in a year or two. This is his brother and Beta, Clark and his wife Charlotte, and his Delta, Timothy." David introduced us. We all nodded with respect as well.

Doris invited us all to sit down to begin the meeting. It started off rather slow, reviewing the past meetings between the Alphas. They discussed Heath's position within the Black Lake pack, what that would entail should we reach a treaty. It appeared that Doris and David had a professional relationship for many years. There was a great deal of trust between them.

"So the treaty would be the first of it's kind between our species. It would make history." Doris began, she rose to carry her voice around the room. "However, making history is not reason enough to write a treaty. It has to be beneficial to both parties. I would like to discuss the terms of this agreement between our packs. I believe we can come to an agreement today."

"Agreed. What are your terms?" David asked.

"We are willing to offer our herbology training to three individuals from your pack, females only who will train alongside our druids to become apprentice healers. This knowledge once possessed may be passed down through generations of other wolves. However, our traditions on the matter must be respected, which means only permanent, mated female members of the Black Lake pack may possess this knowledge. It must not be shared with other werewolf packs you enter into treaties with, there will be no exceptions." Doris said strongly. I found her very proud and mesmerizing. She commanded respect and attention. I had seen the odd female Alpha in werewolf packs, but they were rare. I instantly respected Doris, she had so much to teach us.

David nodded, "That is very interesting to us. What are you asking for in return?"

I stared at Doris, she looked around at her two companions. The shifted in their seats a bit. Her eyes fell to me, we made eye contact for a few moments. Her eyes searched mine inquisitively. I wasn't sure how to take it, so I froze, trying to remind myself to breathe and blink.

"Our pack has grown in the last fifty years, we have swelled to almost four hundred and fifty members. Though this is impressive number for protection we are finding it harder and harder to sustain our food requirements. We are finding it harder and harder to build up enough calories before we hibernate, thus causing many of us to wake too early in the spring. If we don't hibernate long enough we can not shift, we become weak and our souls start to die. No medicine can help it." Doris explained to us.

We wolves looked around at each other. Food was never a problem for us, especially when it came to protein. We were excellent hunters no matter the season. I personally had never gone hungry. I felt a tinge of sympathy for them. If members of our pack were going hungry our Alpha would feel personally responsible too.

"Basically we are requesting enough protein offerings throughout the year to help sustain our pack, especially before our hibernation cycles. We figure six moose, fifteen deer and four elk per year should be enough at our current numbers. However, that may be revisited should our populations change over time." Doris told us, "We are also requesting protection during our hibernation cycles from predators and outsiders. This past year we lost twenty-two of our pack members to rogue attacks while we slept. We want to avoid this in the future."

David nodded, "That is regrettable. Any loss of life from a pack is a terrible loss. I think we can come to a mutually beneficial treaty here today Alpha." She nodded.

"I would like to request that our first druid to be trained would be our new Beta female Charlotte Duffey here." Samuel gestured to me. The werebears all looked to me, straight faced and calm. Doris nodded,

"That can be arranged for the beginning of the summer in July. We can make arrangements at a later date."

My heart was pounding in my chest. I was so excited, I had no idea I was to be chosen to learn the skills of the druids by my pack. It is an amazing honor. I couldn't stop smiling. Clark squeezed my shoulder, I turned to see him beaming down at me. I wondered if he already knew I would be the first selected.

"Do we have an agreement Alpha David?" Doris asked, David stood, "We do. Let us make history my friend. The first treaty between our two species, let us shake on it." The two Alphas crossed to the front of the room and shook hands. It was a monumental moment in were history. I was so happy to be a part of it.

We all chatted amongst ourselves in the conference room while we waited for lunch. I was admiring the wood carvings on the walls when the werebear Gamma approached me. She stood shoulder to shoulder with me. "So you will be the one I am training in July." She muttered, not looking at me. I jumped at her words, she didn't seem pleased by this. I turned and starred at her, bowing my head, "I am Charlotte Duffey, I am so grateful for this opportunity. I love herbology, I consider it a privilege to learn from you."

The Gamma paused for a moment, she took a deep breath and exhaled loudly. She was an older woman in her sixties with long silver hair and cool green eyes. I waited for her to say something to me but she didn't speak. I turned back to the carvings on the wall. I stepped away to my right, the Gamma matched my movements. She sighed heavily, "I am Gamma Rose, I will teach you everything I know. I hope you understand the importance of this training and take it seriously. You are still a child; I would guess no more then eighteen. If I even suspect, you are not taking this seriously I will inform my Alpha and your training will be suspended until I deem it fit that it continue. I hope I make myself clear to you, girl."

I nodded rapidly, "I am so honored to have this opportunity. I won't let you down Gamma Rose." She turned to face me, her eyes very cold. I think she could tell I was intimidated by her. I think she wanted it that way. I forced myself to maintain eye contact with her, I wanted her to understand that I was brave.

Rose took another deep breath. She was smelling the air, she stared into my face, searching it. I inhaled deeply, I didn't realize I had been holding my breath. Rose took a step forward and whispered to me, "Are you sure you want to learn this? The knowledge that comes with it isn't for the faint of heart. Some of it will break your heart."

I starred back at her, I nodded slowly. Rose exhaled loudly, "Alright girl, I am going to tell you something that may make you change your mind. You are pregnant, right now. I can smell that you are about two weeks along. Congratulations."

My mouth fell open, I was shocked. I wasn't sure how to take what she telling me. I wasn't sure she was telling the truth, I wondered if it was a test. "However, I can also smell that this pregnancy won't last. There is something wrong with it, your body will reject it before the next full moon. The pain of this loss will be hard, especially now that you have to go through it knowing there is nothing you can do to stop it."

"Why are you telling me this?" I asked softy, my voice came out almost inaudible. Rose stared at me. She reached out and took my hand, her eyes still cold, "The Goddess does not give us more hardships then what we can handle. This will be a trial for you, with this knowledge that I have told you today. I told you that our knowledge comes with great responsibility. If you accept this, learn from it, grow from it then you may come back for training on July 1st. If you can not, then you are not ready to learn our ways."

I was speechless. Rose let my hand go and moved away from me. I didn't know what to say, I wasn't sure any of it was true. I couldn't tell. My head was spinning, I instinctively touched my stomach as though that touch would answer anything. I felt Clark behind me, he touched my shoulders. I knew he felt my confusion. He asked me through my link what was wrong, I told him the Gamma was just trying to get into my head.

The werebears fed us lunch before we headed back to our pack house. As we were leaving Rose came to me again, reaching for my hand. I gave it to her without hesitation. She stared into my face again, "This is a special kind of tea. When it happens, you will be in a lot of pain. Have your mate make this for you. Only your mate may make this, no other. Drink it three times a day for three days. It will subdue the pain and encourage faster healing. This tea will also heal the heartache faster, for both yourself and your mate through the bond."

I looked down at the brown canvas bundle she had placed in my hand. My eyes lifted slowly to her face, she met my stare, "I hope to see you in July." With that, Rose turned away and went back into her pack house. I slipped the bundle into my pocket. I decided it was time to take a pregnancy test as soon as possible.

## Chapter 12

I spent the next few days in a haze wondering around the pack house. I wasn't really aware of myself. I tried to keep busy with various tasks like helping out in the kitchen, bringing Michael his tea, researching herbs in the library. It was coming up to the middle of May. The spring air was fresh with faint smells of flowers. I took to exploring the close grounds of the pack house on my own, shifting into my wolf and going for runs to escape my own thoughts. I didn't feel any different, but since our meeting with the werebears I often caught myself touching my stomach absentmindedly.

Clark knew something was off about me, but he didn't push too much. I avoided the conversation by avoiding him. I am sure he was hurt by that, but I wasn't ready to talk about it yet. I was coming up to my nineteenth birthday in July. I knew he wanted to celebrate it with me, but I couldn't bring myself to plan anything like that. The words Rose told me repeated over and over in my head like a mantra. By the time I was celebrating my birthday I would be hurting from the loss of this supposed child I was carrying. It felt as though there wasn't much to celebrate.

I had put in a request with Cheryl for some pregnancy tests to come in on the May supply plane. I begged her to keep that information to herself, she agreed only if I told her what was going on. I had to tell her about my conversations with Rose. Cheryl was supportive, hugged me and told me everything would be alright. I had asked her if there was a chance the Gamma was mistaken, she had said there is always a chance, but probably not.

When the plane was unloaded Cheryl brought me the test in a small bag full of our usual monthly toiletries. I was grateful she didn't make a big deal about it. I moved quickly to our bedroom, went to the bathroom and locked the door. I took the pregnancy test and waited for the results. It felt like five minutes took about three lifetimes. I started at myself in the mirror, willing myself to call for Clark but I didn't. I had to hold it together.

When I finally turned the test over, it read positive and a ball felt like it dropped into my stomach. I started to cry. Suddenly I heard Clark on the other side of the bathroom door, "Charlotte, what's wrong?!"

I threw the test across the room and sunk to the floor, I started to rock back and forth, unable to stand. Clark broke the door down and picked me up from the floor. He brought me to our bed, wrapping me up in his body and held me close. I hung on to his chest like my life depended on it, as though I couldn't live without him. I couldn't talk yet; my body could only respond it deep sobs.

"Charlotte, darling you are scarring me, what is it?" he begged, I could feel his sobs start to form. I chocked out, "I'm pregnant." He scoffed, looking down at me but I didn't meet his gaze. I felt his heart sink in his chest, "You are sad that you are having a child with me?"

I shook my head, pulling his face to mine, "No, I am sad because this baby isn't going to make it." He stared down at me, shock on his face.

"What do you mean? How do you know that?" he cried out, almost angry that I would suggest it. I buried my face in his chest again, "Rose told me." I continued to sob, not able to say more then that. Clark cried with me, holding me as close as possible. We stayed like that for hours. Tabitha brought us my mother's mushroom and camomile tea at some point, leaving it for us on the dresser. At some point I fell asleep in his arms, him in mine.

Michael knocked on the door around supper time and brought us in some rabbit stew with bread. We ate it and returned to our bed, holding each other. We were no longer crying, but we could feel the sadness bouncing between us back and forth. I looked up into Clark's face, he met my eyes with his own despair.

"I am sorry honey." I whispered. He kissed me slowly, "You have nothing to be sorry for. Are you sure that the werebear is correct though? How do you know for sure?"

I sighed and rested my forehead against his shoulder, "She is a druid as well. Rose is the one who will train me in July. They can smell it, it would seem. I read about it, I talked to your mother as well. It seems it's all a part of their training."

He shook his head, "Well she could be wrong about this." I pulled him in and kissed him. "Clark, she isn't going to be wrong. You know that. She told me how to take care of us both when it happens." My voice shook as I said the words. He pulled me closer to him, I almost felt like I was going to melt into his chest and we would become one body.

At some point we slept, I felt the morning sun coming through the windows into the window. I was still in yesterday's clothes, so was Clark. I slipped out of bed and changed clothes. I snuck to the library and wrote an email to Marie. I told her about the meeting and about the pregnancy. I told her all about what Rose had told me and how Clark and I were feeling. I didn't even ask how she was. I didn't really care if it was Anthony who read it, I just wanted to get it out to her. I wanted the comfort of telling my twin my heartache and having her share it with me, even it was across miles. I sent the email and went to the sofa to read another herbology book.

The phone ran in the library; it was the pack house phone. I waited for someone to answer it, returning to my book. Amy came in to the library, breathing heavily, "Charlotte, the phone is for you." I looked up, not expecting it. I picked up the receiver and whispered a tentative hello into the receiver.

"Hello Charlotte, how are you?" I heard Anthony's voice. I stood up straight when I recognized his voice. "Hello Anthony, I am alright. Yourself?" I asked.

"Fine, fine. We just received your email. I suggested Marie give you a call, for a chat. That is if you have time for us." He mumbled, almost apologetically. I was taken aback, I wasn't expecting him to call me and offer any kind of support at all. "That would be wonderful. I would love to speak to her." I managed to say, tears started to come to my eyes again.

"Good, I am glad. Here she is. It was nice to say hello Charlotte. Take care." Anthony said shortly. I gasped as the phone was passed between two people and I heard her breath at the other end of the line.

"Charlotte?" she whispered. We both sobbed into the phone for a few moments, just repeating each other's names over and over.

"I miss you so much Char, it is so good to hear your voice." She finally told me through the tears. I smiled widely, "I miss you too Marie."

"I am so sorry about the pregnancy." She whispered, "Are you sure there is nothing to be done to keep it?" I hung my head, it was as though she could see me doing it through the phone, "I'm sure you and Clark are devastated."

"We are; I wasn't expecting to be pregnant this soon." I confessed. Marie giggled suddenly, "Well have you two been practicing?" she asked coyly. I sighed, "Yes, I suppose you can call it that."

Marie laughed, it was good to hear it. She sounded like herself, I was so relieved to hear her voice. "I know all about practicing." She told me, smiling, I heard Anthony shush her through the phone. "It makes Tony blush when I talk about sex. However, it happens to be one of my favorite subjects."

I laughed out loud, surprised she was saying that out loud with him just on the other side of her. I gathered up some courage to finally ask her, "So how are things going with Anthony?"

Marie paused, she sighed and inhaled deeply, "Things are getting better. Tony and I have been talking a lot more. He is coming around to my way of doing things slowly, aren't you sweetie?"

I heard a grunt in the background, followed by a low growl. "Are you sure?" I asked wearily, not sure if I believed that. "Trust me Char. I am doing better here. I have actually been meaning to call mother and father one of these days. I've been busy learning my Luna duties, my days are pretty full." She told me with confidence. She sounded like herself, I was cautiously optimistic.

"Any chance of a visit soon?" I asked. She groaned, "Probably not this year. Maybe next year. One step at a time." I nodded, so he was still controlling and possessive, but I was talking on the phone with her so that was progress.

"I should get going, Tony and I need to get going to a meeting. Charlotte, I want you to call me when it happens," she told me sadly, "We will be here for you and Clark every step of the way, I promise. Right Tony?" I heard Anthony say in the background, "Of course my love."

I sucked in a breath, "Ok, I'll call you." We hung up the phone, I sat back against the coach and mulled over the conversation we just had. Had I imagined it? Was that all in my head? How had I just had a twenty-minute talk with Marie, who actually sounded like herself. Anthony was still there, hovering over her and in control but she was still herself. She sounded happy, content, safe. I adjusted my glasses and opened my book back up, maybe this was a new chapter in Anthony's story.

Clark came to the library about an hour later. He didn't need to link me anymore to ask where I would be. He kissed the top of my head, asking how I was. "Good, I talked to Marie this morning." I told him.

Clark sat down with a thud on the sofa next to me, "Are you serious?" I nodded, "I know I was shocked when Anthony called me this morning. I had emailed her with our news. He called and offered for me to talk with her. We talked for twenty minutes. She sounded like herself, she was happy."

He studied my face with caution, "Are you sure?". "I know I was surprised too, I asked her how things were going with him. She actually called him 'Tony' several times, teased him on the phone. She told me a bit too much about their sex life, which I didn't need to hear and I could tell he wasn't happy she shared it with me." I told him with a laugh. Clark shook his head, "Well that I can understand." I kissed his cheek.

"I'm not sure how to feel about it. I know he is still abusive and controlling. I don't trust him at all but she does sound better then she did in the emails. I actually got to talk to her, she sounded like herself." I told him. Clark nodded slowly, "Alright. Well keep tabs on it all the same. It might be a honeymoon period. Anthony has a mean streak, so it might not last." I sighed and agreed. It could be that. I wanted to hope it didn't go back to the way it was before, Marie deserved to be happy.

Clark's eyes glazed over and I could tell he was getting a message. "What is it?" I asked. Clark stood up and kissed me quickly, "Rogues on the boarders between Ice Water and ours. Timothy says there are about four of them. They need me to go and lead the hunt." This was the first rogue sighting I had heard about since I arrived at Black Lake. I nodded, "Be safe honey." Clark nodded, he mind linked me and told me he would find me later. I knew as a Beta; Clark was way stronger then rogues. He was a very strong Beta, above average size. When he and Heath shifted their wolves were very close to the same size, Heath's just being pure black and Clark's being a very dark grey. It was curious, because when Samuel shifted his wolf was smaller then both his sons. It wasn't unheard of though.

Melanie came to me shortly after Clark left, asking me to join her in the conference room. I followed her, she had a very detailed map up on a bulletin board of our pack territory, she had red pins on it in various places. "The red pins indicate rogue sightings. I leave them up all year long to try and determine a pattern if there is one." She explained. I nodded, it made sense. "Each pin indicates one rogue, so if there are four like today, I put in four red pins. This way we can also indicate strength. If there is one rogue it's very different then if there are a dozen. We want to know if there is a rogue pack coming our way, we don't need that." She went on.

"Have we had rogue packs around here? I thought the attacks were a minimal, a few a year?" I asked. Melanie pointed to her pins, I could see there were about ten on it right now. "I am going to add the sightings from the werebears as well to our map, now that they are our allies. They told Timothy they had over twenty-five sightings since the beginning of this year. With the deaths they had during their hibernation we are starting to suspect the Ice Water pack is being targeted." She explained.

"I can see why they wanted us to enter into a treaty with them. Hibernation would be the perfect time to hit a werebear pack." I suggested, she nodded. "Their territory would be attractive to a rogue pack. It's how werewolves took down so many werebears throughout our histories. I suspect there is a pack, these rogues today are probably just scouts but Timothy, Clark and Heath have been discussing it. I know the Alpha and the Beta believe it is a possibility, that's why this treaty was so important to them."

"Are they targeting all werebears?" I asked, she shook her head. Melanie sighed sadly, "No, not all. Their cubs seem to be the top priority. Of the twenty-two killed so far this year seventeen were cubs or young of some kind." I frowned when she said that, "That's terrible."

Melanie nodded. Werebears carried their young for almost nine months like humans so when they loose a cub it takes well over a year to produce another one. Unlike us, we carry our pups for six months, we can potentially have two a year. For rogues to attack their young could have a lasting effect on their populations, which could greatly damage a pack's vitality. It pained me to ask, "How many have they lost before this year?"

Melanie shrugged, "We are not sure, but the Alphas have talked about it at length. Apparently they are desperate to get some help. Based on the reports I have been getting from the past few years it has been up to fifty per year of cub and young deaths due to rogue attacks." I winced at the numbers, that was so many children lost. It seemed there was probably a plan in place somewhere to effect the werebear populations. It would take a few decades to see the effects but it had already made a dent in their future vitality.

It could be random; I was no military expert but it happened every year it doesn't sound random. That sounds planned, perhaps by rogues, perhaps not. It was hard to say, there wasn't enough evidence.

"Do we have many deaths from rogues here at Black Lake?" I asked Melanie. She shook her head, "The last one was over ten years ago, it happened when an few Omegas were out gathering plants. We don't think they realized how far the had drifted to the boarder of our territory. One was killed, the other two made it back. Since then no deaths, we have rogues run through our territory, but not a large amount usually and not all the time." I sighed, I was relieved we were not being targeted, however it spoke volumes that the werebears were and we were not.

"I am glad we are cooperating with the Ice Water pack. I hope our warriors are able to help them with the rogues." I stated, studying Melanie's map. She was placing blue pins on it, to illustrate the number of rogue attacks in the werebear territory. It was alarming how quickly it areas on the map became concentrated blue. She nodded in agreement, "I believe this treaty will be mutually beneficial. Werebears almost went extinct because of werewolves. It's an honor to be a part of rewriting history and changing perspectives." I smiled at her. Melanie was a kind soul, she had a great respect for life, traditions and family. I was happy she and I would be working together through the years for our pack.

"Are you from Black Lake originally?" I asked her, changing the subject. I turned and sat down at the conference table. Melanie didn't take her eyes off the map, she continued to plug in pins as she answered, "Yes, Timothy and I are both from Black Lake. We grew up together, he is a year older then I am. He felt the pull before I did, when he was fifteen, I was only fourteen at the time."

"What was that like, to find him so young?" I studied her face, she seemed to be listening to me only half heartedly, but she still managed to answer, "It was alright. I didn't really know how to take it at first, as I felt nothing. He was just my friend."

Melanie turned and set the papers down she had been holding on the table and made eye contact with me, "Shall we have some lunch and tea?" I nodded. We left the conference room and went to the dining hall for some food. We filled our plates and sat at an empty table. We sat in silence for a bit before she continued to tell me about her mate, "When Timothy felt the pull, he came to my room and broke my door down, he was like a wild animal, almost losing control." I stared at her, not sure what to say.

She smiled at me and let out a laugh, "Don't get me wrong, I'm crazy for him now, but at the time I was a terrified fourteen-year-old girl who didn't understand why my friend was trying to bite me. Our parents sat down together and had a discussion. A few days later my father explained to me what was going on, at that time I didn't know a lot about the mate bond yet, I was still too young. My father explained to me that in a year or two I would start to feel the pull to Timothy, when I did I was to tell my parents immediately. Over the next year Timothy was only allowed to spend time with me when we had a chaperone present. It drove him crazy, he wanted to be alone with me so badly."

"That must have been intense for you. For him as well." I offered. Melanie nodded, "He kissed me once, I remember biting him and he liked it. I thought it was the grossest thing in the world." We both laughed out loud. Tabitha pulled up a chair to join us, she looked at the two of us confused.

"Oh, I am just telling Charlotte about how Timothy and I became mates." She told her. Tabitha laughed, "Right, I remember that well. He broke your door down. We had to sit through a few lectures about etiquette over the following days because of that, they were very boring."

I smiled at Tabitha. "Anyway, my pull came just before I turned sixteen. I started to smell cumin, I love cumin. I searched the whole pack house for it, it was making me so hungry. When I realized it was Timothy I couldn't stop myself and I leapt into his arms. He was so relieved

I finally felt the bond he marked me right there. My father was not pleased." Melanie told us, laughing out loud as she blushed.

Tabitha sighed, smiling at both of us. "I wish I knew my mate. I am supposed to go to the exhibition next year. I can't wait." I nodded, finishing my plate of lunch.

"I had a very pleasant experience, but that isn't everyone's story." I said dryly. Tabitha raised her eyebrows at me, but I didn't elaborate. "I am sure yours will be a nice story though."

She smiled at me, "I hope so. My sister found hers when was sixteen. I was never so jealous in my life." I giggled, remembering how I didn't want to find my mate. I wanted to return to Red Rose to be left alone with my books and my thoughts. Now that seemed like years ago when in reality is was a matter of months.

"Time goes so fast, I'm sure it is only a matter of time before you look back on this conversation as though it is a million years ago." I told her supportively. Melanie and Tabitha both smiled.

I received a mind link from Clark, telling me they had tracked the rogues to a cave in the werebear territory. Apparently they had been hiding there for a while, as they had a camp set up. The rogues had fled the area when our warriors had caught their trail, leaving everything behind.

I was glad he was safe. I knew he would be, but it felt comforting all the same. I wanted to see him as soon as possible, I told him. Clark said they were combing the camp; they would be back before dinner. I told him I loved him and to be safe. Clark was so kind, he was so good, sometimes I still waiting for the other shoe to drop. I knew that was preposterous, that Clark was not going to turn into a monster overnight but it was still hard to believe I had come so far with him in a few short months. I never thought I would need someone like I needed him. It could be all consuming.

I was in our room when Clark came in. He was covered in dirt and sweat, yet he still smelled so delicious. I smiled at him as he came to me to give me a kiss before he went to the bathroom to clean up. I followed him in, watching him turn the water on, strip down and step in. I followed suit, shedding my clothes and pulling my hair up. I joined him under the warm water.

"I want to wash you, to take care of you." I whispered as I grabbed the soap and a cloth. He smiled at me, but didn't say anything. I scrubbed his back, shoulders, chest and legs. He was completed caked with dirt and dust. There were no blood or marks though, he hadn't been in a fight with anyone. I rubbed shampoo in his hair, massaging his scalp softly. He purred, enjoying that I was taking care of him. I kissed his shoulders as the water washed away any remaining soap, I drew him close to my chest as I encircled him with my arms.

"I love you so much my darling." He whispered. Clark turned around to face me, lifting my face to kiss my lips. "How are you feeling today?" He searched my face, concern in his eyes. I nodded, but did not smile, "I am alright. I spent the day in the conference room with Melanie discussing the rogue issues." I told him.

Clark frowned, reaching behind me and turning the water off. "You know that is not what I mean." I looked into his eyes and nodded. I sighed, "I am devastated. I am sad that I will loose this child to nature. I can't do anything about it and I feel powerless." My confession made me burry my face into his chest, letting myself shed a few tears. Clark pulled a large towel around both of our bodies and stood with me.

"However, I know it will not be our last child. I know what to expect and I am prepared for the pain. I know in my heart that you and I will have children one day, more then one. We will have a wonderful life together and I am not letting this destroy that." I told him sternly. His sadness subsided, he buried his face in my neck and kissed me sweetly. We shuffled to our bed and made love slowly, quietly. We comforted each other with our hands, our lips, our moans. There was nothing else in the world but my love for him and his love for me. We let go of our fears about the baby and embraced our future, knowing the best was yet to be.

# Chapter 13

The summer crept up fast. There were a two more rogue sightings between May and the end of June. Clark and Timothy managed to capture one of them, but he died during interrogation. There was no more information as to the reasoning for these attacks on Ice Water. Thankfully, there were no more deaths this year. I also did a lot of foraging with Tabitha several times a week. I was trying to build up my collection of herbs to take with me to Ice Water for my druid training. Tabitha knew a lot of great spots for mushrooms, plants and herbs. We dried them in the kitchen, labeled them and organized them in my constantly growing pouch.

"I think I am going to recommend that you take druid training next." I told Tabitha one day, when we were making tea in the kitchen. She paused, staring at me with wide eyes.

"Are you serious?!" she shrieked, so excited. Tabitha jumped up and down, almost spilling her tea on the counter. I laughed out loud at her face, she was so happy, I had never seen it before. "Yes I am serious. You are a natural at herb gathering, mixing and creating. I think those of us who love it should learn it first, that way we can teach others later." I explained.

Tabitha starred at me with so much excitement, "It would be an honor to receive that training. I would be so grateful."

I remembered what Doris had said, about who would be allowed to receive the training. I took a deep breath before I told Tabitha, "There may be a catch though. The werebears will only offer their training to mated females who are permanently staying with Black Lake. If you went to the exhibition and found your mate you would not be able to receive the training. But I am going to teach you all I can on my own until you go next year. I think you should know it as much as I do. If you come back unmated, then I will ask the Alpha if you may receive the training next. We will see if they will make an exception."

She looked at me, concern on her face but then she smiled, "I would be honored to receive the training in any way. Thank you." She pulled me in and hugged me tight. I was so happy I made friends with Tabitha, she was a kind soul. I wanted her to be happy, even if that meant she got to become a druid with me instead of finding her mate.

I became a part of the fishing team of our pack house, going out twice a week to catch fish for the pack. I wasn't the best fisherman but I managed to catch three pike on my first week out. There were five of us on a team, all ranks and genders. We went to the nearby river to fish. I found the sound of the running water peaceful. The Omegas taught me how to cure and smoke the meat from the fish. I was planning on taking several pounds of it to Ice Water when I went for my training. I know that fish wasn't in the treaty, however it would be a nice offering to bring with me when I go.

As the end of June came, I was still pregnant. My stomach was starting to show a small bump. Rose had said I would loose the baby before I left for my training. I would leave in three days and I was still pregnant, I didn't understand how this could happen. I instinctively touched my stomach constantly. I could feel the fluttering of movements inside. I waited for my body to let go, but there it was. Growing every day, moving every moment. I was no longer filled with sadness and dread, I was filled instead with acceptance of the things I can not control. I enjoyed this life forming inside me, I loved this little heart beating along side mine. I knew all lives come to an end, some end before they start, I was in love with this life no matter how long or short it was going to be.

Clark came to me the night before I left for training, he set his hand on my stomach and breathed heavily. I stared at him as he nuzzled and kissed our child, it moved me that he would was just as in love with this life as I was. I ran my fingers through his hair as he kissed my stomach, pulling up my shirt, "What are you thinking about my love?"

He kissed my stomach over and over again, so slowly, "I am in love with every single part of you, from top to bottom." I smiled, my eyes heaving as I gazed at him. He looked up at me, "I am going to miss you so much darling. A month is a long time for a mate to be without the other."

I nodded, "I know honey, I will miss you too. I'll be back at the beginning in August, then we can stay locked in our room for a week if you want." He laughed, reaching up to my face and kissing my lips tenderly.

"It's not just about that, I will miss everything about you." Clark told me, looking down into my face, "I will miss your smell, the way you snore at night, the way you feel. I will miss everything."

I felt a tear fall down my cheek, he wiped it away carefully. "Clark, I don't know why I still have the baby but there must be a reason. I am hoping Rose has an explanation for us." I whispered into his ear. He shivered against me, burying his face in my hair as he always did.

"Darling, no matter what happens we love this child and we will love them all. I love you, no matter what happens. I will be here when you return, we will be together forever and beyond." He told me carefully. I searched his face, I loved him so much. I kissed him sweetly, muttering how much I loved him against his mouth. He wrapped me up in blankets and cradled me in his arms as we fell asleep.

The next morning came too soon. I had packed my bags the night before. Tabitha had helped me pack an herb bag as well. She had sewn it for me herself made from the skins of a wolverine. When it rolled out, it had several pouches and pockets for various sizes and shapes. It was a wonderful gift. Clark was going to take me there, Michael packed the side by side for us while we said our goodbyes.

David gave me a hug, "Good luck my dear. You will make all of us proud." I thanked him. My in-laws engulfed me in a hug between the two of them, not saying anything, just holding me. Heath pulled me into an embrace as well, Clark didn't make a sound like he used to do. I hugged him back, "Take good care of your brother." I told him, Heath nodded into my shoulder, "I promised him no more teasing about you. I will keep that promise." I giggled and pated him on the back as I stepped towards the side by side. Michael rushed me and gave me a tight hug, "I'm going to stay until you come back. Thank you for all you have done for me, Char. I'm excited to hear about this adventure." I nodded, "Please, stay as long as you want. We love having you here with us." I promised him. He pulled me tighter, I sighed into my brother's shoulder.

Clark patted him on the back, signaling it was time for us to go. He helped me climb in the side by side. We drove away, waving at them as we left. The drive was rough but I held Clark's hand the entire way. When we arrived, Doris and Rose were waiting for us out in front. Clark helped me out of the vehicle and gave my bags to some Omegas who carried them in quickly.

"Good morning Charlotte, we are pleased to welcome you here for your training." Doris said warmly. I smiled and nodded to her. I gestured to some packages in the back of the side by side, "I have brought a gift from Black Lake, it is twenty pounds of smoked pike for your pack. I caught it all myself, we hope you enjoy it."

The Alpha and the Gamma stared at me, then looked to each other, "That is an unexpected offering. Thank you very much. You say you caught it all yourself?" Rose inquired, taking a few steps closer to us to examine the packages in the side by side.

"I did, I joined a fishing team, I'm not very good at it yet, but I managed to catch quite a bit of pike in the last few weeks. I wanted to bring it with me to show how thankful I am for this opportunity." I told her. Clark smiled at me, proudly. I hadn't really fished before moving to the Northwest Territories, but I was enjoying learning the skill.

Doris smiled widely at us, gesturing for some Omegas to take the packages from the vehicle. Rose handed the packages to the Omegas and turned to me, making eye contact, "You are a resourceful girl, full of surprises. This will work in your favor I believe."

Doris shook mine and Clark's hands, "Beta Duffey, you may pick up your wife in exactly thirty-one days. By then her training will be complete as much as we can train her, the rest is up to her." Clark bowed quickly to the Alpha. He turned to me and kissed me warmly, letting his hand trace around my stomach one last time before he whispered, "I will be back to get you soon my darling. I love you." I whispered that I loved him, holding his hand overtop of my stomach. I kissed his forehead before he turned back to the vehicle. Rose took my hand in hers and guided me into the pack house, "Come young mama, I will show you to your room while you stay with us."

I smiled at her, letting her lead me without another word. I was shown to a small room down an unremarkable corridor. It was quant, but it was warm with a nice bed and adjoining bathroom. "Lunch is in two hours; I will be back for you then. After we have something to eat I will show you our herbology room where we will have training each day. We will begin this afternoon." Rose told me. I turned to her and smiled, "I am looking forward to it."

She took a step forward and for the first time I saw her smile, she placed her hand on my stomach and traced a small infinity symbol over it, "Congratulations." I looked at her with wonder, had she made a mistake? Before I could say anything, Rose slipped out of the room and closed the door behind herself. I was left standing there wondering what the afternoon held.

Lunch was served, it was an assortment of wild berries and sweet breads. I noticed that the portions were smaller then back home, probably to make sure there was enough to go around. I could feel the various eyes on me as I followed the Gamma to a table. We joined a young man around my age, "This is my son, Luca. He will be assisting us with your training. Luca is an excellent forager. He can find just about anything in our dense forests." Rose told me, pride on her face.

Luca was very tall and strong; he could easily be seven feet in height. His dark hair and dark eyes would have been intimidating if he didn't betray them with a sweet smile for his mother. "Thanks mom, it is good to know I am good for something."

I smiled and reached out my hand, "I am Charlotte Duffey, of the Black Lake pack. It is nice to meet you." Luca shook my hand, giving me a small smile, I could tell he was younger then me, he seemed almost shy.

"Nice to meet you, "he mumbled, "My mother has told me a lot about you." His face was kind; I could tell he thought I was pretty. I smiled at him, taking my hand away and continued to eat my food.

Rose cleared her throat before she spoke, "So I thought we would start with the tour and then Luca and I would take you out to the forest for some foraging. We will shift of course, are you up for that?"

I nodded, "You bet, I am always up for a shift."

The herbology room was essentially a large walk in closet full of many different vials, plants and concoctions. It wasn't a huge space, but then it didn't need to be. Rose showed me to a small station that was freshly cleaned and the void of any dust, "This is where you will be doing your studying. We will also be spending some time in the library, but I suspect you had read as much as you could already on herbology."

I smiled sheepishly, "I have yes, I was excited for this training." Rose smiled at me, "The only other thing we will need to do today is make you an herb bag. I am sure we can find some scraps of hide to do that before sundown."

I reached around my body and presented her with the bag Tabitha had made for me, "Actually my friend made this for me."

Rose took the bag, opened it and examined it closely, she nodded with confidence and smiled at me, "Your friend did an excellent job of this one. Is it badger?" she asked.

"Wolverine." I said, she smiled and nodded again. She rolled it back up and gave it back to me, "You are very well prepared Charlotte. I have to say, I am impressed." There was a bit of embarrassment in her voice as she said the words. I smiled and touched her shoulder gently, "As I told you at our first meeting, I am honored to be taking this training. I am thrilled to be here with you to learn all I can."

Rose looked into my face and sighed, "I am thankful for that. I hope you will forgive an old soul for my coldness at our first meeting. I was apprehensive about this treaty, considering our species histories. I apologize for that."

"No need," I told her, leaving my hand on her shoulder, "You had every right to be skeptical. You didn't know me. I understand."

I showed her my grandma Daisy's recipe book my mother had passed down to me. She examined the pages carefully, nodding and smiling as she went through it. When Rose closed the cover she looked at me with pride on her face, "It seems you come from a line of healers already. I am impressed yet again." She handed the book back to me, I smiled.

She smiled at me, reaching out her hand and placing it on my stomach. She held it there for a moment before tracing an infinity symbol over and over again, "When I met you I smelled this child instantly. It was weak though, I could sense that it wasn't a strong beginning. I thought it wouldn't take, the pregnancies like this one rarely do. Yet here you are today, still carrying this child. I can smell its strength now. You have a future leader inside your belly, already has this young one gone through the trials of weakness, now it is strong and hearty. You will give birth to a strong pup, one that will go on to do great things. I can smell it."

Her words took my breath away, I had been prepared for the end of this life inside me at any time. I had accepted it, even though I had fallen in love with it. Clark was the same. I refused to let the pain of my child's loss break me. To hear that I was giving birth to not only a healthy pup but also a future leader filled me with so much happiness. I was so overjoyed, I cried. Rose rubbed my back as I shed tears of relief.

"Come young mama, let us begin your training out in the wilds." She whispered, we walked outside were Luca was waiting. We all shed our clothing and shifted quickly. The werebears were both larger size brown bears, in contrast to my grey wolf. We all moved out into the woods together.

## Chapter 14

The days flew by like minutes. I was suddenly in my last week of training at Ice Water. I enjoyed it so much, I was hardly home sick for Black Lake. I suppose it was because I didn't have time. Rose and her son, Luca were so encouraging. I had learned so many wonderful medicines, potions and concoctions. I was looking forward to applying my new trade to our pack. I knew there would be so many ways I could help to keep my pack strong.

My belly had swelled during my time there. I was now half way along in my pregnancy, my small bump had become a noticeable one now, there was no hiding it anymore even if I wanted to. I was sitting at my work station in the herbology room absentmindedly rubbing it when I felt some tingles in my hand. I stopped, gasping slightly. I wasn't sure what I was feeling. I closed my eyes, taking a deep breath and moved the palm of my hand over my stomach. My mind flooded with light, I could smell my child as though I was touching them right there. I could feel their heartbeat in my hand, it was so strong and steady. I was shocked I could smell and see this, it was all new to me. I realized my druid training had taken over and I was sensing the future of my child. I could feel him, my son, it was a boy. I could smell his strength, his prowess. He was going to make an excellent leader. I could feel him in every pore on my body, he was going to make his father and I so proud.

I broke the trance I was in, letting myself breath. I wasn't expecting this kind of vision but I knew it was a possibility. Rose had told me that once we had started to subconsciously adapt to our druid training we would start to have visions of others, the future, the past. It wasn't magic per say, more of our bodies becoming in tune with nature around us and other living things. This power was another level of consciousness druids would experience, eventually being able to control it and channel it to find and gather information. I was pleased my mind was taking the training so well.

When I sat with Rose and Luca at dinner that night, I told them about my experience in the herbology room. They both smiled and nodded, Rose said, "It is good to see you are taking to the training so well." I smiled, "I have had a great teacher." She blushed and took a bite of her supper.

"Have you thought about anything else you would like to learn?" she asked, changing the subject.

I shook my head, "Not really. I feel as though I have learned as much as I can at this point. It's a process right, so I will never stop learning."

Rose didn't look up but she smiled at her food, "That is the correct answer girl. We never stop learning our skills. We never perfect them, we are all students of nature." I nodded, she was right. I had learned so much in my short time here and I knew it was just the beginning of my training. I looked forward to sharing my knowledge with our pack when I returned.

Finally, the thirty first day came and I was packed and ready to return home. Luca took my bags for me out to the foyer. Rose walked with me. We held hands as we walked, a strange sort of comfort. I took the canvas bundle from my pocket she had given me at our first meeting and handed it to her, "I suspect I won't be needing this after all."

She shook her head, holding out her hand and pushing it back to me, "You may not, but someday you will need to give that to another loved one. Keep it, it is powerful medicine." I nodded, tucking it back into my bag.

"Charlotte Duffey, you have been a delight to train. I never thought I would enjoy the company of a werewolf so much." Rose told me, taking both my hands in hers. I smiled, "Thank you Gamma, your pack hospitality has been wonderful. I am grateful to you all."

"Remember, let the visions come. Don't block them or it will set you back. Remember to drink the waking tea each day, every day no exceptions. It will bring you closer to nature and strengthen your bond to your subconscious. If you need anything from me, just reach out and I will be happy to act as a guide for you. I am always here girl." She told me sternly, a very motherly tone slipping through her lips.

I laughed, "Yes mame." I heard a vehicle pull up outside, I knew instantly it was Clark. I could feel his urgency, his need, he missed me terribly. I could smell it.

I opened the front door to see him sitting in the side by side, the Omegas already putting my bags in the back. Clark didn't even pause before he ran to me, lifting me up and kissing me passionately, heat filling up my entire body. He didn't set me down, instead he buried his face in my neck and hair, taking deep, urgent breaths as though I was air and he was a drowning man. I held on to him, my legs still off the ground, attempting to sooth him by rubbing his back.

"I haven't been able to breath properly for thirty days. My heart was only half with me; it is the worst feeling in the entire world." He whispered into my neck. I kissed his neck softly, "Take me home Beta, I will be happy make up for lost time." He growled possessively into my neck, nibbling on my marked spot. I whimpered slightly, "You have to put me down though."

Clark laughed, somewhat saddened but he set me down on my feet. I turned and said my farewells to Luca and Rose. I promised to be in touch soon. Luca rubbed the back of his neck, a bit uncomfortable with my husband's display of affection. He hugged me quickly and whispered a kind farewell in my ear. Rose offered to be here for the birth of our child, which I accepted happily.

I made my way to the side by side and climbed in, Clark was hot on my heals. We made it back to the pack house in record time, he didn't give me time to climb out myself, instead he lifted me out and carried me into the pack house at a run, passing by his parents, the Alpha, my brother and our friends. I shouted my greetings to them, each laughing as I passed by with a flash, seeming to understand my mate's urgency. Clark ran at a sprint to our room, throwing the door open and slamming it shut. He clicked the lock and took me to the bed. Clark shed his clothes completely, I was shocked at his speed. He wrapped his naked body around me protectively and pulled me close to his chest. I breathed him in slowly, he kissed my forehead over and over again. His hand fell protectively to my stomach and stayed there. He was growling unconsciously over and over again, eyes closed just holding us together.

"Clark, are you alright?" I asked finally, I ran my hand down his check slowly trying to sooth him.

He didn't answer, almost as though he didn't hear me. His hands stayed present, not moving from my body. He didn't try to undress me, he just held me as close as possible in our bed. I kissed his forehead again and slowed my breathing, trying to sooth him that way. Gradually, over time his growling changed to a whimpering, still urgent but less possessive. More like a wounded animal. I moved his face to meet my gaze, he looked into my eyes and let the tears move down his face.

"Clark, honey, are you alright?" I asked again. He nodded, finally speaking, "I was feeling so much loneliness while you were gone. It became physically painful. I talked to my mother about it, she told me she didn't understand it. Betas don't have this strong of a reaction to the loss of their mates, that is only Alphas. She told me my father would miss her when she was gone, but never to the point of loss of sleep or physical pain. David came to visit me; he was concerned as well. We decided not to bother you while you were at your training, that I would go to you on the thirty first day and bring you home. The entire pack house was informed that you would not be coming out of our room upon your return for two full days."

Clark's voice was full of relief, as though a huge weight had been lifted from him. I starred at his face, I could feel his pain lifting as we lay close together. He continued, "I am sure most of the pack house believes I am just having my way with you. A husband in lust from missing his wife. Only a few know the real reason I need you to myself for a few days. That I actually felt as though I might die without you." His voice broke as he finished speaking.

I had no idea he was in such turmoil during my absence. I had missed him a great deal, I could feel he missed me but I had no idea he was feeling physical pain. It was unheard of for a Beta to have these feelings for his mate, Clark's mother was correct. My father had felt sadness when my mother was absent from him for periods of time, but never pain. That was an Alpha reaction, Clark was not Alpha. I mulled the information over in my head, perhaps it was because Clark was mated and Heath was not, neither was David. Perhaps that was why he felt the same level of urgency as an Alpha. I was unsure about it but now was not he time to examine this philosophy.

I pulled myself from Clark's grip, he cried out as I moved away from him. I stood at the edge of the bed, removing my clothing. I climbed back into our bed, pulling the sheets around us. I moved my body overtop of his, taking his hands and placing them on my hips. I kissed him passionately, exploring his mouth with mine, moving my hands through his hair and down his chest. I moaned into his mouth, nibbling on his lips. I let my hands trail down my mate's chest, sliding to his stomach and lower to his manhood. I took Clark in my hand and moved him to my entrance, sliding him into me in one slow motion. We both shuttered as I lowered myself onto his lap, Clark reached up and pulled me down to his chest. We stayed like that for a long time, me on top of him, his body inside mine. I kissed Clark's face and lips over and over again, soothing his anguish with my touch.

"Please my darling, never leave me again," Clark whispered as he moved his hips softly up to mine. I moaned at the movement. "I don't think I could take it again. It's not because I am jealous or possessive, I actually don't believe I can live without you." He begged, moving his hips again. I nodded against his face and kissed him again. Our mate bond was very strong; I already knew this. I had no idea a mate bond could ever be this strong or intense. I moved overtop of Clark, making him moan loudly as I rotated my hips over him, causing immense pleasure for both of us.

We made love on another level that afternoon. We did not just enjoy our bodies, we molded into one soul. I had never experienced anything like it. I held Clark close to my chest as we both came down from our highs. "I had no idea you were so upset while I was gone." I whispered. He flinched against my chest.

"I am feeling stronger now. It didn't happen right away, it was gradual. The longer you were gone, the weaker I became." He told me. I nodded and kissed my mark on his neck, "I promise I will never be away from you again. Where ever you go, I shall go with you."

Clark sighed with relief at my words, "I am sorry Charlotte. I didn't expect to have this kind of physical reaction to you being away. I am embarrassed. I don't like that I am this weak."

I shook my head, "I don't think it is weakness my love. I think you and I being together makes you stronger. It is a known fact that the female mate gives her male strength through their bond. We have a very deep bond; therefore, it does make sense that my absence would cause you to feel withdrawal." Clark shook his head, "It is more then that. I don't know how but it's more then just you make me stronger. I need you more then food or water or sleep." He confessed.

"I will never leave you again. You will come with me and I will go with you. From now on, always." I promised him. It was definitive. I may not understand why he felt this way but I was determined to never make him suffer like this again. Clark kissed me sweetly, he thanked me through our mind link for being so understanding.

I heard a soft knock at the door, Clark groaned not wanting to get up from our warm embrace. "I'll go." I whispered. I moved out of bed, pulling my dressing gown on and went to the door. I opened it to find Tabitha there with a tray of food for us. I took it from her, setting it down just inside our bedroom and stepping out into the hall.

I pulled my friend into an embrace, it was nice to see her. "Charlotte, you are all rosy, it's so wonderful to see you." She said, teasing me.

I blushed as we parted, "Yes, you know a husband and a wife, after a long period, we do have some things to catch up on." I told her, not wanting to give away too much of Clark's feelings on my absence.

Tabitha giggled, she nodded. "After you and Clark have caught up, you and I should have tea and you can tell me all about your training. "she suggested. I smiled, "That will be first on my list, I promise." I told her.

I closed the door as Tabitha left. I turned to see Clark had risen from our bed and was eating his sandwiches with vigor. I laughed, moving towards the tray to take one before he ate them all.

"Sorry darling, I haven't been able to eat much. I am just famished now." He muttered, his mouth full of food. I shrugged, eating my sandwich slowly, enjoying the flavor. After we ate I suggested we take a walk down to the common room, but Clark refused. He pulled me back to the bed, moving his hands over my stomach to caress our child. "I need some quality time with my baby right now. After that, then we will go for a walk." He whispered.

"Your son." I told him, Clark's face shot up at me. His face was full of excitement. "Son? We have a son? We are having a boy?"

I smiled up at him, nodding. "How can you know that?" he asked me, rubbing small circles on my stomach.

"I had a vision. It's from the druid training, it puts me more in contact with my body and nature. I was able to smell him and feel him. I can sense who he is going to be. It was so amazing when it happened. I learned so much while I was there. "I told him. Clark's eyes searched mine, "So he is going to grow to term?"

"Yes. He is strong, he is going to be amazing." I whispered. Clark cried into my stomach softly, I could feel his relief in this body. He wanted this baby so much, he never admitted it out loud but I knew he did. Now that our son was going to be born, he could finally allow himself to want it. I kissed the top of his head and ran my fingers through this hair. I continued, "He is healthy, he is going to be a great leader someday my love. He is strong. Just like his father."

Clark looked up and kissed my lips warmly. He was so happy; he couldn't contain it any more. I pulled him out of bed and forced him to get dressed. He groaned and I made him leave our room with me, going down to the common room and on to the library. We found Michael in there reading a book, he was surprised when we walked in.

"I thought I wasn't going to see you for two days?" Michael asked, putting his book down on this lap.

"She forced me to leave our bedroom. I tried to stop her." Clark muttered, holding my hand up and kissing the back of it. Michael laughed out loud, "Yes Clark, I can see how she overpowered you."

I hugged Michael and sat next to him on the sofa. He wrapped his arm around my shoulders, "So how was druid training?"

"It was amazing. I learned so much about herbology but it's more then that. I learned about channeling energy, listening to nature in a different way. I learned what to look for in the woods, more then just what we can eat but the way a plant grows compared to another one. I learned how to make so many different kinds of concoctions for all kinds of uses." I explained to both of them. I went on and on, telling them both about my time with the werebears. Clark and Michael listened intently to my ramblings. At some point Tabitha came to the library to bring Michael his tea, she wanted to hear all about it as well.

It was a wonderful afternoon spent in the library. I regaled them all with tales about the werebears. We drank tea and they shared the stores of what happened while I was gone. There had been no rogue attacks, which was a relief.

"We are still trying to figure out where these rogues are coming from." Clark told us, "but we believe they are coming from the south."

"Did you find anything from that camp you found before I left?" I asked him.

Clark shook his head, "Timothy found out that the rogues were not real rogues but from some kind of pack. Not as strong as our pack but still from somewhere. They camp was too organized with too many supplies to be ordinary rogues."

I took his hand quickly, concern crossing my face. "We put out a bulletin to our allies to the south. Don't worry my darling, we will be safe." He told me, kissing my hand.

"Mother and father send their love. You should probably call them tomorrow to tell them all about your time with the werebears." Michael pipped up. I smiled at him.

"How are they?" I asked. Michael shrugged slightly, "The same as ever. Red Rose is in full foraging mode right now. Byron even went out this year to help out. He is begging father to let him start training to be a warrior since Clark taught him a few moves while they were here."

Clark smiled broadly at that, "I'm glad my brother in law wants to be a warrior. He would benefit from the training."

Michael and I laughed, it was difficult to pull Byron away from video games, yet somehow Clark had done it. I turned to Michael, "How are you doing?"

He smiled at me and pulled me a bit closer, "I am doing well. I almost feel normal again honestly. The tea has worked wonders, but I think being here at Black Lake helped just as much to be honest."

"I love this place too. It didn't take long for it to feel like home for me." I said, laying my head on his shoulder.

"I will have to go home sometime, little sister." Michael chuckled into my hair. I shook my head, "No rush."

Tabitha smiled at us, "That's right no rush. It's not everyday we get fresh meat up here so stay as long as you want." Michael blushed slightly at her comment. She laughed, knowing her teasing was successful.

"Stella got all her stuff from Red Rose. She apparently had called there looking for me but mother told her I was up here with you." Michael mentioned, "She was happy to hear I was doing better."

"What about Marie? Has anyone talked to her?" I asked, everyone shook their heads. "I know that mother has tried to call a few times but Anthony has told her Marie wasn't available." Michael told me. I knew I needed to send her a message as soon as possible.

"Come my darling, we should go to dinner and feed that little life inside you." Clark whispered in my ear. I nodded. We all walked down to the dining hall together. Clark carried my tray to our table while I stopped to visit with the Duffey's for a round of hugs, kisses and welcomes.

"How are you feeling?" Cheryl whispered to me, pulling me aside from the table. I smiled, placing her hand on my stomach, "Everything is strong and healthy. We are going to be just fine." I told her. Cheryl looked at my stomach then back to my face, smiling brightly. She wrapped her arms around me. "We love you so much sweet girl. Congratulations." I hugged her back tightly.

David walked up to us as we parted, he patted Cheryl's back before she stepped back to her seat. The Alpha turned to me, smiled and asked motioned for me to follow him. I matched him step for step to the edge of the room, Clark looked at me concerned but I waved at him telling him I was fine.

"Welcome back Charlotte. I trust your training was good?" David asked.

"It was Alpha. I am excited to start up here. I learned so many useful things from Rose." I told him.

David smiled, "I am glad to hear that. Clark, Heath and myself put together a herbology room for you on the second floor. It's not huge but it is clean and prepared for you to start your work whenever you want." I smiled at him, "Thank you sir. I will do my best to make the pack proud."

"You already make us all proud." He told me. "Listen Charlotte, I will be making the announcement tomorrow night but I will be stepping down as Alpha at the end of the summer. Heath will be having his Alpha ceremony in September. Which means that there isn't going to be a Luna. You know that the same was with me, Mrs. Duffey filled those shoes a lot over my years as Alpha. I think you should prepare yourself for Heath to ask the same of you."

My breath hitched. I knew there was no Luna, and I did realize Cheryl did a lot of the duties of a Luna over the years. Heath had talked about it briefly when I arrived. I knew this conversation was coming, I wasn't expecting it to be so soon.

"Alright. I understand David. I will do everything I can to help our pack." I told him.

He studied me for a moment before he spoke again, "I also assume you talked to Clark, he told you about his difficulty while you were gone. The way he felt is unusual for a Beta, the strong reaction is more typically an Alpha reaction. I have never felt it personally, but know of some Alphas to have died of heartache when their mates died or left them."

"Clark did tell me about it. We talked about it when I got back this morning. We discussed that maybe it has to do with the lack of Lunas in our midst. How you do not have a Luna, Heath doesn't yet either so maybe that's why he felt such a strong reaction." I told him.

David thought about it for a moment, eventually shaking his head, "I'm not sure if that is what it is or not. It could be possible. I have just ever seen that from a Beta before."

"I will do my best to take care of him as well." I promised, David met my eyes with concern, "And who takes care of you, Charlotte?"

"Everyone here takes care of each other, that is what a pack does. What a pack should do." I said strongly.

He smiled at me, "Spoken like a born Luna. Thank you Charlotte. Please, return to your mate, we will talk more another time." David pulled me in to a quick hug and let me leave to return to Clark.

By this time Heath, Timothy, Melanie, Michael and Tabitha had joined our table. Clark looked at me inquisitively as I sat down. I shook my head at him, signaling not to worry at this point.

"Welcome back Char. It's always great to see you." Heath told me, smiling. I smiled back, "Always a pleasure brother."

We ate our dinner in happy conversation. Heath seemed preoccupied, but based on my conversation with David I could understand why. Becoming Alpha, even if you were prepared for it, would be a big step in Heath's life. The entire pack would know soon enough; I didn't feel the need to share it with our table tonight. As we broke apart for the evening, returning to our rooms I reached out and caught Heath's shoulder. He turned to face me, I pulled him in for a tight hug. I whispered in his ear, "I will help you all I can until you find your Luna. I promise."

Heath pulled me close to his chest exhaled loudly into my shoulder, in much the same way Clark did when he was worried. "Thank you sister." He whispered lowly. We parted, giving each other a knowing smile.

Clark didn't growl at us, but he did stare at the exchange with an uncomfortable expression on his face. I walked to him, smiling at him sweetly and kissed his lips quickly before he could say anything, "Come now big bad Beta. Nothing to worry about, come with me to our room and give me some sugar."

He laughed out loud, unable to remain annoyed and followed me to our room. I kissed him over and over again. Clark melted into my body as we turned in for the night.

I awoke the next morning so happy to smell apple pie for the first time in a month. I saw that Clark had already gone to training so I got up lazily, showered and made my way to the kitchen. I found Amy and Tabitha there preparing breakfast for the pack. I helped them by mixing pancake batter and flipping bacon. The girls seemed happy that I was willing to help. I had missed making food with the girls at Black Lake while I was gone. Even though the werebears were welcoming and kind, it was different to be with family. I drank tea and we laughed about nothing in particular. Cheryl and Melanie came in after a while and joined us.

"So when are we having a new pup join the pack?" Amy finally asked. Clark and I hadn't shared our news very much as we were sure the pregnancy wouldn't take, but now that my belly was in full view it was impossible to ignore. Cheryl gave me a warm smile, she wrapped her arms around me and pulled me close to her chest.

I let her go and turned to my friends, "November will be when this little boy arrives." Shrieks of joy ripped though the room, I couldn't hold back my laughter. Amy, Melanie and Tabitha all threw their arms around me and engulfed my small form in hugs. I heard various congratulations but I wasn't sure who was speaking.

When I was allowed to come up for air, Cheryl took my arm with a pause, "A boy? Are you sure?" I nodded, "One of the things I learned from the werebears if how to channel energy into visions. He will be very healthy and strong." Tears rose in her eyes and she brought me in again for another embrace. I leaned into Cheryl, she had become a second mother to my own. I was thrilled I would be giving her their first grandchild.

We served the pack breakfast, my pancakes were pretty good if I do say so myself. I went to the library afterward to telephone my parents and Marie. I hadn't actually told mother and father about the pregnancy yet, so I was excited to do that now.

"Hello Mom, how are you?" I said into the receiver.

She laughed as she heard my voice, "Oh Charlotte, we are good here. How are you? How was the training?"

I settled down on the sofa sigh a deep sigh, "It was very good. I had a wonderful time with the Ice Water pack. They taught me so much. I'll be sending you some new recipes for some healing salves for your warriors. They work so much better then the ones we already have."

"That's wonderful dear. You got back yesterday right? How are you?" she asked, I could hear she was drinking coffee or tea as it clicked against the phone.

"Well, I am growing everyday now. I have some news. Clark and I are expecting our first child in November. I am pregnant." I said calmly with a smile.

Silence hit the other end of the phone. I was surprised she didn't say anything. I waited, nothing. "Hello?" I whispered tentatively.

"Sorry my darling. I am happy for you of course. It's just so soon, you are still young and I remember how overwhelming it was for me at that age. Are you happy?" my mother finally asked.

"Yes mom, I am very happy. We are very happy, I am thrilled, I promise." I told her.

She let out a sigh on the other end of the phone, "Good, then I am happy for you. Your father and brother will be thrilled. This is our first grandchild. Oh goodness!" I would hear the excitement in her voice now. Always the caring soul, my mother, making sure everyone was alright before her feelings came out. I smiled at her.

"Rose from Ice Water will do the birth with me. You and father should come for it and bring Byron. The birth of your first grandchild is a very big deal. We would love for you to come." I explained.

"Yes, we will be there. I would love to meet the werebears as well. You know, I have never met one. Are their lives much like ours?" she asked.

I mulled over her question in my mind before answering, "Yes and no. They are far more guarded then we are but that is for a good reason considering our histories. However, the Ice Water pack treated me very well, with open arms when I came and they have so much to teach us."

"Yes of course. I am looking forward to meeting this Gamma Rose? Is that her name? I am sure she has all kinds of knowledge." She agreed.

"Clark, Heath and Samuel built me my very own herbology lab so I have all kinds of space to make my concoctions now. I'll show you when you come." I told her.

My mother shrieked when I told her that, "OH I am so jealous! I've always made everything in the kitchen, much to everyone's dismay." We both laughed, remembering how not everything has a nice smell when it is being cooked or prepared for a purpose. I can remember more then once an Omega almost loosing their breakfast because of a smell from the kitchen of Red Rose.

"How is my Michael doing?" mother asked, love in her voice.

I nodded, before I remembered she couldn't see me, "He is doing much better now. His heartache is almost completely healed. I think he will be returning home soon."

"Yes, I know he feels like he should but there is no rush. I am happy he is doing better. Stella has called here twice looking for him. I have told her he is with you; she is happy to hear he is healing. I know the mate bond is hard to come back from. I suspect she thought it would be easier then it has been for herself." my mother told me.

I shifted on the sofa, my stomach getting a bit heavy, "Yes, I believe that. She was always selfish though mom."

My mother sighed, "Charlotte, that isn't fair." I could hear her stern tone in my ear.

"Yes it is, Michael gave her everything she wanted and it wasn't enough. He didn't deserve to go through the pain she caused." I muttered. I could hear my mother tsk down the phone line at me and I rolled my eyes before smiling.

"My sweetheart, that isn't fair and you know it. Your mate bond took immediately and not just that; it was so strong that there was no hint of doubt in either of your minds about it. Not everyone gets that. In fact, most don't. Stella loved Michael, have no doubt about that. She just didn't feel the pull as strongly as he did, but when it ended she felt the pain just the same. No less then he did. Don't be so hard on her, she isn't a villain, Stella is just a girl who was in love but it wasn't right." As those words left my mother's lips I thought they were the wisest of all. I paused for a while before I responded to her.

"That is very true mom. You are right."

"Have you phoned Marie yet?" she asked testily.

"No I was going to after I got off the phone with you actually." I told her. She sighed, "Well I hope you can get through. We have been trying for weeks and Anthony always has some excuse for why she can't come to the phone."

I sighed, so he had shut her off again. "Well he might let me talk to her, I'll try to get to the bottom of it."

My mother choked, "I miss her so much. It's hard to know that she is there and we can't see or talk to her. Sometimes I can feel pain and I know it's hers. Marie is such a sweet soul; I miss her dearly."

"I know mom. I'll do my best to reach her." I whispered that promise to my mother. She sighed and composed herself, "My dearest Charlotte, always the healer and the protector. So loyal, I love you so much my sweetheart."

I smiled, "I love you to mom. Give my love to dad and Byron. I'll let Michael know I talked to you today.

We hung up in light tears. I missed my family but they were never too far away. I had been so busy since I moved to Black Lake that I hardly had time to be homesick. I suspected Michael's presence might have helped with that. I did miss my family but I had found another one here and they were so loving I couldn't really complain that much.

Amy found me and brought me some tea, I thanked her. For some reason she always did that. I knew she didn't do that with anyone else, it made me feel special. I lifted the receiver of the phone with a sigh, knowing I had to try to reach Marie. Amy gave me a quick wink and left me to my phone call, not saying a word. She was a kind soul.

I dialed and waited, on the fourth ring Anthony answered, "Rocky Mountain Alpha Office, Anthony here."

"Anthony, hello its Charlotte. How are you?" I said, letting my voice crack. I heard him adjust in his chair and suck in a quick breath.

"Charlotte, hello. I am well thank you. What can I do for you?" he asked, very formally.

I took a breath and said very calmly, "Well I just got back from my training yesterday and I wanted to tell Marie about it. I'm sure she can I have a lot of catching up to do. I would love to speak with my sister please."

He didn't say a word, he shifted and cleared his throat but he didn't say anything. I waited but nothing came through the phone. "Anthony, are you still there?" I finally asked.

"Yes, I am here." He whispered. I waited another moment, still nothing. I heard his voice crack as he tried to say something but then stopped himself.

"Anthony, has something happened?" I asked, keeping my voice as calm and soothing as possible.

My stomach did a flip inside my body, I could feel my heart race, his lack of reply was making me think the worst. Suddenly the library door flew open and Clark came in, fresh from the shower. He sat down next to me and pulled my feet into his lap, staring at me. I loved that he could sense me and I could sense him, we always found each other. I smiled at him, though I was terrified of what news was going to come down the receiver.

"Charlotte, I am afraid Marie isn't available today for a visit. I will tell her you called and she can perhaps call you back tomorrow." Anthony finally said. His voice was quiet though, I could hear he wasn't very strong in his resolve.

"Please Anthony, has something happened? I would like to talk to my sister. I love her very much." I whispered.

"You think I don't?!" he shouted, "I love my Luna more then anything! She is mine! I take care of her and I decide what happens to her!"

"I know Anthony; I'm not suggesting you don't. I just love her and I miss her. You know I am not trying to take her away. I just miss her, that's all. I wanted to tell her about the training and about the baby." I finally said, his voice caught in his throat.

"What about the baby? Tell me!" he demanded. I sighed and adjusted my stomach again, "Well I am due in November. Clark and I are having a healthy boy. Everything is fine, we are going to be healthy and strong."

Silence hit the phone and I thought for a moment he had hung up on me. Then I realized he was just holding his breath. "That is wonderful news Charlotte, congratulations to you and Clark." He managed to say.

"Thank you. Now, what is going on with my sister? I would love to share this news with her. Please Anthony, let me talk to her." I asked again, remaining calm.

Anthony sighed, "I'm afraid she isn't available just now, she is..." As his voice trailed off my breath hitched. "What?"

"She's down on the training fields in a collar." Anthony finally told me. I shuddered when he spoke those words.

I took two deep breaths before I spoke, to try and calm myself, "You collared her?" I asked. Clark's eyes filled with rage as he shot me a look. Collaring, one of the worst punishments for a werewolf. Often reserved for terrible crimes against a pack. The criminal is forced to shift into wolf form, then a silver collar is placed on their neck to they can not shift back. They are placed on a chain for all to see and left in a public place so the rest of his pack can view their punishment. It often leaves permanent scars on the necks of the victims. It poisons us slowly from the outside in with the silver. It's a terrible punishment.

"Anthony," I asked calmly, "why did you collar Marie?"

His breath quickened, "She was angry with me over some stupid Omega girl. She told me no more messing around and that if I did she would reject me. I lost it, I got so mad, I threw her around our room. I forced her to submit to me, now she's out there, she's been out there for three days now."

I took more deep breaths. I was trying to remain calm, if I didn't I would just make it worse for Marie and potentially her punishment would last longer. I bit my lip and took my glasses off, pinching my nose, "Anthony, you need to go get her. She loves you so much, and I know you love her. Marie just wants you to herself the way you want her to yourself. You know that."

"She makes me so mad sometimes. I am the Alpha; she can't order me around like that!" he shouted. I paused, "Yes you are the Alpha, and she is your Luna. How would you feel if she stepped out on you?"

He growled through the phone, "She would NEVER do that! I would kill them both!"

"Exactly, she would never do that because it would hurt you. She loves you too much to even consider hurting you. When you mess with Omegas it hurts her, she was just trying to tell you that." I told him.

"They mean nothing to me, she means everything." He said coldly, "My Luna is my everything."

"Then why are you punishing her for something you did?" I asked quietly.

Silence filled the line again. He seemed to be thinking about what I had just said. I stared at Clark, he stared back at me. I was holding my breath for Anthony's next reply.

"I love Marie you know. I know what your family thinks of me. I love her more then anything in the world." Anthony said suddenly, a hitch in his breath.

"I know you do. Please Anthony, show her that you love her enough to end this punishment. Go get her. Show your pack that you love your Luna, show them that you have the power and control to forgive her for getting angry with you." I said, stroking his ego. Anthony didn't respond to demands, I had seen from his interactions with my family. It had to be in his favor for him to act. It had to make him look good.

Anthony considered my words for a few minutes, I could hear him weighing what I had said. Finally, he cleared his throat and said, "I will have Marie phone you tomorrow morning. I'll go and get her this afternoon, no earlier. Good day Charlotte."

He hung up the phone and I sat there with the receiver in my hand, finally letting my body shake. Clark took the phone and set it down. He pulled me into his lap and rocked me slowly, placing one hand around my shoulders the other protectively over my stomach.

I didn't cry, I don't know why but I didn't. I just took deep breath after breath, "He collared her because she called him on screwing around with the Omegas. She's been out there for three days." Clark pulled me closer and shook his head, placing his forehead against mine.

"He should be the one out there. What an animal." Clark muttered, "How can he do that to his Luna? I can't even fathom that kind of rage and hostility."

I stroked his face with my hands, "I know honey, because you are not built like that. You would stand in fire for me."

"I would!" he said loudly, Clark kissed me softly. I returned his kiss before leaning back and whispering, "He's taking her out of it this afternoon. She will call me tomorrow morning." Clark nodded.

"I am so angry at him. He has way too much control over my sister. I want to hate him, but I know that anything I do or say against him will make it impossible for me to see her." I said angrily. Clark kissed my neck through my hair and rubbed my stomach lovingly. He didn't say anything; he didn't need to.

We sat together in the library for over an hour. I worked to calm myself down, letting Clark massage my stomach and release the stress. It wasn't good for our baby after all. I decided to email my parents to let them know I had a phone date with Marie the next day, but no other information at this time. I didn't want them to phone and get upset with Anthony, making it all worse and furthermore making it impossible for me to ever speak to her again.

I walked to the window, realizing today as the day David would be announcing to the pack that Heath would be taking over in September. I sighed and beckoned Clark to me, he came to me and wrapped his arms around my waist. "Tonight is about your brother. We need to set this aside for now and be there for him." I stated, Clark nodded and kissed my forehead.

"He will be announcing his team tonight as well." He told me. I nodded, "So you will be Beta now. Will you still get to train the warriors?"

Clark shook his head, "No, I will be in charge of more of the day to day stuff like most Betas. I have requested to still do the scouting missions though. Heath has agreed to allow me to continue that part of my work. I will be doing training on my own as I see fit." I ran my fingertips over his stomach, making him shiver.

"Well we need to make sure those sexy abs don't go anywhere with a desk job, Mr. Beta." I teased. He growled with longing and pulled me closer to his chest, kissing my lips hard. I returned his kiss with a little nip to his lips.

"You drive me crazy Char, how is it this tiny body of yours has complete control over mine?" he whined, I laughed and ran my fingers through his black hair. I pulled him with me to the sofa, placed my glasses back on my face and moved towards the door, "We need to get on with the day my love, save your dirty mind for tonight."

Clark groaned in protest but came with me to the Alpha's office. We found Samuel, David, Heath and Timothy in the office. When we arrived they all stood up as though I were the queen.

"Hello Duffey's how can we help you?" Heath smirked at us.

Clark held my hand, smiling broadly at his brother, "We just came to see what you need from us for tonight?"

"Right, well I will be announcing my retirement as well as the retirement of your father. I will thank the pack for all of their support over the decades. Then I will hand the evening off to Heath. He will thank me and the pack for our confidence in him, accept the appointment and announce his team. After all, that we will announce the date of the official ceremony which we have selected to be September 9th." David told us. We both nodded.

"It's important for you both to be there but other then the announcement of the team there isn't much for you to do." Samuel said, smiling at me. He held out his hand and I stepped towards him. He touched my belly softly, amazement crossed over his face. I laughed as Heath crossed the room to join him.

Timothy smiled, "One thing that would be good is if you could take care of the werebears tonight, Charlotte. Their Alpha and Gamma will be attending as a display of good faith. Since you already have a very close relationship with their Gamma it would be nice if you would make sure they are taken care of."

"Of course, consider it done." I told him, nodding with a smile. "Gentlemen, I am going to leave my husband here with you to prepare for tonight. I am going to see if the ladies need any help in the kitchen."

I pulled my stomach away from the men and kissed Clark goodbye before I stepped out of the room and headed down to the kitchen. I would feel Clark's pride radiating through our bond as I walked away.

The announcement went off without a hitch. David made a lovely speech about family, values and pack pride. He thanked the pack and his team for their support all throughout the years, even making a special mention of Cheryl as his stand in Luna. I smiled as he mentioned her, knowing all the work she put into our pack throughout the years. Heath took over, announcing that he accepted the appointment of Alpha, thanking the pack, David and his family for their confidence and support. We all cheered, even the werebears.

I studied Heath as he looked down at his cards, he seemed nervous. He took a deep breath before continuing, "I am so proud of the people I have selected to be on my team to lead this pack alongside me. I am thrilled to introduce each of them tonight. First, as my Beta, there is no one better suited then my brother, Clark Duffey. I have relied on my little brother for everything over the course of our lives, many of you know him as a notable warrior but he will serve us all as a strong Beta to our pack." Heath gestured for Clark to stand up, he stood and the pack let out a loud cheer.

"Next, we have the Delta position, which shall be awarded to my cousin, Timothy Duffey. We all know him as a man of statistics, maps and mathematics. He is also a proven warrior, defending us time and again during rogue attacks. He will be a very strong Delta to all of us." Clark continued, Timothy stood up, gave a very small bow and sat back down before the applause ended. I giggled, knowing that Timothy was not a public person, he preferred to be behind the scenes.

Heath took a deep breath and met my eyes, "I have not selected a Gamma yet, but I assure you I shall before I accede to the position.

However, there is the matter of the lack of Luna for this pack. It is known that Alpha David never took a Luna, and now I do not have a Luna for our pack either. I know it has been many decades since we have had one, but I will keep my eye open for her." The crowd giggled at Heath's joke, "I would like to introduce my brother's wife, Charlotte Duffey, who will be our Beta female, please stand up Charlotte."

I was surprised he mentioned me, I stood, not sure what to expect. He continued, "Clark went to the mating exhibition in Brandon this past spring and he found his mate, Charlotte Gillies. She came all the way from Red Rose pack in Saskatchewan. My brother, Clark has found a wonderful mate and she has agreed to assist me with many of the duties a Luna would typically care for. I know that Charlotte will love and care for our pack with all her heart the same was she does for my dear brother."

The room filled with applause, I bowed and thanked Heath for his kind words. My brother, Michael let out a loud 'whoop' noise, making me giggle. Heath continued to thank the pack for their support and we eventually turned in for the night.

"I think the pack has embraced your brother as Alpha already." I mentioned, unzipping my dress once Clark and I returned to our room. I dropped it to the floor, stepping out and kicking off my shoes. I tossed my clothes in the hamper and stretched in front of the mirror. Clark smirked in the mirror, standing behind me, "Of course, he is going to be a great leader."

I turned and studied his face, he seemed somewhat disappointed, "What's wrong my love?" I asked. Clark unbuttoned his shirt, tossing it into the hamper, "Nothing, I'm just glad he's Alpha and not me. It's a lot of work, I'm a bit annoyed he will be relying on you to do the work of a Luna." He pulled his dress pants down and threw then in the hamper as well.

I smiled and cross the room, pressing my naked form against his body, "It's no different then what your mother did for the pack." Clark nodded, "I know, it's just different because I am not my father and you are not my mother." I giggled, looking up at him.

"Are you a bit possessive my love?" I asked him, raising my eyebrows. Clark blushed, "I try not to be." I pulled him to the bed with me, laying us down and covering us in blankets.

I snuggled into the crook of his neck and kissed my mark softly, "Don't worry Clark, I will be fine. I am proud to serve our pack. I am proud to be your wife, the mother of our children." He nodded as he kissed the top of my head, "My mate is so strong, I don't even remember what I did before I met you." As we fell asleep in each other's arms, I felt our son gently kicking against his hand that was now always placed overtop of my belly.

## Chapter 15

I woke up before dawn the next morning. I pulled myself out of bed trying not to bother Clark. I pulled on sweats and slippers. As I pulled my hair back in a messy bun, I tiptoed out of our bedroom and made my way to the kitchen to make myself tea and a quick breakfast. It was a deserted space, I had never found the kitchen completely empty before. I made myself oatmeal with apple slices and tea, carrying it carefully to the library where I would wait for Marie's call. Anthony did not give me a time but I wanted to be prepared. I ate my oatmeal and waited for the call. Minutes went by like hours, it felt like the lobby of the hotel in Brandon all over again.

Thankfully, the phone ran at 7:30am, I answered it, "Black Lake pack house, this is Charlotte Duffey."

I heard a rough sigh on the line, "Hi Charlotte, it's me, Marie." I couldn't stop myself from crying out with joy at the sound of her voice. I knew she was alive, but a part of me thought I may never get this phone call.

"Marie, thank god! Are you alright?" I cried out, I didn't control the level of my voice. I pulled the blanket onto my lap as I made myself comfortable on the sofa.

She coughed slightly into my ear, "Not really." Neither of us said anything for a moment. I sighed, "Tell me what happened."

Marie cleared her throat and put the phone down. I could hear her talking to someone else, "Please give me some space. I want to talk freely to my sister... Yes, now... No... I said no Tony... Go, I'll link you when I'm done..." In the background I heard a door open and close softly at the other end of the line.

"Sorry Charlotte, I needed the room." She told me, "Tony is gone now." I lay down on the sofa, pulling the blanket up to my chin. I heard Marie shift as well, knowing she was getting as comfortable as I was for our conversation.

"So how much did Tony tell you?" she asked me. "He told me you got mad at him about an Omega girl. You threatened to leave him. He got mad and collared you for three days." I told her, my voice stumbling over the last remark.

Marie sighed into the phone and coughed again, "Yeah, that's the jest of it. The last time we talked things were getting better between us. He finally let me mark him, I thought he was finally ready to be mine. Then I felt it through the mate bond, he was messing around with someone in his office so I went to confront him about it. I kicked her out, yelled at him told him I was sick of his crap."

"Yeah, I knew you got mad at him." I said, she laughed but it wasn't a real laugh. She sighed and continued, "I went to our room and started packing a bag. I was going to take off for a few days to mother and father's not forever. Anthony followed me, he watched me pack and he lost it. He pushed me down, slapped my face, kicked me. He was so angry, he lost complete control. He choked me until I lost consciousness. When I woke up I was naked, bleeding from everywhere and in a collar on the training field. I didn't even get to shift, so everyone saw I was naked and beaten."

I gasped, I had assumed he had made her shift before the collaring. That is the usual way that punishment is handled. Without the fur of her wolf to protect her neck, Marie would definitely have open sores and welts on her neck. They might never heal properly now.

"Marie, I am so sorry." I whispered. She coughed again, I could tell she was weak. Marie cleared her throat again, "I was out there for three days, no food or water. Tony visited me each day, but he didn't come close enough to talk to me. I could sense his sadness and shame through the bond but I was in way too much of my own pain to care. He finally came yesterday to get me. He took the collar off with his bare hands and carried me to our bedroom. He tended to my wounds himself, apologizing over and over again, crying."

Marie seemed unmoved by his apologetic behaviour. I was glad to see she wasn't as soft as she used to be, yet sad that she had to be. I asked her to continue, she said, "He told me he would never hurt me again. He wouldn't mess around anymore, that I was his everything and he loves me so much. I asked him what changed his mind, he said he talked to you."

I laughed, "As though I would have that kind of power." She snickered, "Well it got me out of the collar anyway, so thank you. I'm so exhausted, my entire body throbs but I'm alive."

"Do you believe he is done hurting you?" I asked her. She didn't reply, Marie was silent for a moment before I heard the door open again on her end of the phone.

"Tony and I would like to ask you and Clark to come for a visit here at Rocky Mountain. I am sick and I need my druid sister here to heal me. I think after all the damage he has caused; Tony won't mind footing the bill for the fuel here. Tell me when can you two come?" she said, I could hear Anthony on the phone as well agreeing with what she had said.

I paused, I wasn't sure Clark would want me to go there but I knew Marie would need some help. "I'll talk to Clark today and get back to you later this afternoon."

Marie seemed satisfied with that, "Please Charlotte, don't tell anyone else about this except Clark. I don't want the whole world knowing about what I've been through." I agreed to keep her secret.

After we hung up I raced to our bedroom as quickly as I could. Clark was in the shower. I ran and opened the door, scaring him. Clark jumped about two feet in the air and screamed, "What the hell Char!"

"Sorry my love, I have to talk to you immediately. I just talked to Marie, she needs me to come to Rocky Mountain, she's very ill." I spoke sternly. Clark faced me, catching his breath. He searched my eyes for a moment before he spoke, "When do we leave?" he asked.

I smiled, "Today? This afternoon?" He nodded, "I'll let my brother know. I'll talk to the pilot and arrange the flight for us. Can you pack us up for a week? Get your kit ready." I ignored the water pouring down on him and jumped into his arms. I got completely soaked but it was worth it. He knew me so well, he always knew what I needed and he never stopped me. I loved him so much. I let him go and ran to our room dragging out our bags, frantically packing what we would need. I called Anthony and let him know we would be at their pack house before nightfall.

I went to my herbology lab after I packed us up and made a variety of healing salves, stamina mixes, teas and vitamin boosters. I knew Marie would need all kinds of things to heal and I wasn't exactly sure what shape she was in so I made a bunch of different things. Michael came and found me when I was in the middle of making them, he was annoyed that I hadn't told him I talked to Marie.

"What's going on Charlotte, why are you and Clark leaving in such a hurry? Tell me!" he demanded. I was scurrying around my lab, trying to get everything ready.

"I'm sorry Michael, but Marie asked me to come and help her. She doesn't want everyone to know her business." I told him, trying to keep quiet about what had actually happened.

Michael grabbed my arm gently, pulling me to his chest, "Is she dying Char?" I hugged my brother and shook my head. He sighed heavily, relief on his face. Then his eyes turned dark again with fear, "Does he hurt her?" I flinched, I didn't answer but he knew what that meant. Michael hugged me tightly. He murmured into my ear, "Take care of her and if she will come, bring her back with you."

I nodded. I knew she wouldn't leave him. The mate bond can be strong, even the toxic ones. Marie and Anthony had a very unhealthy relationship but she loved him with every fibre of her being. I would bring her back with me if she would come willingly, but I doubted she would agree to it. Michael stayed in the room with me while I readied everything. Once it was all done I hurried to the lobby where Clark was waiting for me.

"Tell her I love her, Char." Michael said, rubbing my shoulder. "I will." I promised. We said our goodbyes to the Duffeys and headed out to the side by side. We took the short journey to the air strip. We didn't say anything the whole way to the plane or on the flight. While we were in the air, Clark wrapped his arm around my shoulders, holding my hand. With his other hand he rubbed my belly. The flight seemed to take forever, even though it was only about six hours. The sun was down by the time we landed at Rocky Mountain. Anthony had sent a car for us which I was grateful for.

As we drove up to the pack house I saw it was very large compared to ours. Their lands expanded far out beyond where ours did. If I were here for any other type of visit I would have been impressed, but I was only thinking about Marie and what she was going to look like. Right now this land only looked like a prison designed to keep my sister from her family. I needed to see her.

We pulled into the drive, I jumped out of the car before the engine was even cut. I didn't wait for Clark, I ran to the front door and opened it myself. I could feel her pain now that I was here, and it was intense. As I walked through the pack house doors I was met by Anthony and his mother. They both looked at me shocked that I ran in.

"Take me to her now please!" I demanded. Juliana touched her chest in mock shock, but Anthony didn't bother to feign anything with me. He didn't meet my stare as I moved my eyes over him. I heard Clark come up behind me at a jog. He handed me my herb bag, I didn't even realize I had left it in the car.

Anthony gestured for me to follow him, we did. Juliana tried to pull Clark with her but he growled, "I go where my wife goes. She doesn't leave my sight." She took her hand from his arm and stepped back. Anthony sighed, "Just take care of their luggage mom. Don't make a nuisance of yourself." Juliana nodded and turned to the chauffeur.

Anthony lead us up several flights of stairs and down a long corridor to a large room with oak double doors. He unlocked the door with a key, I stared at him and grabbed his hand, "You are locking he in?" I demanded.

He met my eyes, shame twinkling in the corners of his, "I didn't want her to leave. She said she would leave me." I pulled the key from his hand and put it in the pocket of my dress.

I placed my hand on his shoulder and gave it a squeeze, "You have to trust her not to leave you. Locking her in won't keep her here. Loving her will." Anthony searched my face, I held a cold expression.

"She's inside," he whispered, "our healers have done all they can do. They said because she wasn't shifted when she was collared that the silver poisoning is too extensive. They told me she might be too weak to regenerate." Anthony let out a deep moan and he cried into my shoulder. I held on to him, not wanting to, but he reached for me and I had no real choice.

I motioned for Clark to come to my side, I pulled Anthony off of me and Clark pulled his arm over his shoulder, "Go with my husband. Don't come back tonight, I will need time and space to take care of Marie. Clark will keep you company if you want."

I kissed Clark on the lips and mind linked him 'Thank you.' He nodded and linked to me, 'Once he is passed out I will sleep outside this door.' I smiled and slipped inside to my sister.

The room smelled of blood, silver and despair. There was only a small fire lit in the hearth. I walked over to it and placed another log on the flames. It wasn't warm in here either, we needed to change that. The bedroom was royal purple and gold, fit for a king and queen. I saw there was an attached bathroom, two large closets and a wardrobe. My eyes continued to scan the room, I saw a small figure laying on top of the large king size bed. I could tell Marie was sleeping, I walked up next to her side of the bed and touched her shoulder. She flinched, I pulled back and noticed blood had soaked through the back of her nightgown.

"Marie, it's me. It's Charlotte." I whispered. She moaned in pain and tried to roll over on her back but I could tell it hurt too much. I decided to turn on some lights and get a look at her. I moved and turned on the bedside lamps. It was like a horror movie. Marie's face had three huge claw marks across her left eye. She had a fat lip, a broken nose a large gash on her forehead. "Hey sweetie, how are you feeling?" I asked.

Marie opened her eyes to look at me, her left eye was bloodshot. "Thirsty." She whispered. I grabbed a glass from the bathroom and brought her water. She could hardly sit up but she drank it all down.

I grabbed the phone from the wall and called down to the Omegas, "Hello, yes this is the Luna's sister. I need you to bring up half a dozen clean towels, two hot water bottles, a kettle and a bucket of ice. Right now."

I got Marie some more water and gave it to her, she drank all that down as well. As she swallowed I go a better look at her neck. There were welts on top of welts. Her entire neck was raw, still bleeding with no signs of healing. I opened my herb bag and took out the strongest salve I had made. "Marie, this is going to hurt but I think it will help once it soaks in." I told her.

I rubbed some of the salve into her neck and face, she screeched in pain but she let me rub it in. I went into my bag and pulled out an adrenalin stick, which is a mix of licorice root and ginseng. I put it between Marie's teeth and told her to chew it up and swallow. She did as I said, keeping her eyes closed. "The adrenalin stick will kick your body into overdrive which will hopefully give it the push it needs to let the salve start to soak into your skin and pull it back together." I told her.

I heard a soft knock at the door. I went to let the Omega in with the supplies. She set it down on the table in the corner of the bedroom. I grabbed the kettle, filled it with water and set it in the fireplace to boil.

"We need to change your nightgown. It's soaked with blood." I whispered, she nodded slowly. I found them in the wardrobe and brought one back to the bed. I forced Marie to sit up, she moaned with pain. I pulled off the blood soaked one and replaced it with a clean one. I had a better look at the rest of her body. I noticed her right arm was broken and healed incorrectly, I knew I would have to re-brake it. Her legs were bruised but not broken. She had a rib or two out of place, but it appeared to be healing alright. I touched her right arm, "Honey, your arm isn't healing properly. I am going to have to re-break it and set it properly."

Marie groaned, but she nodded slowly, I told her to brace herself before I snapped her arm and reset it. She didn't make very much noise when fixed her arm. The kettle started to boil. I pulled it from the fire, filled the water bottles and set them on either side of her body. I took some tea leaves from my bag and made a cup of it to drink. She drank it all down. I took out another jar of salve and rubbed it all over the rest of her wounds. I wrapped Marie up in the blankets and tucked her in for the night.

She fell asleep quickly, I wrapped some towels around her head to keep her warmer. All through the night I stayed at Marie's bedside tending her wounds. I ordered up some soup for her the next day to give her a protein boost. I kept Anthony out of the room, though that was a very difficult task. Clark tended to Anthony, taking him to train and tracking with their wolves to keep him away from Marie's bedroom door.

By noon the next day I saw her arm had set nicely, healing up well. I moved the towel around her head and the salve was working. I force fed Marie another adrenaline stick and reapplied the salves to keep up the process. At some point after lunch I fell asleep for a few hours on the other side of the bed from her.

"Wake up Char." She whispered into my ear. I was sound asleep, Marie rubbed my arm to wake me. I moaned as I rolled over to face her. The slashes over her eyes were closed now, as was the gash on her forehead. They were still red and scabbed but at least closed. Her lip was completely healed. She smiled at me. "Hello sister."

I smiled at her and pulled her close, "Hey Marie, how are you feeling?"

She moaned a bit, "I'm ok, I still hurt all over but I can tell I'm healing." I nodded into her shoulder, not letting her go. "Don't worry, I have some pain killers I can give you in my bag." I told her.

"Where is Anthony?" she asked. I leaned back and looked into her face, "I asked Clark to keep him away. Do you want me to get him?"

She shook her head, letting her eyes fall to my belly. Marie ran her hands over me and giggled as she felt a kick. "You look so beautiful, Char." She told me. "Thank you.", I whispered.

I looked into her face, I could still smell the blood on her from the wounds but they were healing so that was dissipating. I could smell something else though, I wasn't sure what it was yet but I could smell something on her. Maybe it was just the combination of salves, teas and remedies. I dismissed the thought, I shouldn't' be distracted right then, Marie needed me.

"Are you hungry?" I asked her, she nodded. "Ok, I'll give you something for the pain and then I'm going to go and make you some homemade soup in the kitchen. Mom's recipe of chicken noodle should add some comfort."

I swung myself out of the bed, going to my bag to get some camomile and peppermint leaves. I mixed them together into a tea which she drank down quickly. I lifted her hair up to see her neck, the wounds were still very prominent, closed but taking a long time to heal. I pulled a vial of tea tree oil from my bag and applied it liberally to her neck, she flinched at the contact.

"You need to keep resting. Here, lay this lavender on your pillow. It will lull you to sleep. When the soup is done I will bring it to you." I told her, handing her the small branch. I kissed her forehead, noticing that wound was also taking a while to heal. Marie didn't say anything, just taking the branch and setting it down next to her pillow. She did as I said, inhaling deeply.

I tiptoed out of the room, not locking the door behind me. I almost fell over my husband who was laying down in front of the door in his wolf form. He smelled like outside, I smiled, he was so tired trying to keep Anthony preoccupied. I rubbed his head lovingly, he woke up and stared into my face. He was exhausted. I rubbed Clark's snout and kissed his nose, "Go to our room and sleep my dear. You are worn out. I am going to make Marie my mom's chicken noodle soup. She is fine, you don't need to be on guard duty." He whimpered, protesting that he should stay. I shook my head at him, "I will link with you if I need you. Go on big bad Beta, I'll bring you some soup too, ok."

His ears lifted and he wagged his tail, I laughed. Clark nuzzled my stomach before he rose to stretch, he licked my face and walked slowly down the hall to our room. I realized I hadn't even seen it yet; I had been too busy taking care of Marie.

I found my way to the kitchen and found three Omega girls in there preparing various foods. They all stared at me like I was royalty when I walked in, they also looked frightened.

"Hello, I am Charlotte, Luna Marie's sister." I said smiling, introducing myself to the room. The three girls all bowed to me, not making eye contact. The one closest to me opened her mouth tentatively, "We know, Beta, welcome to Rocky Mountain pack house. How can we help you?"

I smiled at her, no one had ever called me 'Beta' before. I wasn't exactly sure how to take it, though I knew she meant it as a form of respect, "I'm here to care for your Luna while she heals. I want to make her our mother's homemade chicken noodle soup for comfort, I just need to use the kitchen with you here for a bit."

They all bowed and started to exit immediately, I raised my hands, "No, ladies you don't need to go! I just wanted to share the kitchen with you if that's alright with all of you."

The one furthest away looked up at me, astonished. She then lowered her head again as I tried to make eye contact with her. The one closest to me whispered, "You want us to stay while you are in here?" I nodded, "Of course, I don't want to interrupt your work, it's important. Just as important as what I am doing." They all looked at each other, speechless. I was astonished that Omegas were treated so poorly here like they were second class citizens.

"What are your names?" I asked with a smile. The one closest to me raised her head a little, still not making eye contact, "I am Danielle, this is Rachel and she is Vayda. We are all Omega." I nodded, "It is lovely to meet you all. Just call me Charlotte ok? None of that Beta silliness. I don't get that at home so I won't be used to it." I giggled.

I moved closer to Danielle, she stepped back slightly. I could see her arms had scars, all very healed but still present. I examined the other girls as well from a distance. They had scars, corporal punishment was alive and well here at Rocky Mountain. It made my stomach churn. I noticed Vayda was shuffling her feet, uncomfortable. I moved to the other side of the kitchen towards her, "Vayda, can you tell me where the pots are?" She moved towards a large cabinet and opened it up for me. I pulled a soup pot down and placed it on the counter.

"I'm just going to ask you ladies where things are since I don't have any idea if that's alright. Just bear with me." I laughed, they all looked at each other and nodded in unison. I felt sorry for them, so terrified in their own home, "It's alright, I am not going to hurt any of you. I promise." Danielle nodded to me and moved back to her station, slowly the other two did as well. We settled into a comfortable rhythm of working together in the kitchen. After about an hour they were laughing as though I wasn't even there, talking amongst themselves about the day to day happenings of the pack house. They were all sweet girls, still not of age. All of them were fifteen, but seemed younger.

I was stirring the soup when Vayda came over to me, "God that smells so good." She sniffed the air deeply. I smiled at her, "Would you ladies be my taste testers?" They all nodded happily, I laughed. It was coming along nicely, just needed a bit longer at a low boil. "I cook a bit back home, when the Omegas deem it acceptable." I joked. Rachel and Danielle looked at me with awe, "You cook at your pack house? But you are Beta." Rachel shuttered, Danielle lightly touched her shoulder as though to try to stop her from saying anything.

"Oh yes, breakfast is my usual shift. We are a lot smaller up where I come from then you so we all pitch in. Though Tabitha and Amy are far better cooks then me. My mother in law is excellent with meat seasonings." I told them. Vayda smiled at me, "Are Tabitha and Amy your personal Omegas?"

I shook my head, "No they are my friends. Their ranks don't matter to me. I don't have a personal Omega." Danielle cocked her head to the side and looked at Vayda then me, "You are friends with Omegas?" I nodded, "They are my dearest friends back home." Rachel took a step towards me, "How is that allowed?" I shrugged, "It's just how we do things at Black Lake. We were similar in Red Rose where Marie and I were born, in Saskatchewan."

Danielle nodded, she cleared her throat to bring the other two girls back to their tasks. We all returned to a content silence. When the soup was ready I asked Rachel to bring out four bowls so we could try it. I served them all some soup, which was an adjustment for them, I could tell. I took the first spoonful to show them it was alright to eat with me. It was pretty close to my mother's but it was missing a bit of rosemary. I turned back to the pot, putting a dash of the herb into the pot and stirred it up again. The girls all took a spoon of the soup, eating it slowly. "So, what's the verdict?" I asked.

"It's perfect madam." Danielle told me, without even thinking. I laughed, "It's not, it's ok Danielle, I know it's not. You won't make me angry to say so. It's pretty good, but not perfect." Rachel smiled at me, "It's very good Charlotte." The other two girls turned to her, both with scared eyes as Rachel had called me by my name.

"Thank you Rachel. I appreciate it." I told her, touching her shoulder lightly. She nodded and took another spoon of her soup. I turned to the pot, turning it on a simmer and stirred it up a bit more. "Thank you for sharing this with us." Vayda whispered, I turned to face her, "Of course. Thank you for trying it for me." Danielle cleaned up the bowls when we were finished. Clark linked me asking where I was, I told him. A few moments later my mate walked in. The girls all froze, trembling when he entered the room. He didn't respond, just walked right to my side and kissed my forehead, "Hello darling. What smells so good?"

"My mother's chicken noodle soup. I'm making it for Marie. Would you like some my love?" I asked him, melting into his chest. He nodded,

"Sure where are the bowls?" Rachel produced a bowl immediately and bowed to him, Clark looked at her then me, he took the bowl, "Thank you..." I smiled at him, filling his bowl. "These lovely ladies are Danielle, Rachel and Vayda. They have been helping me navigate the kitchen. Ladies, this is my husband, Clark."

Clark started to eat the soup, "Nice to meet you all. I'm sure my wife has been having fun in here with all of you. She loves to cook in our pack house kitchen back home." He leaned with his back to the counter next to the stove while I stirred the pot. He drank down the soup without a spoon. I laughed at him, playfully threatening to hit him with my wooden spoon. He pretended to duck. The girls all looked at each other, not sure what to make of our familiarity.

"Char, this is pretty good you know." He told me, I nodded. I took a Tupperware container and filled it up, "I think it's ready for your Luna, girls." I set the bowl to the side and took the pot off the burner. Vayda stepped up to me to take the pot, I shook my head, "It's alright Vayda, I will take care of the messes I made. You don't worry a moment about it. You can all have this soup and give it to your families if you like." Clark stepped forward to fill his bowl again, "I want one more bowl before you give it all away darling." I laughed and kissed his cheek.

I took the bowl for Marie and stepped towards the door, Clark stayed behind, "I'll clean up from the soup darling. Don't worry, I won't let these ladies do it." He winked at me, I thanked him with my eyes. "Thank you girls for all your help today, you all made me feel welcome. I'll see you all later, ok." I told them, the girls all made eye contact with me this time and smiled. They still bowed to me but it was an improvement from the terror in their eyes just a few hours ago when I walked into the kitchen.

I went back to Marie's room to find the door ajar. I stepped inside to see Anthony at her bedside. I was about to yell at him to leave until I noticed what he was doing. He was licking her neck and face wounds, as wolves do to heal themselves and each other when they are hurt. I walked to the opposite side of the bed to him, setting the soup bowl down on the end table. He glanced at me, but we didn't speak. He was curled up next to her, whimpering into her neck and face. I studied what he was doing. I could sense Marie's warmth towards him as he did this for her. Anthony was behaving very tenderly; I wasn't expecting to find him in here like this.

"Is Charlotte here?" Marie whispered, her voice muffled by Anthony's face. "Yes Marie I am here." I told her. Anthony looked to me, his eyes full of tears. I handed the soup bowl to him, "Feed her this, it will bring her so much comfort." I told him. He looked at me, letting the tears fall. He took the bowl from my hand with a spoon, thanking me silently. He helped Marie sit up, spoon feeding her the soup. I rose and took my herb bag to the table and took stock of what I had left. I listened to Anthony gently feeding my sister in the background, making sure she ate the whole bowl. I was getting low on the strongest salve I brought, but I had enough for one last application to her neck and face.

When Marie had eaten all the soup I returned to the bedside, taking the bowl from Anthony. I handed him the jar of salve, he took it eagerly and stared at me. I held a cold gaze, "Apply the rest of this to her neck and forehead. Don't lick it after its on, let it soak in. Once it's on, just hold her while it sinks into her skin." Anthony nodded, apply it over her neck and face. Marie winced, but accepted his touch. She moaned a little. I stepped back, watching Anthony caring for my sister.

I went to the bathroom to fill up the kettle and went to the hearth to tend the fire. I decided to make some tea for Anthony, a heart healing tea. He hadn't been sleeping since he took the collar off, I could tell. He looked terrible himself, nothing like her but still hollow and exhausted. His inner pain reflected on her body, as though he inflicted it on her because he was in turmoil himself. What a toxic situation I thought to myself. I linked Clark and told him Anthony was in here with me, he could come in with me. He was there a few minutes later, coming in quietly. Anthony growled when he saw Clark walked up next to me by the fireplace. "It's fine, he isn't here to take you out of here. He is here to be with me." I told him. Anthony sighed with relief. He went back to snuggling into Marie's body like she was his only source of life.

Clark pulled me close to his chest as we watched the fire. He kissed my head and buried his face in my hair. We didn't speak, I just pulled his arms as tight around my stomach as I could and leaned back into his chest. As the kettle boiled, I pulled it off the fire. I poured it into a cup, stirred up and tapped Anthony on the shoulder. He looked at me, I handed him the cup. He went to move Marie, but I stopped him. "No, Anthony this is for you. This will help your heart to heal. It will help you to forgive yourself." I whispered. He whimpered, his face breaking into a sob, pushing the mug back into my hand. He sat up, running his hands through his hair as he growled low in his throat, "I don't deserve that."

I stepped back, setting the cup down on the end table. I sighed, "Anthony…" I began but he waved his hand towards me, "No Charlotte, I don't deserve to heal from this. I almost killed my Luna, if you hadn't of come she would have died. I know that. I hurt her in so many ways and I can't take any of it back. She will never forgive me; she will leave me when she is strong enough. I deserve that, to feel her rejection break me and kill me. I don't deserve her; I know that now. She isn't my right, her love was my privilege and I beat it to hell." His voice broke as he spoke. Anthony started to shake on the bed, Clark moved towards him, touching his shoulder. Anthony growled slightly, but it was short lived and replaced with trembling and sobs again. Clark sat next to him and rubbed his shoulder, offering a small comfort.

"I know you will take her back with you when you leave," Anthony whimpered, not looking at me, "I won't try to stop you. Just let me be here with her so I can have a little of her before she leaves me and I die of heartache. I know I don't deserve it, I know you hate me and you have every right to. Please just give me a little time before she's gone forever."

I took the mug again, "She isn't going to leave you. Marie loves you and she doesn't want to leave you, she told me that already." His face whipped around to stare at me. His eyes were so blood shot they looked pained. "Drink this down, we will leave you here with her tonight. Just call our room if you need me." Anthony reached out a shaking hand and took the mug, he started to sip it slowly.

I leaned down and kissed my sister's forehead, she was sound asleep. Clark and I left without a word, he led me to our room. Clark carried me to the bed, taking off both our clothes and tucked us under the covers in silence. It didn't hit me how exhausted I was until I was wrapped up in his arms were my walls came down. He pulled me close to his chest, snuggling into our favorite position to sleep. I let the land of dreams take me away.

## Chapter 16

I awoke the next morning to a knock at the door. I rose up in the bed, rubbing my eyes. The dawn was just breaking through the windows. I moved to the edge of the bed, stretching my tired muscles. Clark didn't even stir at the knocking; it was too soft to rouse him. I raised myself up and shuffled to the door, putting on my housecoat along the way. I quietly opened the door to see Rachel standing before me, "Hello, what can I do for you?" I asked her.

Rachel shuffled her feet, seemingly nervous. She raised her eyes slowly to make eye contact with me, "Alpha Anthony asked me to come and get you. The Luna is awake and asking for you." I smiled, "Thank you Rachel. I'll go straight away." She turned and left quickly. I got dressed, not bothering to shower. I kissed my mate goodbye, whispering in his ear, "Marie is asking for me my love. I'll be with her." Clark stirred slightly and kissed my face, rolling over onto my side of the bed. I giggled at him. I left quickly and made my way to Marie's room.

When I entered her room she was sitting up in bed. Her eyes were closed, but she was talking to Anthony who was laying next to her. He was still in his clothes; I could tell he had changed Marie's night gown at some point. Anthony rested his head on her shoulder, looking up at her face. It was endearing actually. "Good morning, you asked for me." I said, stepping into the room and closing the door behind me.

"Thank you Char, come here." Marie chocked out, her voice still not fulling returned. She gestured with her arms to come to her. I crossed the room quickly and pulled her into an embrace. Anthony leaned back, giving us some room. I breathed her in, trying to hold on to her as long as I could. She released me, I pushed her hair back on her neck to examine it. The welts were still persisting, red and angry. It hadn't occurred to me before, but Marie may never fully heal from the collaring. I went to my herb bag, grabbing a jar of salve and brought it back over to the bed.

"It is good to see you are getting your strength back. Have you got an appetite?" I asked. She nodded, I asked Anthony to call down for some breakfast for her. He nodded, going to the phone. I began to rub the salve into her neck. She didn't flinch this time, which was a great sign. "How are you feeling?" I asked her.

She opened her eyes, they were still red but they were starting to turn back to green. She managed a weak smile, "I am alright. Still in a lot of pain but I am much stronger now." I finished rubbing the salve in, "I'm not sure these wounds on your neck will ever fully go away my dear sister." Marie stared at me with sadness, "I know. If I would have been in wolf form they wouldn't be so stubborn, but because I was in human form the wounds went deeper."

I nodded, "Almost down to the bone." Anthony shuddered at my words. She looked up at me, pushing the covers off herself and stretching her back, "I am still weak but I'm feeling like I should move a bit. I need to go to the bathroom." I helped her up and to the bathroom, closing the door behind her.

Anthony got off the bed and smoothed his clothing. He was still in the same clothes as last night. He cleared his throat, "I ordered up breakfast for all three of us." I studied his face, not smiling, "Alright." Anthony smiled at me but I did not return it. I sucked in a deep breath before I told him, "Anthony, just because I want you to forgive yourself does not mean I am going to forget what you did. What you did is undeniably the cruelest thing I have ever heard an Alpha do to his Luna.

I want you and Marie to move past it if you can, but don't think for a second that I will ever condone or understand what happened here."

He stared at me, lowering his head with shame. Anthony nodded, "I understand that Charlotte. I expected it actually. I am not going to pretend that I didn't do any of the things I did to my Luna." He paused, giving me time to soak up his words, "However, I do vow to you and your sister that I will never lay a hand in anger on Marie again. I will spend the rest of my life making up for the hurt I did to her, hoping one day she will forgive me."

Anthony waited for me to say something, I didn't. I got the impression he was used to making grand speeches and getting a round of applause at the end of them. Promising not to hurt my sister any more wasn't exactly something that warranted applause. I turned to the bathroom door, "Marie are you alright in there?" I shouted through the door. "Yes, I'm just having a sink bath. I'll be out in a bit." She replied. I turned back to Anthony, still not smiling. "Actions speak louder then words." I muttered, staring into his eyes. He sighed and lowered his gaze again, turning towards the chair in the corner and sinking into it.

I started to strip the bed, replacing the soiled sheets with fresh ones was a good idea for her. I pulled fresh ones out of the closet and tossed the old ones in the laundry hamper. Anthony didn't make a move to assist me, I could tell he had no idea how to change bed linens. I thought to myself, 'What a spoiled little brat.' Clark mink linked me, 'Who's a spoiled brat?' I giggled to myself, I must have thought that louder then I intended to. I filled Clark in on my little chat with Anthony, he was equally unimpressed with the promises my sister's husband had made. Clark came to the bedroom a short time later, knocking before he came in.

"Hey darling how is she doing today?" he asked me, closing the door behind himself. Anthony didn't lift his head when Clark stepped towards the fire place.

"She's in the bathroom. Anthony ordered up breakfast for us, she's alright. It's the first time she's been out of bed in about 4 days." I said, tucking the sheets under the mattress. He nodded, coming over to help me put the quilt back on the bed. When it was made Clark came around and wrapped his arms around my waist. I pulled his head to my neck and snuggled into him. He reached around to rest his hand on my belly, it was the greatest feeling in the world.

Marie opened the door, Clark and I turned to face her. She looked dizzy, stumbling as she stepped out of the bathroom. Clark reached forward and caught her, causing Anthony to growl. I turned to him frowning, "Oh stop it! She can barely walk, she's so weak and he caught her so she wouldn't fall. She could have hurt herself again! What is wrong with you?!" I couldn't help it; I was shouting at him. I never shouted, but this Alpha was getting on my last nerve.

Anthony shrunk back into the chair, shocked at my tone. I turned back to Clark, he was holding Marie up. She was exhausted, I could tell she over did it by taking a sink bath. "Clark, please put her back in the bed. I'll make her some tea." I muttered. He did as I asked, then stepped away from the bed. I pulled the covers up to her chest, making sure she was comfortable before I made the tea. What I was doing that, Clark filled up the kettle and put it in the fire. He added a log. I smiled at him, so sweet.

"Charlotte, I'm going to go and find some grub for myself. I'm also going to give Heath and Timothy a call to see how things are going back home. Just link me if you need me darling." He told me, kissing my forehead. I nodded, remaining silent. He nodded to Anthony who was still in the corner sulking like a child. I grabbed the mug from the bedside table and took it to the bathroom to wash it out. While I was at the sink Anthony followed me in. He leaned on the door frame and stared at me.

"What?" I asked, not looking at him. He sighed, "Your husband really adores you." My eyes shot to him, "Yes he does."

Anthony shuffled his feet, putting his hands in his pockets, "I can see how he looks at you, it's very sweet. The two of you make it look so easy. He knows how to show how he feels about you." I nodded.

"Does he ever get mad at you?" he asked. I tilted my head to the side, "Like does he yell at me?" Anthony looked down at the floor, "Does he ever loose his temper?"

I dried the mug off and walked past him to the bedroom. I pulled the tea from my herb bag and shook the leaves into the mug, waiting for the kettle to blow. "Of course we have arguments. All couples do. He looses his temper and so do I. We aren't perfect." I told him.

Anthony's eyes moved to Marie's resting form. He was very pained; I could see it. "Has he ever hurt you?" he asked. The kettle blew, making me jump slightly. I pulled it from the fire and poured the water.

"No he has never hurt me. Not once." I said clearly, emphasising the last word. He sighed again, running his hand through his hair, "My dad used to hit my mom. My grandfather hit my grandmother. My uncles hit my aunts. It's how it's always been done in my family; it's how we show we are in charge. I didn't even think about it when it happened the first time."

I raised my hand up to Anthony as I walked past him to Marie's bedside. "I am not interested in your confessions. I'm not your therapist, Anthony. You have anger issues; you know your behaviour isn't acceptable. I am not going to feel sorry for you. I'm not attending your pity party. If you want to change, then you need to do it yourself." I muttered.

"I'm not asking for pity, I'm just trying to talk to you, Charlotte." He said sternly. Anthony reached out and grabbed my shoulder, turning me to face him. I pushed him back from me and shouted, "Don't you dare touch me!" I heard a loud growl, it rocked through the house. Within seconds Clark burst into the room, crossed it and lifted Anthony up in the air by his throat. Anthony looked down in shock at Clark. My mate's eyes were black, his canines were extended, he was growling, "Do not touch my mate, EVER!"

Anthony's hands went to Clark's on his throat, he was trying to free himself. Marie sat up, suddenly aware of what's going on, "Anthony what did you do?!"

"Clark, put him down." I whispered, reaching out and touching his arm. He turned to face me, his canines retracting. Slowly, he set Anthony down and removed his hand from his neck. Clark pulled me to his chest urgently and kissed my lips.

"That animal will not touch you." He said, still growling into my hair. I nodded, "It's ok my dear, I wasn't expecting him to touch me and it startled me. I don't believe he meant anything by it."

Clark pulled back to look at me, his eyes still black, "He has a record for hurting women. I don't care if he didn't mean anything by it, he will not touch you again! Do you hear me Anthony, if you touch her again we are going to have more then words!" I nodded, rubbing Clark's back slowly to sooth him.

Anthony cleared his throat trying to steady himself on his feet, "I am sorry Charlotte, I didn't mean to scare you. I really didn't." His eyes were pleading for me to believe him. I glared at him but nodded, "I know, I believe you."

Marie lay back down and moaned in pain, I pulled myself from Clark's grasp and moved towards her, grabbing the mug as I sat next to her. She drank it down quickly. I rubbed her hair softly, soothing her back to sleep. Before she dozed off, Marie whispered to me, "I'm sorry Charlotte. I'm so sorry I didn't listen to you." I kissed her forehead and let her fall asleep.

I turned to see Clark staring at Anthony with rage on his face. Anthony leaned against the wall holding his throat, staring at the ground. I moved to Clark, gesturing for him to sit in the chair in the corner. I took the salve from the nightstand, opening it to Anthony, "Here, put this on. It will sooth the pain." He took some on his finger and rubbed it over his throat.

I walked around the bed to Clark, I lowered myself into his lap and leaning into his chest. He embraced me quickly and nuzzled my neck from behind. The two couples in this room were such a sharp contrast, it was almost unbearable.

# Chapter 17

The next two days were less eventful at Rocky Mountain. Marie continued to heal, she was able to move around a lot faster without assistance anymore. She still tired easily but she was getting stronger each day. I gave her salve several times a day but her neck had a permanent red ring around it like a necklace. Though it had healed well, it didn't seem that the marks would fade. It bothered me that Anthony had left such a mark on her body.

We decided to take a short walk to the gardens one afternoon. Marie was enjoying the fresh air after being cooped up in her bedroom for so long. We sat down on a blanket and drank some fruit punch in the sunshine. "It really is beautiful here." She told me, "I love this place. Even though it isn't Red Rose I love the mountains."

I smiled, "I know what you mean. I miss home sometimes, but I have fallen in love with Black Lake." Marie nodded, "It's so far though. You can't just pick up and go shopping like I can do in Calgary. That must be a pain sometimes." I laughed, "No I can't go shopping on impulse I didn't do that anyway. I think I'm better suited for the wilderness then the city." She laughed, agreeing with me.

As we sat talking I caught a whiff of something from Marie. It was faint but I could smell it more clearly now that she wasn't covered in blood and puss. It was a different sweetness that I had never experienced before. I leaned closer to her, almost in her face and took a keep breath. The smell was radiating from her, leaking through her pores. Marie stared at me, quizzically, "What's up?"

"You smell different. I can't place it. It's not from your injuries, it's not my salves or remedies. There is something going on, are you feeling alright?" I asked, placing my hand on her forehead. Marie waved it away and laughed, "No I'm not sick. I am alright. I know what it is." I stared at her, urging her to tell me.

Marie's eyes twinkled, "I'm pregnant." My face fell. She was radiating happiness; I couldn't hide my sadness. "Oh come on Char, I'm alright. This is happy news; you should be excited. We are going to be pregnant at the same time." She said, holding my hand.

I shook my head, "Are you happy about this? You know that he will never let you leave now that you are with pup." She smiled, "I know he's made some mistakes but we are having a family."

I sighed and put my face in my hands, "Marie, are you hearing yourself? I'm not talking about mistakes; I'm talking about abuse."

She looked away from me, I could see her closing off. "I want you to be happy for me, Char. I am happy, please be happy for me." I sighed and reached out, turning her face towards mine, "I am happy you are having a baby. I will be there for you and your children always. Alright?" Marie nodded, her smiled returning.

"Have you told Anthony yet?" I asked, trying to keep the conversation upbeat. She shook her head, "No, I was going to tell him but then the whole incident happened. I was scared I would loose it with how bad I was, but my sister is a miracle druid." I smiled softly at her. "I'm going to tell him tonight." She admitted.

I sighed, forcing a smile and nodded. "Let's get you back to your room for a bit more rest. I'd rather not push our luck just yet." "Yes mame." Marie said, teasing me. I took her back to her room and set her up in the bed. I wanted to be happy for her, like she was happy for me. I knew Marie had always wanted a family of her own, I knew this was her greatest dream. I knew Anthony had said he wanted to change his ways but I wasn't convinced that was a possibility. I decided I needed some time away so I went to my room.

I lay down on the bed, taking off my glasses and closing my eyes. My chest felt tight, everything with Marie was starting to take its toll. My head started to hurt, I sighed heavily. Instead of taking something I decided to try and breathe through it. I let the smell of Clark fill my senses. I mind linked him, asking him to come to our room for some private time. He arrived in a matter of moments, locking the door behind himself.

Clark smiled at me laying on the bed, he wiggled his eyebrows at me. I laughed out loud, and beckoned him to me with my arms. Wordlessly Clark stripped down to his birthday suit as he crossed the room to me. He lifted me up to and pulled my sundress off quickly. He removed my bra and my underwear gently before shuffling me up the bed. Clark lowered himself next to me, I gazed into his eyes. He kissed my lips slowly, softly over and over again. The taste of his lips made me weak, the sweetness of his mouth. His hands ran through my hair down my arms and rested on my hip. I deepened the kiss as I shifted on top of him, running my hands over his chest.

Clark reached up, cupping my face with his hands to see my eyes. He kissed me lips again tenderly. I trailed kisses down his face to his throat and over to my mark on his neck. I bit down hard, Clark let out a loud growl. I could tell I surprised him, I licked my mark over and over again. I shifted moving his member to my entrance, lowering myself onto him with a deep sigh into his mouth. Clark moaned, raising his hips as I sunk down onto him. We made love slowly that afternoon, over and over again. I needed something good to hold on to, something pure and loving. I needed to be reminded that love didn't have to hurt. I needed my husband's strength and warmth, he gave me everything I needed and more.

Afterward Clark held me close to his chest, purring into my hair. I rubbed my hand over his chest lazily, listening to his heart beat. My head no longer hurt, though I was exhausted from the afternoon's activities. I felt a sudden hard kick in my stomach, the baby was moving. It hurt more then I expected, I had to move onto my back, let out a loud groan.

Clark sat up quickly, helping me to sit up, "Darling what's happening?"

"I don't think it's much of anything, just a very active baby." I muttered, trying to breath through the kicking. I knew it wasn't a contraction but there was a lot of activity in there.

"Maybe he doesn't like what I just did to his mama." He said with a chuckle. I glared at Clark, "Mama liked it so this little man can chill out. My body, my decisions."

He shifted over to my side and placed his hand on my stomach, moving in large circles. It seemed to relax the baby. I sighed, contented, "He knows his daddy."

Clark sucked in a breath, he turned his head to meet my eyes and smiled like a manic, "Daddy… I'm going to be a daddy. You made me a daddy." He kissed me with urgency. I smiled against his lips, "You are a wonderful daddy and he's not even here yet." I ran my fingers through his hair.

We lay down together again, unwilling to let each other go. "Marie is pregnant." I whispered. Clark pulled me closer into a hug. I squeezed him back. "Does he know yet?" I shook my head into his shoulder. "Is she going to tell him soon?" he asked me.

"I think so. She's so excited about them becoming a family." I muttered, the words tasted toxic in my mouth. Clark kissed my forehead and sighed, "I'm sure Anthony will be excited. When I was keeping him preoccupied he asked me all kinds of questions about pregnancy."

"I'm not sure how I feel about it." I told him. Clark nuzzled my hair, "That is understandable Char, he's not my favorite person either."

"I know Marie loves him so I am trying to be supportive. I want to help her, but I'm scared for her." I confessed.

Clark's arm tightened around my shoulders, "You love your sister, I know that feeling well. I love my brother the same."

"True, but Heath hasn't done anything to make you worry about him." I said bitterly. He chuckled, "Not yet. He's over due though." I giggled.

"Char, all you can do is be there for her. I know it's cliché but it's true. Maybe Anthony will clean up his act and be a better mate. If he doesn't then we will be there to help her pick up the pieces." Clark told me.

I sighed into his neck, "I know, you are right. It just drives me crazy that I can't do anything about it." He chuckled, "Oh my darling, I know. Maybe it's time for you to have a bit more stress relief."

He snuck down to the end of the bed and started to rub my swollen feet. I moaned with pleasure, I didn't even notice my feet were as sore as they were until Clark started touching them. Slowly my stress melted away as he rubbed. I moaned and groaned at his touch, I heard Clark growl once in a while at my sounds. After about twenty minutes he couldn't take it any more, climbing my body and having his way with me one more time before supper time.

## Chapter 18

After a week in Rocky Mountain it was time to go home to the North West Territories. Though I had missed my sister it was a relief to be going home. Our bags were packed; the plane was waiting to fly us out. Anthony and Marie saw us off in the foyer. She was looking so much better. Marie's smile was back, her body head healed but her neck would never loose the scar.

I held on to her for dear life, "If you want me to come when the baby is coming I will do the delivery." She nodded into my shoulder as she returned my hug, "I will let you know."

I leaned back and smiled at my sister, "I love you Marie. Take care of yourself. I am just a phone call away." She smiled at me and let a few tears fall down her face, "I can't thank you enough for all you have done for me. I love you so much, I wouldn't be here without you."

I pulled her close again, squeezing her tight again. A sudden fear of never being able to see her again shot through me. I knew it was irrational and likely false but it still hit me hard. I felt Clark rub my lower back, sensing my tension. I buried my face in the crook of Marie's neck and shed tears. She did the same. When we finally let go I turned to Clark. He and Anthony were staring at each other, both with their hands in their pockets unsmiling. They did not shake hands.

I crossed the room, taking a deep breath to gather my courage. I extended my hand to Anthony, he looked at me with huge eyes. "Goodbye Anthony. Take care of my sister and yourself. Until next time." He smiled broadly and shook my hand heartily, "Yes of course Charlotte. Thank you for coming!"

Clark nodded to Marie and Anthony, he placed his hand on the small of my back guiding me out the door. We walked to the car to take us to the air strip. Clark wrapped his arm around my shoulder, we were ready to go home.

By the time we landed at Black Lake I was exhausted. Once I stepped out of the plane I took a deep breath. The symphony of the woods and waters filled my whole body with an undeniable feeling of home. I had missed this place so much. Clark laughed at me as he loaded our luggage in the side by side. His brother Heath had come to pick us up. They embraced tightly, smacking each other on the back.

"It's good to be home." Clark grumbled, separating from Heath.

"Welcome back little brother. Char, it's great to have you back home." I hugged Heath tightly. "Thanks, it's great to be back."

"She's exhausted." Clark pipped up, I sighed and waved him off but I knew he was right. We drove back to the pack house. Supper was just being served when we walked in. A couple Omegas took our bags to our room while we joined the line for lasagna night. I took two pieces and found Michael, Melanie, Timothy and Tabitha. They rose and welcomed me back. Clark and Heath followed and joined the table as well.

"Oh my Char, you must be hungry." Tabitha teased as she looked at my plate. I giggled, "I guess I'm finally eating like a pregnant woman." The whole table erupted in laughter, I couldn't believe how good the garlic bread was. I stole Clark's right off his plate, he held up his fork like a sword when I started eyeing the rest of his plate. Melanie smiled and put her garlic bread on my plate, I smiled and mouthed 'thank you' to her. After supper we went to our room, I fell asleep in a matter of minutes.

The weeks flew by like minutes and before we knew it Heath's Alpha ceremony was just two days away. Cheryl, Melanie and I had been busy planning a wonderful evening. We had a wild bore flown in to roast for the occasion. The ceremony was a lot of reciting on Heath's and David's part, a small speech by Clark and myself followed by the pledge and the run. Heath had to pledge his life to the pack, to forever serve us all until his last breath. After that he would shift into his wolf, his Beta, Delta and Gamma would follow and lead the run of the rest of the pack around the territory.

Heath wasn't on edge or nervous at all. He was ready, calm radiated from him which was wonderful considering his mother was exactly the opposite. Cheryl was worried about the meal and the speeches, even though this event wasn't really a social one. She was also worried about the delegates from the surrounding packs of the North West Territories. It was more of a right of passage, a political ceremony. I did my best to help Cheryl stay as cool as possible, but I wasn't winning that battle. As the days inched closer we were all ready for it be over and done with.

I was starting to feel very pregnant. My feet hurt all the time now, so did my back and hips. The skin across my stomach was so tight I was becoming very uncomfortable. I was officially walking with a waddle, having to rush to the bathroom several times each hour. My sleep patterns were not very steady, I woke up each night several times to pee or to shift in bed to try and get more comfortable. Because I am only 5ft3 I didn't have a lot of places for this baby to go so my belly felt so big and heavy.

I took some herbs and drank some tea for sore muscles but it didn't help much as it was all to do with pregnancy. It mellowed my uncomfortable feelings but it didn't last long. I phoned Gamma Rose almost every day. She offered a lot of comfort to me, sent me over some bath salts to soak in full of lavender and tea tree oils. I enjoyed her mentorship, Gamma Rose was an amazing woman. She was going to be my midwife for the birth. Then afterward she was going to teach me so I would be Marie's midwife.

Clark was a saint. He rubbed my back, feet, legs, hips. He listened to my complaining without a word and never stopped bringing me comfort food. I did catch him laughing at me a few times when he saw me waddling which I had to admit was probably pretty funny. Clark was still obsessed with my belly, especially now that I was so big. Whenever we were in the same room his hand was on it protectively. It was like a reflex for him, already protecting our child before he was even born. Clark was going to be a great father; I could feel it through our bond.

I was in the library that afternoon, two days before the Alpha ceremony when Tabitha came rushing in out of breath. I was sending Marie an email when she startled me.

"Charlotte, I need your help!" she cried, kneeling down in front of me. I took her hand and rubbed it, "What's wrong?"

She was crying, tears running down her face. "He's here, my mate. I can smell that he is here."

My eyes went wide and I smiled at her, "That's exciting!" I rubbed her shoulders, but Tabitha kept crying. I didn't understand why.

"Why are you so upset?" I asked her. Tabitha lay her head on my knees, I ran my fingers through her hair to try to sooth her. She was weeping, I wasn't sure what happened.

"If he is here then I will have to leave. Only Alphas and Betas are here for Heath's ceremony so I will have to go back to their pack with him. I won't be able to take the druid training. I used to be excited to meet my mate but now I don't want to leave. I want to stay here and work with you. The werebears won't let me if I go to another pack." She wailed into my lap. My heart sank, of course. She had been spending so much time with me in my herbology lab. I was teaching her some of the things I had learned from Gamma Rose. I was going to recommend her to be the next in line for druid training if she came back from the mating exhibition next April.

"When did you start to feel it?" I asked her. Tabitha didn't look up, "About an hour ago. I thought you were making some lavender tea so I went to the kitchen but no one was there. The scent filled my entire body, then I felt the pull. I went to my room for a while but I was afraid he would find me there so I started searching for you."

I nodded, continuing to rub her head softly. "We should try to stay calm. He might not try to take you away. You need to meet him, I'm sure he is looking for you. The Moon Goddess works in mysterious ways."

"I could reject him if he tries to take me away." She whispered. I sighed, "Don't plan on that. Just meet him before you get ahead of yourself." Tabitha nodded, still in my lap. We sat like that for a while, her crying softly. I was sure he would be looking for her, if she smelt him he could smell her. Werewolf males seek out their mates when they catch their scent, they track like mad until they locate them.

Tabitha's body suddenly tensed, she started to pant and looked up at the door to the library, "He's coming. He caught my scent. He's scared, I can feel it. He shouldn't be scared; I am the one who should be scared."

I heard running in the hallway outside. I turned to face the door and stood up, pushing Tabitha behind me. I didn't want him to come in a clobber her when he came through the door. We heard growling and panting before the door swung open almost coming off it's hinges. It was Michael.

"MATE!" he growled, crossing the room and coming right up to my face. Tabitha was shaking behind me, she whispered, "Mate." My mouth was open in surprise, I held out my hand to his chest to stop him from knocking me over. Michael was able to hold himself back, if only barely. His eyes were black with lust and excitement.

"Tabitha, why have you been avoiding me? I've been searching for you since I caught your smell downstairs! I was worried something happened to you!" he shouted. She didn't respond, she just trembled behind me and whimpered.

"Michael Gillies calm yourself down!" I told him sternly, "You are scaring the poor girl. She has never experienced this before. Tabitha is terrified and you need to take a step back right now."

He shook his head, as if he heard my voice through a fog. Michael ran his hands through his hair and took a step back, he growled with frustration. "I'm sorry. I'm blowing this. I get a second chance and I'm screwing it up."

Tabitha took a tentative step forward moving past me, "You aren't screwing it up." Her voice was so quiet I almost didn't hear her. Michael rose his eyes to meet hers and suddenly I wasn't even in the room. I sat down at the computer trying to relax.

Michael held out his hands to her, letting Tabitha come to him. She took slow steps towards him, taking his hands in hers. He pulled her close to his chest, resting his forehead on hers. They were both breathing hard. He reached out and touched her face, rubbed his nose with hers.

"Please don't run from me baby. I need you so much. I can't go through another heartbreak again." Michael whimpered, tears going down his face. Tabitha placed her hands on his cheeks and wiped the tears away, "No I won't run. I won't reject you, I want you."

Michael sighed, relieved. He kissed her quickly, just a peck but she returned it. "Michael, I don't want to leave Black Lake. I want to be able to stay here and take the druid training like Charlotte did. If I leave with you I won't be able to do it." Tabitha told him.

He stared into her eyes and smiled, "I will renounce Red Rose and join Black Lake. I would follow you anywhere baby. Nothing will keep me from you."

I smiled at them, I knew Michael would love Tabitha and follow her to the end of the world. She smiled at him, "Are you sure? I know you love your home." He took a deep breath, "I love you more. I can make a life here with you, be a part of your pack."

Tabitha smiled, wrapping her arms around his neck and kissing him deeply. Michael wrapped his arms around her waist and lifted her up. He swung her around and she giggled against his lips. It was beautiful. I started to clap. They both turned and smiled at me.

"Let's go somewhere more private." Michael suggested, I laughed as he took her and lead her out of the library. Tabitha smiled back at me, all fear had vanished from her face. They left the library door open as they took off in a flurry of romance. I struggled to my feet and went to close the door behind them, sighing and turning back to the sofa where I could put my feet up.

Michael and Tabitha didn't come to dinner which didn't surprise me. Heath and Clark were curious about where they were. I giggled to myself, "I don't think we will be seeing them until your ceremony."

The looked at each other puzzled, Clark's face lit up and he turned to me, "Oh my god! No way!" I smiled and nodded. Clark started to laugh, "Michael and Tabitha are mates. Amazing."

Heath's eyes got big, first he smiled, then he looked a bit sad. Yet another male finding his mate while he was left behind again. It must sting terribly.

"Michael is going to request to join Black Lake. Tabitha wants to apply to take the druid training at Ice Water and she can't do that if she leaves us. Michael offered to leave Red Rose and stay here with her." I told them.

Clark nodded, "Michael would be an excellent addition to our pack. He is a great warrior." Heath was distracted and didn't respond. Clark nudged him with his elbow. Heath looked at Clark, then me, "Sounds good. We will make it happen. Please excuse me."

Heath got up and left. He looked so sad, my heart ached for him. I watched him walk towards his office. "I think your brother needs some company." I said.

Clark looked at me and nodded, he kissed me softly before taking off after him. I smiled, reaching across the table to steal the remainder of his plate. I couldn't let it go to waste.

Cheryl came over, sitting next to me in a flurry of nerves. I smiled, continuing to eat Clark's plate of food while she went over the details of the Alpha ceremony for the seventh time today. She was so excited; I didn't have time to interject with my own thoughts. Cheryl prattled on for a while about the food, the delegates, the decorations, the speeches. Details were her obsession; I knew she wanted it to be perfect for her son. Little did she know that he was in a sullen mood.

I started to rub my stomach absentmindedly, the baby was moving around, making me regret eating so much. Cheryl reached forward and touched my shoulder, "Charlotte, are you alright?"

"Oh yes, fine. He's just rolling around in there. I feel enormous now." I confessed. She laughed knowingly, "Yes I felt that way with Clark as well. Heath not as much, he was smaller but Clark was a big baby. He was twelve pounds, three ounces."

My eyes popped out of my head as she said that, "Oh god. Really?" Cheryl gave me a soft smile, "Yes I'm afraid so." I exhaled loudly, thinking about how my little frame would be handling a birth of a potentially giant child in just over a month and a half. I suspected I would be yelling profanities at Clark during that time. She helped me stand up before we said our goodnights as I went off to my room.

Early the next morning I went to the Alpha's office. Clark had come in after I was asleep and left before I was awake so I didn't get the chance to talk to him about how Heath was doing. I thought I would just find out for myself. I knocked on his door, going in when I heard him invite me.

Heath sat at his desk staring out the windows. Papers were neatly stacked around him. He was resting his cheek on his fist, turning to smile at me when I stepped in.

"Hi Charlotte, what can I do for you?" he asked, sighing. I smiled, shuffling up to the chairs across from him and taking a seat.

"I actually came to see if there was anything I could do for you." I told him. Heath smiled at me but it didn't reach his eyes. They were still sad and lonely. He shifted in his chair, resting his arms on the desk.

He turned back to the window, sighing again, "I don't think there is much for you to help me with. I'm twenty-three, still unmated. I've looked everywhere in the North West Territories and she isn't here. I'm lonely and I want my mate, I want to start a family but it's not happening. I keep watching everyone around me find their mates, becoming happy and I am left behind. I'm in charge yet I am left behind again."

My heart ached for him. Heath wanted so badly to be a husband and father. Anyone would be lucky to have him; he was a great catch. I wanted to help him but I was not the Moon Goddess. I couldn't just pull a mate out of thin air for him.

"I don't know Char. Maybe I should just take a chosen mate. Then I could start my life, have a little control over it." He muttered. I knew he didn't really mean that, we had discussed it before. He didn't want to just pick a Luna, he wanted his destined mate.

I shook my head, "Then what will you do when you find her? You will have a wife and children and she will have no place in your life. That would just make everything harder." He chuckled at my words, "You act like I will ever find her."

"You will Heath, I know you will. I can feel it." I told him. I could feel it, that his mate was out there. I knew he would find her and love her. They would have a strong bond and it would be everything he ever wanted. The waiting was the hard part.

Heath stared at me for a moment before looking down at his lap, "I wish I was as sure as you were. It feels like she doesn't exist. David told me he has felt the same way over the years. Maybe that's just how he Alpha of Black Lake has to be, alone and lonely."

"You don't really believe that." I muttered. He shook his head, "No I don't but I wish I did. It would make being alone a lot easier."

I shifted in the chair, my body couldn't stay in one position for too long, "Michael went through a lot of heartache with his first mate. I'm sure you are aware of that. He got a second chance and it is a blessing. I am sure if he gets a second chance you will get a first."

Heath's eyes shot up to mine, "I hope you are right. I remember when Michael arrived, how devastated he was. While you were away at training and Clark was going through his… stuff Michael and I spent some time together on the field. He is quite a strong warrior."

I nodded, he was indeed. "I'm sure it was a good distraction for him. It probably helped him to heal faster." Heath agreed.

"I will be asking him to become my Gamma today. I am sure he will accept. He will be excellent with training the warriors and I like to keep my family close. Since you are my sister Michael is my brother as well. I know he is trustworthy." Heath told me, I smiled broadly. I was happy to hear that.

"You are a good man Heath, one of the best." I told him. He chuckled, "Yeah alright. I'll try to remember that."

I stood up, walked around his desk and hugged him in his sitting position. I pulled him tight and rocked slightly. Heath rocked with me, sighing at the comfort I was offering. He needed it, I sensed he did.

I was his sister and I loved him like my own blood. I felt his pain, I wanted to ease it as much as I could.

"Clark had a terrible time when you were at Ice Water you know." Heath told me, I leaned back to meet his face, nodding. Heath stood up and set his hand on my shoulder, "It is very uncharacteristic for a Beta to need his mate that much you know. It was as though his heart was breaking. Even my father never went through that with our mother."

"Yes, David and I talked about it when I came back. I had no idea how hard it was for him. If I had, I would have come back sooner." I confessed.

Heath shook his head, "No, he didn't want us to contact you. Clark wanted you to finish your training, it was important to you. He knew you would be back, he told himself that constantly. What he went through made me terrified though. I know that if I ever do find my mate I will be worse then he was if she leaves. It would tear me in half."

I sighed, forcing a small smile, "Yes I am sure it would be. I promised Clark after I returned that I would never go anywhere without him again. If he goes anywhere I go with him. I vowed that when I came back. You may just have to do the same." Heath nodded, satisfied with what I had said.

"You take very good care of my brother." He stated. I laughed out loud, "Well he takes very good care of me too." Heath chuckled, he agreed.

I left a short time later, heading to the kitchen to give Amy a hand with breakfast. I knew Tabitha would still be unavailable so I wanted to offer my help. Melanie and Amy were in there with another Omega when I arrived, they seemed happy to have my help. I mixed my classic pancake recipe and got to work.

The delegates from surrounding werewolf packs had started to arrive the day before, the rest would come today. There were five packs in total attending the Alpha ceremony for Heath. I helped to serve the breakfast that morning as we had extra mouths to feed, plus with Tabitha unavailable I wanted to help out as much as I could. I wasn't really paying attention to the man standing in front of me, I just put two pancakes on his plate absentmindedly when he snarled at me loudly and bit at the air, "I will tell you when to stop filling my plate woman!"

My eyes snapped to his face, shock filled them. He was a young man in this late twenties with blonde hair and brown eyes. He was tall and thin, maybe six feet with a tattoos on both his arms. He met my eyes and glared at me with warming, "More pancakes now!"

I placed more on his plate, my hand steady. He studied me, seeming confused that I wasn't afraid of him. Suddenly he grabbed my wrist and twisted it towards his body, I whimpered, "You dare to make eye contact with me Omega?!"

"Take your hand off of me." I warmed him calmly. He twisted my wrist harder, it hurt and I cried out. "How DARE you!" he shouted. The entire pack house erupted in growling, he looked around himself surprised to see all of our members standing up eyeing him with anger. I heard a crash break through the front door with a loud snarl, it was Clark. He leapt to the man, lifting him in the air and throwing him against the wall hard. I walked around the table and pushed against his chest, making him step back.

The man stayed there on the floor. There was a large hole in the drywall where the impact of his body had happened. His face was shocked, I moved closer to him and knelt down, "What is your name?"

"I am Gamma Brett from Midnight pack house to the east." He said, is voice shaking. I nodded, "Well Gamma Brett, you have met my husband, Beta Clark of Black Lake pack, I am Charlotte, the Bata female here. I would like to inform you to kindly keep your hands to yourself, here at Black Lake we do not treat our Omegas with any disrespect. All ranks help out each other in this pack house so while you are here I will insist you abide by our rules."

Brett rubbed his hand on his throat, I could see the claw marks and bruises Clark's hand had left. He looked up at me with terror in his eyes, "I am so sorry Beta, I had no idea of your rank!" I shook my head, "That should not matter, and it does not matter here."

Clark walked up behind me, placing his arm around my shoulders and his other hand on my belly, "Could you not see she is pregnant? Do you enjoy hurting women? I have no patience for that bullshit!" Clark had been through enough of that with Anthony too recently. I knew he hated men who hurt women, it filled him with such rage.

Brett didn't meet Clark's eyes, he looked down with shame. Clark roared at him, "You did notice but you just didn't care!" The rest of the pack house roared with him, I could feel the rage in the room. I pulled myself from Clark's arms, turning my back to Brett and facing the advancing crowd, "Everyone please calm down. We do not respond in kind to this kind of violence. I ask that you all return to your seats. Let us find the Alpha of the Midnight pack and we will handle this situation appropriately."

Everyone stared at me for a moment, looked to Clark then back to me. Slowly the pack house settled down, everyone returning to their seats and eating their breakfast. I moved up and touched Clark's face, "Calm Beta, calm." He exhaled slowly, I could feel his rage flowing out of his body. A man approached Clark and cleared his throat, "Hello Beta Clark, I am Alpha Duke of Midnight pack. I am sorry for my Gamma's behavior."

Duke was a tall broad man in his forties. He held his head high with greying blonde hair and brown eyes. He was a striking resemblance to the young Gamma. His eyes fell to me, he bowed, "Charlotte, I am terribly sorry for my Gamma's behavior. He will be dealt with." I nodded, turning back to Brett.

He was still sitting on the floor, shaking. I held out my hand to him, he looked at it wearily then to my face, "Come on, you can't sit down there forever." I muttered. Brett took my hand and rose to his feet. "Th-thank you Beta." He stuttered.

"What happened?" David shouted, coming into the dining hall with Heath and Samuel. I sighed knowing this was not going to be good.

"Office now!" he commanded. David, Samuel, Heath, Clark, Duke, Brett and myself all followed to the Alpha's office. Though Heath had essentially taken over all the work it was still technically David's office. He sat down in his chair and demanded an explanation.

I explained the incident at breakfast, Clark's reaction, and the reaction of the pack house. I stayed calm throughout my story. I didn't want to further the tension by putting excessive emotion into it.

"How dare you lay a hand on a member of our pack!" Heath shouted. Brett was shaking beside Duke. I could see he was genuinely afraid for his life at this point.

David lifted his hand, signaling Heath to stop, "I think it is best for you and your pack members to leave Black Lake territory immediately. You are no longer welcome here."

Duke made eye contact with him and sighed heavily, "Alpha please reconsider. We have had a strong alliance for decades now. Let us not throw that away over a misunderstanding."

"A misunderstanding?!" Clark roared, "You think laying a hand on my pregnant mate is a misunderstanding? You and I are about to have a misunderstanding outside on the training field right now!" Clark stood toe to toe with the Alpha. He was not backing down; he was not scared to challenge him. Duke's eyes went wide when he realized Clark was serious.

"I'm not attempting to disrespect your mate or your pack. I would just like to work through this with your Alpha. We have had many casualties to rogue attacks in the last few years, our numbers have suffered. We need this alliance to continue, it is imperative to my pack." Duke told Clark calmly. Clark didn't move, he didn't step back. David did not command him either.

I stood up, lifting myself with a tad of difficulty. I stepped forward, maneuvering my body between Duke and Clark, I put my hand on my mate's chest and pushed him back slowly. Clark looked down at me and followed my touch, exhaling a breath he had been holding. A low growl came through his throat as he shot a glare at the Alpha and Gamma.

I took another step forward towards Clark, soothing him with my slow breathing. He followed my breaths and took another step back. I turned around to face the Midnight pack members. Their Alpha's eyes met mine. He was surprised by what I had just done. My small, swollen stature was a sharp contrast to the tall muscular men standing around me. I stood my ground, forcing a calming aura into the room.

"This mate of yours is very impressive." Duke stated, looking from me to Clark. "I am very aware of that." He muttered, setting a protective hand on my shoulder.

"Alpha David, I would like to make a request." I said, not taking my eyes off the Midnight pack members, "I would like for the alliance between our packs to remain in tact. I don't believe the Gamma's behavior should wound the entire pack. Perhaps he would be willing to learn from his transgression and educate himself on how to treat others."

David rose from his chair, he hummed slightly considering my words. He looked to Heath who nodded at him, "Alright," he finally said, "if that is your suggestion Charlotte then as the wounded party we will respect your request. However, if any other incident happens like the one this morning, I will not hesitate to dissolve this treaty, nor will my successor, Heath."

"Thank you Alpha David." Duke said, sighing with relief. He searched my face, "Thank you Charlotte, it is very kind of you to give my Gamma a second chance." I smiled a him, extending my hand to him, "I believe in redemption. I am sure your son will not make a mistake like this again."

"How did you know he was my son?" he asked, his breath caught in his chest. Brett looked at me, surprised I had figured it out. I shrugged as he took my hand to shake it, "I could sense it."

They both nodded, bowing quickly and left the room as fast as they could. I leaned back into Clark's waiting embrace. He lowered his head to my neck and buried his face in my hair. He growled, "I don't like this. He would have hurt you very badly darling."

"I know, but he didn't get the chance to. We need to remember that no one is perfect and we have to try and give others the benefit of the doubt to improve. I think we made a pretty good impression today." I told him. The men in the room chuckled, they seemed to agree with me. I turned to the others, "If you will excuse me gentlemen, I need to go and help Amy clean up that kitchen. She will need an extra pair of hands."

They said their various goodbyes, Clark gave me a kiss before I left the office, shutting the door behind myself. I waddled down to the kitchen as quick as I could, Amy was indeed in the midst of an avalanche of dishes. Melanie was there as well with another Omega but it looked like they needed some help.

I didn't say a word, I just started to dry dishes next to Amy. She smiled at me, "You don't have to help me you know. I'm sure that ordeal this morning took its toll." I shook my head, "No, I am not leaving you ladies to do all this by yourselves. With the extra bodies in the pack house we all need to lend a hand."

Melanie smiled at me and nodded. Amy looked down at the dish water, washing a plate, "I can't believe he did that to you. He had no idea you were the Beta female."

"Rank should not matter. In this pack it doesn't matter, it should be like that everywhere. No one deserves to be treated like that." I told her. She didn't make eye contact, just set the clean plate on top of the others. I touched her hand, "Amy, it's never ok. You are just as important as Melanie or myself to this pack. We all need each other." She turned to me with tears in her eyes, "I know, it just scares me that my mate might be from another pack who will treat me like that when he finds me."

I saw the fear in her eyes, it was true that was a possibility. Amy was an Omega; she hadn't found her mate yet but she hadn't turned seventeen just yet either. She might not find them here at Black Lake, it was possible she would find them in a different pack house. It was true not all packs were as community oriented as ours, I hoped she wouldn't have to go somewhere to be mistreated. I pulled Amy to my chest even though both of our hands and arms were wet. I held her close to wordlessly let her know she was never going to be alone or forgotten. She was important, I was determined she wouldn't forget that.

By the time we were done the dishes the lunch shift entered the kitchen shooing us out. I went to the library to use computer to email Marie. It had been about a week since I had seen her so I thought I should touch base. Mary was in the library muttering to herself when I walked in. She raised her eyebrows at my prescience but didn't stop shelving the books. I sat down at the computer and sent off a message. I sighed to myself, I was tired. My body was so sore and uncomfortable; I wasn't sure how I would handle this until November. I forced myself to my feet and started waddling again to my room. I thought a bath with some of Rose's home made salts would do the trick.

I made it to the staircase when I saw Brett on the banister. He seemed startled when I started to pass him, heading to my room. He opened his mouth to talk, then closed it again, perhaps trying to come up with the right words to say.

"Good morning Brett. Is there something you need?" I asked, perhaps if I started the exchange it would make it easier for him. He looked at me, his eyes moving up and down my body, "I am very sorry for my behaviour this morning Beta. I should not have acted like that. I don't have a good reason for it, I know it was unacceptable. I hope you can accept my apology."

I smiled softly, "I accept. Don't call me Beta though, my name is Charlotte Duffey. You don't need to apply my rank to it." I took another step up the stairs. Brett cleared his throat, "I was very impressed the way you stood toe to toe with myself and my father. I have never seen a female do that before. Not even my mother."

"Perhaps she should." I turned, smirking at him. He chuckled, looking down again at his feet. "Your mate is a very powerful wolf. He is bigger then his brother, very large and strong for a Beta. I was shocked he challenged my father."

"Clark has very little tolerance for violence against women. He feels very protective of the women in his pack and his family. We don't tolerate that here at Black Lake." I told him dryly, Brett nodded.

"Yes you are quite right. It isn't acceptable." He agreed. "So your pack has been having rogue issues yes?" I asked, changing the subject.

Brett looked up at me, he seemed relieved I was willing to move on from the conversation, "Yes it's been quite extensive in the last few years. They have killed off several of our warriors. We don't have many

Omegas left, they seem to pick them off when they go out foraging or trapping."

"Come with me, I'll introduce you to Delta Timothy and Melanie, they are currently tracking the rogue attacks in and around our area. Maybe they have some insights to offer." I suggested, gesturing him to follow me to the conference room. Brett was quick on my heels as we headed upstairs.

Timothy was studiously working on the map in the conference room. I introduced him to Brett and explained about his rogue attacks. I left them together to discuss some strategies. It felt like I was never going to get to my bedroom for my bath. I suspected Melanie was with Cheryl so I took advantage of that to take my bath. It felt so nice to have some time to myself for a while.

# Chapter 19

The night of Heath's ceremony went on without a hitch. The wild boar was delicious. The night lasted what felt like a long time. Heath did a wonderful speech as did David. Clark, Timothy and Michael all took the stage with Heath as he announced his team. There was much cheering at his choices. When it was finally time to shift Heath and his team did first, then we mates followed, then the rest of the pack. We all ran our territory together until well after midnight. The pack had a wonderful night.

It was a lot simpler to move around in my wolf form while pregnant. I stayed in wolf form as I walked through the pack house and up to my bedroom. I was completely exhausted, I curled up on my pillow, trying to fall asleep. Clark came in just after me, laughing out loud when he saw me on the bed.

"No way darling. You are not sleeping in the bed like that. It will be full of fur!" he told me. I whimpered at him and stretched out across the bed. "Come on Char, no way is this happening." I sat up, staring at him. I snorted before I flopped back down and rolled all over the bed.

Clark laughed out loud, dropping his clothes and shifted into his wolf, pouncing on top of me and rolling us around the room. We nuzzled and played together for a while. It was the first time we did that inside the house. Balls of our fur flew around the bedroom as we played together, tossing and jumping. We had so much fun.

I don't recall when we fell asleep but we woke up tangled in each other's naked forms a little past 6am. Clark had me wrapped in his arms, I was tucked up against his side. I moaned when he tried to move me, so stiff from pregnancy. "Come on darling, we should get up." He said with a husky voice. I shook my head, refusing, "Nope, I don't think the baby will let me move." He chuckled, kissing my forehead, "I have to get to training. Today is your brother's first official day with us, I don't want to be late." I held him in place, muttering against his chest.

Clark sighed at me, frustrated, "Pregnancy makes you difficult." I laughed, kissing his neck sensually, I bit down on my mark. He growled at me, trying to fight the urges I was tempting him with. "It also makes you horny." He whispered in my ear, sucking it into his mouth and nibbling. "I know, I'm a trouble maker." I whispered. Clark nudged me onto my back and got up quickly. I grumbled but he just laughed at me, "Sorry darling, usually your little vixen behavior would work but I can't be late for Michael's first big day." I nodded, rolling over and attempting to get out of bed. We had a quick shower together before Clark was out the door. I went to the kitchen to make some tea before going to the library.

A few hours later I heard some shouting down the hallway, I got up and went in search of it. It was coming from the conference room. I walked in to see all our senior pack members gathered around Timothy's map. There was a lot of commotion, I was having a hard time sorting it all out. Clark and Michael came rushing in behind me, "How many were spotted?" Clark yelled.

"The patrol said three but they didn't get a good look at them." Heath told him, he pointed to an area on the map. Clark went to it, studying the terrain and nodded. "We will have to go now, maybe we can pick up the trail and hunt them down." Clark motioned for a few warriors to follow him. He walked up to me quickly, kissing me good bye and rushing out the door.

I went over to Melanie, "What's going on?"

"A patrol spotted some rogues between Ice Water territory and ours. We alerted the werebears immediately and now we are sending a warrior squad to hunt them down." She told me, not looking away from the map.

"They saw three right?" I asked. Melanie nodded, "It's only three rogues which won't be a problem for our warrior team. However, if they are just a small part of a larger group, which we suspect they are then that is more dangerous."

I sucked in a deep breath, for the first time since I arrived at Black Lake I was worried about Clark's safety.

"Don't worry we are sending out more patrols around the pack house and a warrior team has gone to Ice Water to enhance their warriors. We will be fine." She assured me. I nodded, but I was not afraid for my safety. I decided to go to my herbology lab and mix up some salves. It was better to have extra around then to not have enough. I made six large jars for the extra strong salve before I ran out of tea tree oil, I made a note for myself to get more.

The afternoon came and went, moving into the evening. I couldn't link with Clark yet; he was too far out of range. I went to the library again, trying to distract myself from worrying too much. I knew he was strong and perfectly capable to defend himself, but as his mate I wanted to protect him in any way I could. Just after supper time Tabitha and Michael brought me some chilli to eat. I was grateful for the company.

"It's wonderful to see my brother like this." I teased. Tabitha blushed, as she tossed her hair over her shoulder I saw a fresh bite mark on her neck. I didn't draw attention, but I smiled sweetly. It was nice to see. "He is wonderful isn't he." Tabitha suggested, beaming at me.

Michael blushed, "I'm not so sure about that but she is certainly the most amazing woman in the world." I couldn't stop smiling at them. Their joy was infectious.

"I have you talked to mother and father yet?" I asked, finishing off my chilli. Michael shook his head, "I was going to do it tonight before the rogue attack but now I'm going to wait until all this is over. I'm sure they will be excited for us."

"I am sure they will. Now they have two reasons to visit us here at Black Lake." We all nodded together at my words. Tabitha stood up slowly, giving Michael a sweet kiss before she walked towards the door, "I'm on kitchen clean up duty tonight. Amy will kill me if I don't pitch in after being absent for two full days." I chuckled as she left.

Michael turned to me, running his fingers through my hair, "Oh my god Char, I can't believe this has happened!" I burst out laughing as he slumped back on the sofa.

"She is perfect! Tabitha is sweet, kind, funny, sexy. She thinks I am amazing. She wants me to be her mate, she actually wants to spend time with me!" he told me. I leaned forward as if to whisper, "That is how it should be for two mates. It should feel like you belong together, made for each other."

"When she was hiding from me I thought the worst you know. I thought it was Stella all over again. I couldn't find her and I ran all over the place looking for her. I was desperate. I was surprised she was so young, just seventeen. I didn't think of that when I caught her scent, I was sure she was just playing games with me." Michael explained, I rubbed his arm. He was so afraid of being hurt again, I could under-stand that based on how things had been with Stella.

"Tabitha is just seventeen. She wasn't sure how to handle the situa-tion, she was scared. That's why Tabitha came to find me." I whispered. Slowly I moved myself on the sofa a bit, readjusting my hips and back to make myself more comfortable.

"She loves me Char. I can feel she loves me, through the bond. It was never like that with Stella. She always held herself back from me. Tabitha doesn't hold anything back. She gives me everything she has. I love her more then I loved Stella already, after two days. Is that pos-sible?" he confessed. "I believe anything is possible now Michael." I ad-mitted.

"I'm sorry Charlotte, but I have to tell you, the sex is amazing. Like, I can't even believe it's possible to feel this good. She does this one thing…" Michael started to tell me, but I pushed my hand over his mouth, "There are some things I really don't want to know big brother." He nodded, laughing through my hand. I wrinkled my nose at him and stuck out my tongue.

Michael left my side to grab a book, I adjusted again, sliding my feet up onto the sofa. I suggested he rub them for me but that didn't seem to appeal to my brother. We sat and read together for another hour before Tabitha came back to get him. Michael went with her eagerly, I giggled as they rushed out of the library.

It was after 8pm, still no word. I tried to link with Clark but he was still out of range. I left the library and returned to the conference room. Timothy and Melanie were the only ones left in there. They both looked exhausted. Luckily I had been carrying my herb bag around just in case I needed it when the warriors returned.

I went to Melanie first, "Here, chew on this. It's like a caffeine boost but healthier." She smiled at me and took the stick from me. Timothy was engrossed with the map so I just tapped his shoulder and handed him his, he chewed it absentmindedly.

"How's it going?" I asked Melanie as I lowered myself onto a chair. She shook her head, "No word yet. We sent out another warrior group after them. It's been a bit long." I searched her face, Melanie was concerned. I rubbed my belly, praying to the goddess for their safe return.

"When were you expecting to hear from them?" I asked. Melanie paused a long time before she answered, she met my eyes carefully, "Four hours ago." My eyes welled up with tears, I was terrified. That was a long time to be missing.

"I'm sure everything is alright. They are probably on their way back now." She told me, but I could see in her eyes she was worried. I felt as though something was wrong, I wish I could just link with Clark to know he was alright. "Is there anything I can help with?" I asked, I wanted to make myself useful to keep my mind busy.

She shook her head, "Not really. You could bring us some coffee if you wanted, but these caffeine sticks probably did the trick." I nodded, standing up to head downstairs. I could do that; I could make the coffee. Even though I'm sure it would have them climbing the walls I needed something to do so off I went.

As I was preparing the tray I suddenly felt the worst pain come over my back. It shot through me, forcing me to my knees. I screamed in agony as the intense anguish ripped across my spine, it felt as though a whip made of daggers crossed my back. I became woozy from the shock, I was panting. Rolling to my side, I tried to get up but I started to loose consciousness. I heard voices around me, I couldn't make out faces, they were trying to get me to focus. My eyes were heavy, my senses fading, I floated away from everything into the abyss.

I wasn't sure how long I had been unconscious but when I woke up I was in the infirmary. There was a bright light on the ceiling, my eyes had a hard time focusing. Then I realized I didn't have my glasses on, I felt a bit silly that I hadn't noticed that. Cheryl was sitting next to me in a chair on one side, Michael was leaning against the window sill. I moved my tongue around the inside of my mouth to try a relieve the cotton feeling, "What happened?"

Michael jumped as I spoke, running over to the bedside, "Oh thank god, you are awake. Char you scared the hell out of all of us!"

"Thank goodness girl. We were worried." Cheryl whispered, squeezing my hand. "What happened?" I repeated.

"We aren't sure. You screamed so loud it shook the walls of the pack house. We thought you were being attacked or you went into early labour. The medic looked you over but there was nothing wrong with you. They couldn't find anything wrong at all." Cheryl explained. She rubbed my hand she was holding with her other hand.

"The baby?" I asked quickly, touching my belly. He was still in there; I could feel his movement. Michael smiled at me softly, "He is fine Charlotte."

I sat up slowly, my back no longer hurt. I looked back over my shoulder to see if I could see any blood, nothing. I shook my head, "I felt a terrible pain across my back, it knocked me to the floor. I had never felt anything more painful in my entire life."

Cheryl rose, toughing my shoulder to lean me forward to see my back, "There is nothing there my dear. Not a mark on you."

I gasped as it hit me, "Clark… it was his pain… he's been wounded."

Cheryl's eyes shot to mine, fear and panic crossed between us both. "I felt something when I heard you scream but I thought it was just my concern for you." She whispered. I reached up and touched her face, offering comfort.

"Michael, go and get Heath. Meet us in the conference room, we need to find him now!" I said calmly, with force. I was commanding him kindly. He nodded and ran out of the room. I swung my legs over the edge of the bed, wrapping a dressing gown around my body. I threw my herb bag over my shoulder and made my way to the conference room.

Timothy was still at his map; Melanie had finally passed out on a chair in the corner. The clock on the wall read 1: 45am. Clark and his team had been missing for ten hours. "Timothy, I know Clark has been wounded, we need to find him now." I told him. Timothy's eyes shot to me, his face went white with dread.

"The second team came back with nothing; I send out a third team about an hour ago. How do you know he has been wounded?" he sighed, crossing off sections of the map.

Melanie moved in the chair, rubbing her eyes, "Charlotte, what's going on?"

"I could feel Clark being attacked. He is hurt somewhere. We need to find him." I explained to her. She jumped out of the chair and ran to me, "Are you sure?" I nodded.

"Where have the warriors searched so far Timothy?" I asked, moving to the map. He pointed to two different sections, looking to be about one thousand acres each. I studied it, red X's through the searched areas. I looked to the pins in the map, wondering if there was a correlation.

"Where was the rogue camp?" I asked him. Timothy showed me, I put my finger on the pin. It was out of range of the searched areas. Clark had found it before; it was where they found evidence of very strong rogues. I thought about it for a bit. Heath, Michael and Samuel rushed into the conference room. I was concentrating hard on Clark; I knew he was somewhere close to that camp. I could feel it.

I turned to Heath and Michael, "I want you to take me here." I pointed to the rogue camp. They both looked at me like I was insane. "You are not going out there." Heath told me. Michael stepped forward to see where I was pointing.

"Listen to me, I can feel him. I know he is there. He is badly wounded, he will die. Heath, let me save my mate, take me there. Clark needs us." I begged. "Charlotte you are pregnant!" Samuel cried. I nodded, "I know, but I need my mate. I know exactly where he is. I can channel into him. We will find him faster if I go with you."

Heath's face was cold, stern. He shook his head at me. Tears fell down my cheeks silently, "Please Heath, let me save him." I begged. The room was silent; the only sound was the crackle of the fire in the hearth. Heath was loosing his resolve; I could see it. "Please." I repeated softly.

"I will take you myself." He whispered. Samuel roared loudly, "Heath, you can't take her out there! She could be killed!" Heath turned to his father and hugged him hard, "I will bring them all back. That is what the Alpha does."

Michael and Timothy stepped forward, awaiting orders. "You two stay here. I will bring a dozen warriors with us. If we are not back in three hours signal the alliance packs and get reinforcements sent here." Heath commanded. Both men nodded, Michael went to gather the warriors, Timothy to retrieve the alliance contact information. I studied Heath, he turned to me, "Downstairs in ten minutes. You will guide us, Char. Let's go."

# Chapter 20

Wolf form was so much easier to maneuver in while pregnant then human form. I followed Clark's scent. It was faint from the day before but I would know it anywhere. Heath brought a dozen strong warriors with us. It took us twenty minutes at a run to get to the old rogue camp. I sniffed around it carefully. Apple pie was here recently, Clark. I lifted my head in the air, sniffing hard. He had passed by here not long ago. I moved north, the warriors followed me. There was a cliff edge where his scent ended, I looked down, nothing but rocks and trees. We followed the cliff edge east a few kilometers, Clark's scent got stronger.

I yipped, he was close. I smelled him as I moved east, apple pie and… blood. 'Clark!' I screamed in my mind. 'Charlotte.' It was a whisper. I spun around in a circle, looking for a hiding place. I kept moving, moving, smelling. There it was, a small cluster of rocks with a bush growing out of the top. His hiding place. 'Clark, I'm coming in, I'm here.' I linked to him.

I ran to the tiny cave; it seemed too small for a man of my mate's size. I stuck my head inside, blood filled my nose so deep I could taste it. I licked his face and neck. Clark, thank god, he was alive. I shifted to my human form as I pulled out of the small crawlspace, "Heath help him out of there!"

Heath and another warrior grabbed onto Clark's shoulders and pulled him from the cave. He had bite and claw marks everywhere. He had fought a number of battles, but his back was where the carnage was. There were five deep red slashes about twelve inches long, all the way to the bone. These had not begun to heal at all. I leaned over to lick the wounds, spitting after my tongue came into contact with them, "SILVER!"

I pulled out my strongest salve and rubbed it deeply into his wounds, stinging my own hands in the process. I would have to wash the silver residue out of the slashes when we got home, but for now he needed as much help as he could get. I opened his mouth and put some dried camomile under his tongue. "Come on baby, you are strong." I whispered into his ear. Clark moaned as he heard my voice.

"Pick him up, get him back to the pack house now." Heath ordered. Two warriors lifted Clark's body and made off towards our home. I took several deep breaths before shifting back into my wolf form. Before I could start running after then Heath reached out and touched my back, "Be careful on your way back, don't run ahead of them." I yipped in agreement and took off after my mate.

The sun was coming up by the time we made it back home. Clark was conscious though in a huge amount of pain. I requested he be brought to our room so I could treat him there. The warriors complied, carrying him up the stairs. "Please put him in the bathtub, I will wash his wounds." I told them as I ran the warm water. It took two of them to lift my mate into the bathtub. The warriors left immediately, Heath had stayed back in my bedroom. As the water ran I walked to the doorway to Heath, "Ask Michael to come here in about an hour please. We will move him from the bath to the bed for him to fully heal." He nodded, rubbing my shoulder to comfort me before leaving silently.

I turned back to Clark. He was rolling his neck on the edge of the bathtub, moaning softly. I pulled a wash cloth from the vanity, soaked it in the water and started to wash him. His entire body shuttered at my touch, small gasps escaped his lips as little shocks from our mate bond passed between us. He tried to talk, I brought my fingers to his lips, "SShhh Clark, don't try to talk yet. You are in so much pain I can feel it. Just let me take care of you. We need to get the silver out of your wounds first." He nodded, his eyes closed. I rested my forehead against his and sighed, relieved I found him alive.

I moved behind him, gently pushing him forward to have access to his back, he cried out in pain. I washed the deep wounds out with soap and water. The salve was already starting to work while we were on our way back home, but with the silver still in the wound it was taking longer then normal for him to heal. Now that it was all washed out these deep gashes would disappear in a day or so. I washed his hair of leaves and twigs, he moaned as I touched his scalp. I heard Michael come into our bedroom, I called him to come in.

Michael helped me dry Clark off and get him to our bed. We set him on his stomach gently, Michael was shocked at the damage to his back, "Oh god, Char what do you think that was?"

I rubbed the salve into the wounds slowly, "Whatever it was, it was laced with sliver. That's why he couldn't just come back, it was killing him out there." Clark cried out in pain as I massaged the salve in gently. Michael's eyes studied us, he sighed as rubbed the back of his neck. I pushed an adrenaline stick into Clark's mouth, "Bite down honey, this will make the healing happen faster." He did as I requested. I turned to Michael and walked into his arms. He held on to me as I cried quietly into his chest. He stroked my hair slowly, not saying anything just letting me cry. I had been so afraid I wouldn't see Clark again. Michael kissed my forehead as moved away, back to Clark's side.

"Call me if you need me, I'm just in my room." He told me as he left. Exhaustion hit me suddenly. I noticed the sun was coming through the curtains, it was about the time Tabitha and Amy would be waking up to start breakfast. I crawled into bed next to Clark, staring at his face. His hair was like silk through my fingers, he purred at my touch. "I was so scared Clark, I thought I might never see you again." I whispered. He groaned, "Nothing will keep me from you, not even death." He reached out slowly, resting his hand on my belly.

"SShhh," I whispered, "I love you my dearest. Rest, I will watch over you." I leaned forward and kissed his face. He pecked me cheek as he fell asleep next to me. Closing my eyes, I let myself drift off to sleep next to him, breathing in apple pie and healing salve.

Waking a few hours later, I noticed a tray had been placed in our room for us. It was toast, eggs and bacon with juice and milk. It was cold by the time I ate it, but the food tasted so good. I hadn't eaten in almost a whole day; it had slipped my mind. Before I could stop myself I ate Clark's portion as well, I would blame it on the pregnancy cravings. I moved next to Clark, the gashes on his back had closed. He was healing quickly. Rubbing more salve into the wounds he stirred, "Charlotte, are you alright?"

I giggled, "Honey, I should be asking you that." Clark rolled over to face me. Slowly he sat up on the edge of the bed, wrapped his arms around my waist and brought me close to him. He leaned his face into my chest and breathed deeply, "Thank god you found me. I tried to call to you, but I was too far to link. I crawled into that hole, praying you would sense me."

As I stroked his hair gently I could feel our baby responding to his voice. "I felt your pain. It cut through me like a hot knife through butter. I fell to the floor in agony. After that I had to find you." I whispered. Clark looked up at me, his face almost completely healed from his ordeal the day before, "I love you Charlotte." I leaned forward and kissed him passionately. He stood up quickly, pulling my body as close to his as possible, exploring my mouth with his tongue.

I broke the kiss, breathless. Pressing my forehead against his I grasped his face, "I vowed to never leave your side, and I never will." Clark growled, pulling me in and kissing me again, harder this time. There was urgency in his kisses, he was terrified he was going to die out there, alone. To sooth him, I stroked his hair slowly. I moved my lips against his mouth gently, he responded in kind. Clark's heart stopped pounding, he was allowing himself to relax.

"I ate all your breakfast." I whispered against his lips. He chuckled, gazing at me, "Of course you did." Pulling him to his feet we got dressed and made our way down to the kitchen. It was deserted so I made him some toast with eggs and fruit. Clark ate it quickly, so I had to make more eggs. His body needed the protein to heal. Though he was a bit sluggish he was healing very well since I washed out the silver from his wounds. I wanted to know what kind of weapon was used to inflict that kind of damage. Clark was an extremely strong werewolf, it had to be a weapon of considerable power to do that kind of damage. When you add the silver, it just increased the devastation.

Moving behind him, I lifted his shirt up and ran his hands over the gashes. Clark didn't move, he welcomed my touch. I focused my mind on them, trying to understand what had done it. I slowed my breathing, "Clark baby, focus with me on the wounds. I want to see if I can feel anything from it." He nodded, slowing his breathing down while I pressed both my hands on his back.

My eyes were closed tightly as I focused all my energy into my mate, he matched my slow breathing. I felt a tingle start in the back of my neck, flowing though the rest of my body. I started to see lights behind my eyes as my focus continued. There was a faint smell, I tried to make it out but it was still too light. In my mind, I reached for it. The smell, it was… it was some kind of animal. It wasn't a normal rogue wolf; it was something else.

I released my hands, smoothing Clark's shirt down over his back. "Are you going to tell me what happened?" I asked.

He turned around on the chair and looked at me, "My team followed the scout to where the rogues were last seen. We could smell they were close, so we were prepared. There must have been fifteen of them, we were outnumbered but we were holding our own. It was a rough fight but we were alright until I felt some horrible pain shoot across my back. It knocked me out of my wolf form and onto the ground, I must have gone into shock. A roar ripped through the air unlike anything else I have ever heard before. My warriors started to get ripped to shreds around me, one after another. I crawled, trying to help them but the rogues tore them apart." He told me, I pulled him to my body for a tight hug as he let his tears fall. "In the battle they must have forgotten about me as I crawled into that hole. They took the bodies. I saw the wolves; they should have been no match for our warriors but they tore them apart in no time. They were just rogues, average size rogues yet they had a power."

I rubbed his back slowly, "Did you see the one who knocked you down?" He shook his head, "No I didn't, but I felt the power of it knock me down. Whatever it was, it is stronger then any wolf I have ever seen." Nodding, I pulled Clark as close to my body as I could. I knew one thing for certain, he did not escape by accident. Whatever this thing was, it let him survive, it wanted Clark alive. The question was why.

# Chapter 21

After the rogue attacks everything went silent. There were no more sightings. All of the packs in the Northwest Territories banded together to increase patrols. Training increased all over the territories, each pack was sending warriors from one pack to another to spread tactics. Our scouts tried to track down the scent but it was too faint to find a trail. Red Rose and Rocky Mountain both joined the alliance, spreading the word about what had happened to Clark throughout their territories.

Days turned to weeks, things started to back to normal though guarded. There hadn't been an alliance like this between pack territories in centuries. We were on edge, but it had forced us all to be aware that there was something else out there stronger then us alone. Packs we admitting that they needed more allies, we had to work together to protect ourselves. The stories of my mate's survival and recovery were becoming folktales now. Heath was so proud of his baby brother.

My due date inched closer, my stomach continued to swell even more. I could no longer shift without hurting myself or the baby, so I was stuck in my human form which made me a bit irritable. Clark and Cheryl did their best to keep me comfortable but I was ready for the baby to come out. Rose was coming to stay with us the day after tomorrow to be close by when I went into labour. My parents were flying in today; Clark was going to pick them up at the air strip in about an hour.

I went to the library to call Marie. I was able to have a short visit with her after Clark had been attacked but that was weeks ago. It was time I spoke with her. Dialing Anthony's office, I waited while the line rang. Anthony answered, "Good Morning Rocky Mountain Alpha speaking."

"Good morning Anthony, it's Charlotte. How are you?" I smiled when I heard his voice, though I still hadn't warmed up to him completely I was trying to be supportive.

"Ah, hello Charlotte. I'll ask the Omega to get Marie for you." He told me, not even trying to fight me on it. I was relieved he didn't try to keep her from me anymore. I waited on hold for Marie, it took a few minutes until I heard her sigh at the other end of the phone.

"Hi Char, how are you?" she asked coldly. I was taken aback; her tone was very uncharacteristic.

I stifled a sigh, "What's wrong?" Marie exhaled loudly, "Sorry, I'm just having a bad week. Anthony and I got into it last night. He makes me so mad sometimes."

"Did anything happen?" I asked carefully.

She adjusted herself in her seat, I could hear it, "No, nothing like that. He's just trying to control my movements since the attacks that happened up by your way. He's all worried something will happen to me and the baby so no I am not allowed to go outside at all without a guard. It's frustrating."

I nodded, "I understand. If it makes you feel any better, I'm not allowed out of the pack house at all." Marie giggled, "I suppose it could be worse. We are pretty far south though Charlotte. I don't think we are under threat here."

I furrowed my brows at her words, "We thought we were so safe because it's so isolated up here, but we were wrong. It could have been anywhere and no there is no trace of the rogues who attacked us." She sighed, "I know, I know you are right. I shouldn't complain I just wish it wasn't happening."

"I know Marie, me too." I whispered. "How are you feeling?" she asked me.

I chuckled, leaning back into the chair, "I am as big as a house now. Everything hurts all the time and I can't wait for him to be born. I'm not able to sleep for very long periods of time so I'm grumpy as hell."

She laughed out loud, "Yay more things to look forward to." Smiling, I stood up needing to move around a bit, "It's pretty wonderful though, despite all the uncomfortable times right now. He will be here soon so I am excited for that."

"So how are things with Anthony these days?" I asked her. Marie chuckled and sighed heavily, "He is fine. Still possessive but he's stopped messing around on me so that is a plus. He's excited about the baby, but he's made it clear he wants a boy so if this one isn't Anthony has told me he will be getting me pregnant again as soon as possible."

I groaned, "Uh, he is a controlling one isn't he." She laughed, "He's been better with me. Since everything that happened he has been more gentle. I think he likes it when I'm pregnant. He seems to find me very sexy like this."

"I don't need to hear this Marie." I begged, but she went on, "Seriously, he is so much more gentle with me now. He's calmed down, it's as though he finally believes I won't leave him."

"I'm glad to hear he has improved; you deserve to be treated well." I reminded her. She snorted a little, "Yes I know. He is better, Char I promise. Believe me, I would tell you if he wasn't." I didn't respond to her, I wanted to believe that. I wanted to believe that Anthony had changed.

"How is Clark?" she asked after I was silent for too long. I smiled, "He is great. Healed up nicely. He's been heavily involved in the alliance here in the Territories with Heath so he's been busy. I think Clark would rather be down on the training fields with Michael but alas he's in an office now."

"Oh yes, how is Michael? Do you like that new mate of his, Tabitha?" Marie assed, realizing she hadn't asked how he was in some time.

"Michael is doing very well; he is happy here. Tabitha is wonderful, I really like her. She is good for Michael." I told her. Marie chuckled, "Anyone would be better for him then that Stella girl."

I sighed, "Yeah, they were not well matched. Michal and Tabitha have moved quickly, they plan on having their mating ceremony while mother and father are here for they baby's birth. Tabitha is sweet, she adores Michael and makes a fuss over him. It's a vast contrast between what we saw with Stella and Michael."

"I should hope so, she basically broke his heart." Marie scoffed. I bit my lip, "Marie, perhaps you shouldn't be too hard on Stella. It wasn't her fault the match didn't take. Not all matches are smooth sailing as you know."

She breathed into the phone, "Yes, perhaps you are right, sorry. It was just hard to see him so unhappy with her." I didn't respond, but on that point I had to agree.

"Have you told mother and father about your baby?" I asked. "Yes, just yesterday. They were not enthused but I told them all was well. I could tell you haven't told them about your visit to Rocky Mountain two months ago. Thank you for that." She whispered.

"I didn't tell Michael either. I didn't want to upset everyone. You know if it happens again though, I will." I told her. Marie sighed, "Yes, we have been through this. I know."

I sighed, it seemed our conversation was coming to an uneasy end, "Do you still want me to come for your birth?"

"Yes please. I wouldn't have anyone else." She declared. I giggled, "Alright, well I should go. I need to start moving again before I seize up. I'll call you soon. I love you, Marie."

"I love you too, Char. Talk soon." She sang into the receiver. We hung up on a happy note, which I was grateful for. Marie and I has spoken a few times since I had been back at Black Lake. Sometimes our conversations were difficult when I didn't come across supportive enough of Anthony. Marie wanted me to love him, which I did not. I found it very difficult to have affection for him after all that had happened. She continued to tell me he had changed, which I was grateful for. However, I didn't sugar coat how I felt, she knew my concerns as much as she tried to ignore them. Marie knew my love for her was unconditional. I would be there for her through the good and the bad, no matter what.

I was suddenly exhausted, so I went to my room for a quick nap. I woke up to my mother fluttering around the bedroom with Cheryl discussing what the birth plan was. I sat up with a grumble, reaching for my glasses, "What's going on?"

"OH Charlotte, you are awake, wonderful. Cheryl and I were just discussing what your birth plan was. Are you giving birth in here? It would certainly be the most comfortable." My mother asked, but didn't really wait for me to answer. She put down a bag she was carrying, opening it. Cheryl and her started pulling things out of it. "Oh Dorothy, these blankets are beautiful."

"I made them six for the new baby. I also made some booties and toques. I know how cold it can get up here." She said, smiling. I waddled over to them and took one of the pairs of booties, setting it onto my belly, "It looks like they fit mother."

Both mothers started to wail, reaching out and pulling me into a hug between them. I thought it would be funny, but apparently my joke was incredibly touching. I smiled to myself while being engulfed by grand-motherly hugs. At that moment Clark came rushing in, "What's going on, I hurt loud crying?"

I did my joke again, which caused him to wail and run to engulf us all. Oh goodness, there was way too much estrogen in this room. I rolled my eyes, "You know, I could go in to early labour if I'm squeezed too hard."

Everyone broke apart from me, wide eyed. I laughed out loud, "I'm just kidding. Everyone needs to relax."

My mother scoffed at me, "Charlotte that is not funny!" Cheryl nodded in agreement.

"I beg to differ, I am uncomfortable and grumpy, if I can't laugh then I'm going to get very irritable." I warned. Clark smiled, "Yes, she will get irritable. That's not a threat, that's a promise."

I glared at him, "Don't you start mister. You are the one who did this to me." He hung his head sheepishly. I could see a grin spreading across his face.

"Charlotte, where are you planning to give birth?" Cheryl asked, trying to change the subject. I shrugged, "I'm fine with wherever Rose wants me. Either in the bedroom or the herbology lab. Maybe she will suggest the infirmary, I am not sure. If anything goes wrong, we may want to be in the lab to have everything ready and on hand."

"Go wrong? What could go wrong?" Clark asked, uneasy. He stepped forward, placing his hand protectively on my stomach. I put my hand on top of his, "Nothing yet, but births can be difficult, especially first births. I'm not saying anything will go wrong but it is a possibility."

Clark shuttered and pulled me close to his chest, "Nothing will go wrong." I sighed, "Probably not, everything has been healthy and normal so far. However, we will need to prepare just in case something does go wrong."

He started to rock me back and forth, comforting himself more then me. "Clark, honey, you need to try and relax. I won't be able to relax when the birth is happening so you will need to be the calm one."

Cheryl and my mother giggled before my mother whispered, "I'm sure he will be fine when you go into labour. We are both here as well."

"You never said I needed to be the calm one." He whispered in my ear. I giggled, "Everything will be fine honey. Rose has delivered many babies; I trust her completely." Clark nodded, he didn't stop rocking me but he seemed less urgent about it.

"Come Dorothy, we should leave these two for a bit. I will show you to your room and then I'm sure Michael would like to introduce you and James to Tabitha." Cheryl suggest to my mother.

Mother stepped forward and hugged Clark and I before quickly following Cheryl out the door, shouting over her shoulder, "See you two later!"

As the door closed Clark picked me up and carried me to our bed. He began rubbing my sore feet, it was heavenly. "You know, if you are not careful I will get used to this." I teased. He laughed, "That's fine with me, I like to pamper you."

"I'm so sore Clark. I just want the baby to come out. I'm tired of being pregnant." I told him, whining. Clark looked back at me with a sad face, he could feel my pain through our bond.

"Has he moved at all? Do you feel like he's on his way?" Clark asked. I shook my head, "Just the usual rolls, no descending activity."

"He will be here soon. Any day now." He reminded me.

I nodded, sighing "I know, I just want it to be done." I stretched my hands over my head trying to move the knots in my back around.

"You know, honey, there are some things we can do to bring on labour." I started, "Like eating spicy food, going for a long walk, sex..."

His eyes went wide as his head spun to face me, "What?!"

I shrugged, "That's what they suggest." I put on an innocent face but Clark wasn't falling for it, "I am not sure how I feel about that last one darling. The other two maybe."

I giggled, "Oh you prude." "I'm no prude," he protested, "I'm just not sure it's really safe to do that when you are so pregnant. What if it hurts the baby?"

I scooted forward, reaching to my mate. "Clark, sex has been the recommended way to bring on labour for decades. It's not new, it's actually doctor recommended." I told him.

Clark leaned forward and kissed my lips tenderly, "Yeah? Are you sure?" I reached my hand to his face, I deepened the kiss. He didn't move back, moaning slightly as I moved my tongue into his mouth. Suddenly he moved away quickly, "Oh you clever minx, you are far too sexy for your own good."

I chuckled, "I don't feel very sexy right now." I flopped back on the bed. He climbed up beside me slowly, resting next to my body. Clark ran his hands up my hip and over my stomach, "Oh Char, you will never stop being sexy. You could be the size of ten pregnant women and still be sexy to me."

I kissed him again, slowly. Clark ran his fingers over my stomach softy. "I'm so lucky," I whispered, "You are so good to me, I love you so much honey."

"I love you too Char." He whispered back against my lips. He leaned back to star into my face, "Come on darling, lets get you moving. Maybe exercise will move labour along. Let's go for a walk downstairs and outside."

As he rolled of the bed I sat up with a grunt, "Yes Beta." Clark waddled with me around the pack house, out to the grounds and across the training fields. Our warriors were running laps with Michael, waving as they went by us. Byron had found Michael on the training fields, matching the warriors step for step as best he could. Michael slowed to a jog, coming over to us, "Hey Duffey's how are you doing?"

"Alright. Have you seen mother yet?" I asked. He nodded, "Oh yes, she is in a whirl of energy. She's got Tabitha all worked up about the details of our mating ceremony. I have told her it is going to be beautiful but Cheryl has her all worked up about the caribou."

I laughed, turning to Clark, "Oh yes, I remember the caribou. It's a very big deal here to have caribou at your mating ceremony. They are rare though so when we couldn't find one for ours I just suggested we go with moose. I don't think Cheryl had slept in three days before I told her it was ok to skip the caribou."

Michael's eyes went wide, "Yikes. Perhaps I should offer a similar suggestion. I don't want everyone to be all upset before the ceremony." With that he jogged of toward his warriors demanding push-ups.

Clark put his hand on my lower back, "Come on Char, it's getting a bit cold out, we should head back inside." I nodded, it was getting colder. It was November after all. We went to the kitchen where Clark made me some tea. Tabitha, my mother and Cheryl were all there going over details. I enjoyed the excitement and chatter, mostly that it wasn't my ceremony.

We ate dinner with my family, Clark's family and our friends that evening in the dining hall. There was much laughter and celebration. The mating ceremony, the baby on the way, there was much to be thankful for in our lives. I looked around the table at every face sitting with us, each one more precious a soul then the last. I became very aware of how blessed I was to have such a wonderful network of people who cared about me. The best part was they would all be here for the birth of my first child. It was humbling.

"I brought Saskatoon berries for the crisp Michael." My mother chimed. Michael and I spread large smiles across our faces. "Oh yes!" he said, doing a celebratory hand gesture.

"I'm sure Charlotte will be happy to help me make it for your ceremony right my dear?" she asked, I nodded enthusiastically. Tabitha started to tear up, "Oh, this is so wonderful. I'm feeling a bit overwhelmed." Michael rubbed her back softly, kissing her temple. I remembered feeling like that, Clark easing my stress.

"So little brother, are you getting up with me at 5am tomorrow for a run?" Clark asked Byron. Byron shrivelled his nose, "Do we have to go that early?"

My father chuckled, "Hey you have been talking non-stop about Clark training you while we are here. If he gets up at 5am to take you, you go with him."

Byron nodded, turning to Michael, "Will you come too?" Michael smiled, "Sure. Heath? Shall we make it a family affair with all of us in-laws going together?" Heath smirked over his glass of water, "Sure why not. I could use a good run. However, we may need to do some sparing afterward." Byron's eyes went wide at that word, he nodded excited.

"Dad, are you going to come too?" Byron asked. My father smiled but shook his head, "Nope, not going to happen son. I am retired and I like it that way." Samuel patted my father on the shoulder, "I second that James. We can have coffee while we watch these young warriors and reminisce about how we used to be that active." The two older men laughed out loud.

After dinner Clark decided to pick me up and carry me to our bedroom. He ran me a nice warm bath with the relaxing salts from Rose. After easing me into the tub, Clark massaged my feet and legs. It was absolutely heavenly; I couldn't stop myself of moaning. After a while Clark cleared his throat, "Darling, do you have to make that noise? You are driving me crazy."

"How else will you know how good it feels?" I murmured, opening one eye to look at him. He smiled, rolled his eyes at me and moved around the tub to rub my shoulders next. I was able to sleep soundly for a whole six hours that night, it was excellent.

I awoke the next morning well rested, it was a welcome change. The clock read 6:44am, I decided to get up and help out Amy down in the kitchen. I got dressed slowly, very aware of how heavy my body felt. As I pulled out a clean pair of underwear I felt an odd popping sensation inside me, when I looked down I thought I had urinated. I thought for a moment, realizing my water had broken. Grabbing a towel from the bathroom, I rubbed it over the fluid with my foot. I wasn't feeling pain yet so I went to the bathroom to clean myself up. I decided to put on a long, comfortable dress with a sweater. Slowly, I made my way to the library to telephone Rose.

I sat down on the sofa, dialing the number for Ice Water backhouse. I waited as the Omega brought her to the phone.

"Hello dear girl, how are you doing? Are you ready for me to arrive tomorrow?" Rose asked jovially.

I sighed, "Hello Gamma Rose, I am doing well. I am thrilled for you to arrive, but I was hoping you might be able to come today instead of tomorrow? My water just broke about ten minutes ago." Rose laughed through the receiver, "Oh Charlotte, only you would be so calm at a time like this. Have you started contractions yet?"

"Not yet, I just cleaned up the water from my bedroom floor and called you." I told her.

"Alright girl, you need to continue to stay calm. I will let my Alpha know I will be leaving shortly, one of the Omegas will run me over." She said calmly.

"Where would you like me to be?" I asked. She sighed, "Oh, don't worry about that part just yet. You just go about your day, labour can take hours, sometimes even days so don't get ahead of yourself just yet. No food though, just water and tea if you must. I am sure your herbology lab is fully stocked but I am bringing some birthing concoctions with me. I made them up just for you, girl."

I smiled to myself, "Wonderful. I will go and let my family know. They are all here, my mother can't wait to meet you." She laughed, "I'm sure you've exaggerated my charm, Charlotte." I giggled, "See you soon."

After I hung up the phone I decided to go to the kitchen and take her advice to make some tea. I shouldn't eat anything but some chamomile tea would be great for the nerves that were building in my stomach. Amy was there with Tabitha making breakfast for the pack house. They greeted me slightly, busy with their morning tasks. I made myself the tea and began pitching in at the stove, flipping bacon. After about an hour my back started to ache a bit, I moved around the kitchen a bit.

Tabitha's eyes followed me, "Are you alright Char?" I nodded, "Yeah, I'm just a bit uncomfortable because I'm in labour." Both women stopped what they were doing and stared at me. "Oh god," Amy began, "We should get you to bed and call the Druid!" Amy ran around the counter to my side, Tabitha moved slower the kettle to boil some more water.

"I've let Rose know already, she is on her way. I'm supposed to continue acting normal until my contractions start to get closer. I haven't had one yet actually. Labour can be long, especially with your first child so I'm trying to stay calm." I explained.

Tabitha nodded, "Have you let Clark know yet?" I shook my head, "He's out with the boys this morning. I'll tell him when he gets back. There is nothing for him to do just yet, besides I would rather he be focused when he's in the forest right now."

They nodded, after the attacks a couple months ago no one went out in the forest alone now. It was important to have your wits about you due to recent events. As the kettle boiled Tabitha fixed me another cup of tea, she was at ease which was refreshing.

We finished bringing breakfast out to the dining hall. I sat down at a table, Amy and Tabitha joined me with plates of food. As they ate I attempted to make myself as comfortable as possible. My back and hips were aching more. I felt a small pinch in my belly, I could tell it was a contraction. The pain didn't last long but I noticed it. There was no time to breath through it, the contraction was over quickly. I was sure Clark had felt that, I could sense his heightened tension. He would be coming shortly.

I went to the kitchen again to help with the dishes, I didn't want to just sit around waiting so I may as well make myself useful. After a few minutes Clark, Michael, Byron and Heath came trampling into the kitchen all covered in dirt and sweat. Clark ran to me, pulling me to his chest, oh he smelled good yet terrible all at the same time. I ran my hands through his sweaty hair, "Sshh it's alright I am fine."

"You are in labour darling! Why are you walking around?" he demanded.

In that moment Rose entered the kitchen with a suitcase, she patted Clark on the back playfully, "Because it is good for her and the baby. She's not doing to sit in bed and wait, that is just silly. Leave her to move around, if anything it will make the labour go faster."

I smiled, walking to Rose and bringing you into an embrace. She hugged me back tightly, I had missed her. Breaking apart slowly, Gamma Rose smiled at me, "Now girl, we might want to figure out where you are giving birth. I suggest the herbology lab for your first birth just in case."

I nodded, "I agree. We should get a bed set up in there." Clark spun around, gathering Heath and Michael to go and take care of it. I smiled, "Perhaps it's time to tell the parents they are going to be grandparents today."

## Chapter 22

For the first couple hours I was able to wander around the pack house unfazed by my labour until I came to hour six, then the contractions started to get stronger. I made my way to my bedroom and changed into a loose cotton nightgown. I grabbed an extra one along with my herb bag and started waddling towards the door. Clark burst in, his face completely white, "Where have you been woman!?"

He never yelled, I was taken aback. I stared at him with annoyed eyes, "I just changed into something more comfortable. I was just going to go to the herbology lab to get settled in. My contractions are coming more quickly now."

Clark let out an annoyed sigh, "For god sake, Charlotte, I've been looking for you all over the place for an hour!" I made a pensive face, "Why didn't you just link me?" I asked. He opened his mouth to argue with me, then closed it again when my words sunk in.

I smiled knowingly at him, "I'm going to the herbology lab now. I've got everything I need; Rose is ready for me." He didn't ask, he just picked me up and started to carry me. "You shouldn't hide from me, you scared me half to death." He muttered.

I rolled my eyes, "Why are you scared? I'm doing fine. Everything is progressing safely, the way we want it to." Clark paused and looked at me, he pulled my face closer to his face. "I'm scared there will be complications. I'm terrified." He whispered.

"Honey, you need to relax, "I told him calmly, "I am fine, the baby is fine." Clark raised his face to meet my eyes, "I can't loose you. It would kill me." Tears raises in the corners of his eyes, I reached up to touch his face.

"Clark, I love you so much. I am going to be fine. The most important thing for you to do right now is to stay as calm as possible. I am not going anywhere; I promise you that." I whispered against his lips. He kissed me back, holding me close. I could feel his pulse through our bond. He was releasing his anxiety slowly.

Suddenly I winced in pain, a contraction ripping through my stomach. Clark held on to me, carrying me quickly to the herbology lab. I pushed my face into the crook of his neck, squeezing his shoulder to move through the pain. Our families were outside the doors of the lab, collectively waiting for us to arrive. Clark rushed past them and into the room, he set me on the bed gently. He adjusted the pillows behind me, helping me to be as comfortable as possible.

"Oh good Beta, you found her. See she didn't take off to a cave and have that pup the old fashioned way after all." Rose teased.

I studied Clark's face, he went red and refused me make eye contact with me, "Yes you were right." I stroked his face, he was so worried. I wanted to take it all away.

Rose moved to my feet, "Alright girl, let's see how far along you are." She checked how far I was dilated. She made a face while removing the glove, "You are about half way there. I'm impressed you are moving along quickly. Keep this up and we will have this baby here before supper time." I laughed.

Clark moved over to my shoulders and started to rub them, trying to relax my muscles. As the hours ticked by my contractions came faster and became more painful. Clark did a great job of keeping everyone out of the room which I was grateful for. He boiled the water, fed me tea and herbs and massaged my body as much as possible. It seemed as my body started to display the stress of the birth more, he felt able to be in control.

Rose sat calmly at the end of the bed reading a book. I smiled at her, asking "Gamma Rose, how many babies have you delivered in your lifetime?"

"Oh gosh, girl let me think." she sighed, setting her book down on her lap, "Probably close to five hundred."

"Wow, that's impressive." I told her, she shrugged returning to her book, "I suppose. When you've been at this as long as I have they kind of run together."

I laughed, "I'm grateful you are here with us today." She smiled at me, "Me too." After that she just checked on me when I had a contraction.

I lay back on the pillows, Clark resting his head next to mine. We kissed lightly, smiling at each other. "I'm board." I whispered to him. He giggled, "I'll be sure to tell him that his mother was such a rock star that she found his birth boring."

"The birth isn't boring; the waiting is boring." I whined. "Would you like me to get you one of your books?" he asked. I nodded. Clark handed me Persuasion by Jane Austen. It helped fill the time.

A few more hours passed by, my contractions were three minutes apart. The pain was intense but I was able to breath through it. Gamma Rose checked my cervix, "Well girl, it looks like you are ready. Only thirteen hours since you called me, you are doing great."

"Ready?" I asked through clenched teeth. She nodded, "Yep, time to push Charlotte." Clark and I looked at each other, I took a deep breath and pushed with all my might.

The pain seared through me. Nothing I had ever experienced compared to the force of pushing my son from my body. I squeezed my mate's hands as tight as I could, screaming when I needed to. Clark was a trooper, taking my assaults and sharing my pain. Just when I was becoming exhausted I pushed one last time, feeling as though I was about to pass out. Then I smelt him, the most amazing scent in the entire world. Fresh basil filled the room along with loud cries. I had never sensed anything more amazing in my entire life. Rose cleaned him up and passed my son to me. Clark curled up next to me in the bed, pulling his arm around my shoulders to pull us close to his chest.

"Oh my god, hello there." I whispered to him. His smell overwhelmed us, I cried for the first time all day. He was perfect, absolutely perfect. Ten fingers, ten toes. Small little button nose and dark black hair like his father. I kissed him on his forehead, the feeling in my heart was indescribable.

"Hi buddy, I'm your daddy." Clark said to our son, he wrapped his tiny little fingers around Clark's thumb. In a moment, there were more tears. I kissed my husband, "I love you honey. Thank you so much for this wonderful gift."

Clark kissed my forehead and ran his fingers through my hair, "Thank you Char for this wonderful family. I love you so much."

"What are we going to name this little man?" he asked me. I stared at our son, trying to think but nothing seemed to fit. I shrugged, "You pick."

"Hayes William Duffey." He said without pause. I giggled, "You've been holding on to that I can tell."

"I had been thinking about his name for a while." He admitted. I kissed Clark tenderly, we gazed down at our son, "Hayes William Duffey, welcome to Black Lake. You are so loved."

The next week went by with in a flash. Clark and I took turns getting up with Hayes in the middle of the night. Diapers, baths, feedings, crying, cuddles and sleeping. He filled our lives with so much happiness in such a short period of time. Our mothers took great care of us by doing all the laundry each day. I tried to help out with Michael and Tabitha's mating ceremony celebration but I was a bit preoccupied for obvious reasons.

The night before their ceremony Michael came to our room to see Hayes. He was a bit nervous.

"I hope I can be everything she deserves." He whispered. I smiled, "Michael, you are everything she has ever wanted." He sat on our bed while I walked around the room with Hayes in my arms.

Michael sighed, "Maybe I'm just nervous." Clark smiled at him, "It's all good. I was too. We have all been there."

"I don't know; I just hope I am good enough for her." He muttered, "I already had one chance, I don't know what I would do if I messed this up."

I moved in front of my brother and stared down at him, "You didn't mess anything up with Stella and you won't mess anything up with Tabitha. You were meant to go through that heartache to find your true mate. That was the journey you were meant to go on. You deserve to be happy, Michael."

"Listen to your sister." Clark chimed, stepping up behind me to wrap his family into his arms. I leaned back and kissed his cheek.

"You are right; I know you are right." He said, smiling. Michael went to bed shortly after that.

Clark took Hayes for his evening cuddle before bed. I took a quick shower, taking advantage of the free time. When I returned to our bedroom I saw Clark laying our son down in his crib, kissing him goodnight. I smiled, shedding a small tear at the sweet scene before me.

After we lay down for the night I curled into my mate's arms, "I am so happy, I can't even express it." Clark kissed my face, "I know darling. I love you."

"He is so perfect. How did I get so lucky?" I asked, stroking his chest. He chuckled, "Hey, that's my question for you." We snuggled together for a while, enjoying some quality couple time. Hayes started to fuss after an hour so I got up to sooth him.

"We got an invitation to attend a conference in three months as key note speakers in Vancouver. It's a Pack Summit, there are going to be about two hundred territories represented across Canada." Clark told me, sitting up on our bed to look at me.

I turned around, glancing at him as I soothed Hayes, "What's it about, the summit?"

"Well, since the attack in our territory there has been a lot of cooperation among packs. Enemies have become allies, wolves are working together like never before so the summit has been called so packs across the country can compare strategies and planning programs in case of attacks." He explained.

"Alright, that is exciting. It sounds awesome." I murmured, pulling my son up to rest his head on my shoulder.

Clark rose and crossed the room to us, he stroked my face with a smile, "They want you and I to give a talk about our encounter. About the attack, how you found me and the evidence we have discovered about the creature and rogues responsible."

I nodded, "It's in three months? Vancouver?" My mate nodded. Hayes had fallen back to sleep; I slowly lay him down in his crib kissing his face. I turned to Clark and wrapped my arms around his neck. He pulled me close to him around my waist, nestling his face into my hair.

"Will it be just you and I?" I asked. "No, Heath will join us. Alphas and Betas are mandatory for this summit. He told me about it yesterday, I said I would talk to you before we agree to go." He whispered, slowly kissing my neck. I purred at his touch.

"Alright, I'll go with you if you want me to. Always." I murmured as he rubbed my back lovingly. Clark nodded, "We have time to prepare. The summit isn't for three months so Hayes should be big enough to stay with my parents by then."

"Mmm sounds good. I'm sure by then we will be ready for a mini vacation." I said with a giggle, "Besides it's good to have things to look forward to."

THE END